
★

I walked around the car, carrying my manuscript in one hand and my purse in the other. I juggled the manuscript, finally putting the bulky thing under my arm until I could reach up for the rope to pull down the garage door.

A sound came from behind me.

I whirled around, letting go of the cord. "Jeremy?"

No answer.

Just a cat, I told myself, reaching up again.

I got a solid grip on the cord and gave it a yank. There was a thunderous clattering as the door closed. Then there was another sound behind me. I spun around one more time, but I was too late. Something hit me and I went down hard.

★

"...the story is briskly told, the characters well rounded and Purple Sage promising as a rich setting for future tales from this talented newcomer."

—*Publishers Weekly*

Writers

OF THE

Purple Sage

BARBARA
BURNETT
SMITH

WORLDWIDE.

TORONTO • NEW YORK • LONDON
AMSTERDAM • PARIS • SYDNEY • HAMBURG
STOCKHOLM • ATHENS • TOKYO • MILAN
MADRID • WARSAW • BUDAPEST • AUCKLAND

For my father, who marvels at my persistence. Some people might call it hardheadedness, and I think it's hereditary. With much love, I dedicate this to him.

WRITERS OF THE PURPLE SAGE

A Worldwide Mystery/September 1996

First published by St. Martin's Press, Incorporated.

ISBN 0-373-26214-0

ACKNOWLEDGMENTS

I don't think you can reach a dream all by yourself. It takes the support of others, and I was lucky enough to have that. There was the assistance of two wonderful groups of writers. First, there were the TPWs: Dinah Chenven, Sally Helen Reid, Susan Wade and Mary Willis Walker. Thank you. Then came the Black Shoes, to whom I am especially grateful for their good judgment, good advice and great friendship: Susan Rogers Cooper, Jeff Abbot and Jan Grape.

I also wish to thank Elisabeth Story, who took a chance on me, and I am grateful to Elisabeth and Karen Pilibosian Thompson for the miraculous gift of good editing.

Most important were two very special people who not only read and coached, but who also never stopped believing in me, even when I gave up: Caroline Young Petrequin and Susan Rogers Cooper.

And special hugs go to W.D. and Martie Smith, Carol Ruff, Bruce Burnett and Gary Petry, who loved me through it all. I needed that.

ONE

My FIRST STOP on the way to the jail was the bakery on Main. A brass bell was stuck to the door with months-old Christmas ribbon and it jangled merrily as I went inside. The wonderful fragrance of freshly baked bread wafted toward me.

"Close the door, Jolie," a voice said. "Cain't stand when them bugs start comin' in."

It was IdaMae Dorfman, the owner, who was almost as old as the city of Purple Sage. I could barely see the top of her white hair over the glass display case.

"Sorry, IdaMae."

"Oh, don't mind me," she said. "I been cranky lately, waitin' for spring. So, what can I get for ya?"

I glanced at the piles of homemade cookies, rows of cakes and fluffy cream pies, then over at the loaves of plump brown bread. "Just a dozen of the shortbread cookies, I guess."

She reached for some white tissue. "Must be Tuesday. You girls are having your writers' meeting."

"Right as always." I loved the way she referred to us as "girls." The ages of the women in our group ranged from twenty-seven to sixty-four, and I was personally closing in fast on thirty-nine. Not exactly major users of Stri-Dex, but I guess to IdaMae Dorfman almost every female was a girl.

"Do me a favor," IdaMae said. "You tell June Ingram to get busy on her writing. I finished her last book months ago and I need something peppy to read."

June Ingram was Purple Sage's claim to fame and half the town seemed to live for the release of her latest book. She wrote cozies—gentle mysteries with a middle-aged couple doing the sleuthing. She had published more than a dozen and had garnered almost as many awards for them.

"I'll tell her," I said. It was no use explaining to IdaMae that June had finished writing two books and there was a lag time between writing and publishing.

"And what about the rest of you girls?" IdaMae demanded. "When are one of you going to finish a book?"

We *had* finished books. Twice I had tried convincing IdaMae that the time between finishing a first, or second, book and finding an editor willing to take a chance on it was even longer, but she'd always waved away my explanation. IdaMae believed in results that you could see, touch, and check out of the library.

"Soon," I promised.

IdaMae put one sack on the counter and began filling another as she cackled, "Can't wait to see what June's cooked up for her next murder!" She picked up a loaf of bread and set it beside the two white sacks already in front of me. "I gave you some extra cookies and some homemade bread and I want you to eat every bit of them. You're gettin' too skinny, Jolie Wyatt."

Divorce, America's most effective diet plan, had struck again. Still my weight was lurking around the 110-pound mark, which on my five-foot-three frame was hardly what you would call wasting away.

"Thank you," I said as she took my money.

A siren sounded in the distance and I felt a slight chill slither down my spine. When you know everyone in town a siren strikes a sensitive chord. You begin to wonder where all the people you love are at that particular moment.

IdaMae straightened up and handed me some change. "I hate that sound."

I nodded.

"Well," IdaMae went on, "I'll just hold the thought that it's someone I don't much like. Figure there's plenty of them around."

I smiled. "I guess I've got one or two like that, too. See you later."

I stepped outside into the twilight and saw Rhonda Hargis whizzing by on her racing bike. I waved but she didn't look up;

all I saw was blond hair and the flashing of tanned calves as she peddled up the hill.

Besides being a member of our writing group and a reporter for the Purple Sage *Tribune,* Rhonda taught an aerobic dance class three times a week. She lived and worked with the single-minded fervor of a Marine drill sergeant. Usually she had just enough time to end the class, race home, and shower before she showed up for our meeting. Obviously she was late, so why was she going in the opposite direction of the old jail where the group met?

By the time I had decided not to worry about Rhonda, I was in the Mazda and almost at the square. The huge courthouse stood as placidly as it had for over a century; the tall pecan trees around it were optimistically putting out the first of their spring green leaves. The shops that bordered the square had closed for the night, leaving the streets empty. I felt a pang of regret. Despite all my complaints about small-town living, I was going to miss Purple Sage.

Two blocks away I pulled up to the old jail. It looked like a small medieval castle against the reds and purples of the setting sun. As I got out of the car I admired its crenelated tower and wondered for the millionth time why jail builders in the Old West had created such romantic-looking places to keep their criminals.

Beside the front door were dusty gray purple sage bushes, without the tiny lavender flowers that gave them their name. According to local folklore they only bloomed when it was going to rain, a good omen for a community that depended on agriculture for its economic health. Since there were no blossoms I assumed the dry spell wouldn't be broken anytime soon.

The door was newly painted, but still warped, and it creaked ominously as I swung it inward. With a flick of the wall switch the room lit up, dispelling the ghosts of long dead murderers and thieves. Old or not, the jail, now a museum, had most of the modern conveniences.

I'd always considered it the perfect place for our writers' group to meet. Most of us wrote mysteries or suspense novels, so the proximity of the gallows two floors above added a nice flavor to the gathering. A noose still hung there, but not the same one that was used the only time a murderer had been executed. Now the whole building was merely an attraction for the tourists who wandered off the beaten highway and ended up in Purple Sage.

The room we used functioned as a reception area where visitors paused before climbing the stairs to the cells. Here there were a number of relics carefully collected by the museum committee, including an antique regulator clock that ticked rhythmically from its place of honor on the wall to my left. Overhead was a green- and clear-globed chandelier that sent light bouncing off the glass cases that displayed old-style barbed wire. A shiny rolltop desk covered almost all of the back wall. Taking up the center of the room was a heavy antique oak table with six matching chairs, but I veered around it and went to the closet to get our own battered but serviceable card table. We had decided that putting a wet glass on the silken surface of the oak table would have been sufficient cause for the museum committee to reinstate the gallows. It was bad enough that we had the gall to sit on the antique chairs.

A blast of fresh air swept around me as the door creaked open and Maria Chavez hurried in, carrying a heavy notebook and a half-gallon Thermos. "Hey, Jolie," she said. "How's it going?"

"Just grand," I said, battling and losing to a table leg that refused to stand firm. "What am I doing wrong here?"

"Let me help." She dropped her things on the polished wooden floor and grabbed the metal leg. "Just hold the table and I'll pull." With a quick snap the leg locked into place.

"You should have been a chiropractor," I said.

"No, thanks. I aspire to moderate fame and extreme wealth without the aid of work."

I looked at her manuscript, which was slowly but surely coming along. It was her second book. Both were western romances filled with calico-covered bosoms heaving with unbridled passion, and lean tanned men fighting over the sod. Someone said that she was like the Judith Krantz of the 1800s. Since I've never read Judith Krantz, and since I'd never read a western before hers, I didn't feel qualified to judge. I do know that she keeps me turning pages and sometimes she has a line that I want to write down and slip into my next book. Of course, I don't.

"That's not work?" I asked, pointing to her manuscript.

"A labor of love."

Maria was the youngest member of our group and had graduated from the University of Texas three years before. She'd been headed for her master's degree when her mother was diagnosed as having Alzheimer's disease. Even though she had two older brothers, it was Maria who'd been elected to come home. In dutiful manner, she had.

If anyone in town had bothered to think about it, they probably would have said that Maria would end up working as someone's secretary, at minimum wage. Maria, however, rarely did what people expected of her. Instead she got a business license, calling herself Maid for the Day, and then hired crews to do the actual labor. Maria supervised. It was rumored that she had an eye so keen she could spot a floating dust mote and whisk it out of the air before it landed on a windowsill.

"What's in the jug?" I asked.

Maria looked at the Thermos as if it had somehow offended her. "Oh, that. It's my latest and I spent most of the afternoon working on it. It's for the political reception tomorrow. I want you all to taste it tonight and tell me what you think."

"Now you're doing catering?" I asked, realizing that her normally golden skin looked pale. "When? In your spare time between midnight and dawn? Give yourself a break, Maria. You look exhausted."

"I've got to make a living in this rotten town! You figure a better way."

"I can't," I said. "Which is why I'm leaving as soon as school is out, remember?"

It's nearly impossible for a woman to support herself in Purple Sage, and there was no way I could support myself and continue to feed my fifteen-year-old, Jeremy, in the manner to which he had become accustomed. Jeremy thought a ten-dollar roast made a great appetizer. (And, naturally, he never gained an ounce!) There was another reason why I had to leave Purple Sage: you can't live in a town of 5,000 people when your ex-husband's family has been there as long as dirt.

"Damn," Maria said. "I forgot. Just ignore me."

It was impossible to ignore Maria, especially when she was in one of her moods, but I did decide to overlook her outburst. "So this is some special punch?" I asked, pointing to the jug.

Maria nodded. "It was first served in the White House during the Ford administration."

"Really? How did you get the recipe?"

"From a book!" she said with a snap. "I can read, you know."

Most people attributed Maria's temperament to the load she carried or her artistic streak; I considered it pure self-indulgence.

"You read?" I said. "Impossible! You mean people who graduate summa cum laude have to be able to read?"

"I'm sorry," she said. "I don't mean to keep snapping at you." She dropped her head and tried to make her shoulders sag, but her black eyes were still radiating a kind of nuclear fury.

I had no idea what her problem was and I thought it wiser not to ask in her present mood. "Maybe you should run around the block before the others get here. Blow off a little steam."

She picked her manuscript up off the floor and it looked like she was fighting the urge to slam it on the card table. After a moment she put the manuscript down with great care. She seemed to deliberate, then said, "I've had some customer problems." She stopped herself and gulped in air.

"You want to talk about it?"

"No!" She put her keys in her purse and said, "God, if I didn't need the money, I'd tell him to take his house and shove it!"

"Who?"

"It doesn't matter."

"Not to me, but it obviously does to you," I said. "Besides, it's Tuesday, and every Tuesday afternoon you have a crew at the Judge's house. And you usually supervise."

She stared at me for a moment. "How do you remember things like that?"

"I'm a writer. So what happened with the Patron Saint of Purple Sage?"

Maria tried to sound casual, but casual isn't really in her repertoire. "He called me this morning and said that he didn't like the job my crew was doing. Not only that, he decided that he didn't trust them. 'Those people steal, you know. It's just their way.'" Her imitation of the Judge was cruel and nearly perfect. "Because they're Hispanic, that's why he didn't want them."

"So what did you do?" I asked.

"I went over and did his damn house all by myself, that's what I did! And then he had the gall to complain that the windows weren't clean and it was so important that everything be perfect. But I was cool. I very politely offered to send a special crew, with me along to watch them, at some convenient time for him." She looked at me and suddenly became calm. "I'm already planning to go out tomorrow and we'll make those windows sparkle. I'm not cut out to deal with the public; I just don't have the patience, especially not with people as picky as the Judge. But I don't have to tell you about Judge Osler. You've had a run-in with him."

And much more publicly than Maria had. "He's old," I said. "You have to make allowances, especially since he's done so much for the town. Everyone loves him. Well, except you and me, I guess."

Maria took a deep breath and seemed to shake off some of her anger. "Yeah, well, thanks for listening. Guess that will teach you to be early."

"Doubtful, but it was a good try."

"So, now that I've told you my troubles," Maria said, "how are you doing? Any luck with the job hunting or is that another touchy subject?"

"Not touchy, just slow. I've only been gone from Austin for three years, but everything has changed. People treat me like I've come back from the dead, or something. No one is interested in hiring me. I feel like I'm marooned here." I'm a great believer in the philosophy of self-fulfilling prophecy—you get what you predict—so I attempted to predict a rosier future. It felt a little like lying. "I'm really not all that worried; I'll find something. A good job, I'm sure."

"I'm sure you will," she said. "How's the writing coming?"

"Uh, fine." Fine if you like the last chapters of a book to have a slow pace, contain terrible clichés and characters who suddenly become as deep and complex as birdbaths. "Just a few pages this week, but I've been busy," I said.

Maria looked at the clock. "Where the hell is everyone?"

"Diane is walking the district," I said.

"She's doing what?"

"You know, going door to door. Asking people for their vote."

Maria cocked her head, her expression shocked. "Diane is going door to door? You've got to be kidding."

"No. She's had lots of experience with all those charity things she's done."

Maria snorted. "She chaired those committees. She never actually did anything."

I was about to disagree, and probably really get Maria going, but the door opened and it was Diane. Her glossy dark hair was pulled back in a sophisticated chignon, and not even one hair was out of place despite her wary expression. Her normally flawless skin seemed to have a grayish tinge.

She stopped just inside the room and struck a pose; her smile was several watts lower than usual. "Hello. I'm Diane Atwood, and my husband, Trey, is a candidate for mayor. I'd like to leave you this brochure, which will explain his stand on the issues facing Purple Sage." Her voice became sing-song. "I'd also like to invite you to the political reception tomorrow at the Community Center. Trey will be there and will be happy to answer any questions you might have. Your vote is important to us, and we want to do everything in our power to earn that vote."

"Sounds like you've said that a few hundred times," Maria commented.

Diane sagged visibly. "Only forty-eight, so far."

"Come and sit down," I said, pulling out a chair for her. "Are you okay?"

Uncharacteristically Diane collapsed into the chair, letting her purse and briefcase drop to the floor beside her. Diane and Trey were the Di and Charles of Purple Sage. Or like Di and Charles had been when they'd reigned as the fair-haired hope of the sovereign nation. Actually, I suppose Diane and Trey had lost some of their sheen, too. Oh, not through anything they had done, but because Judge Volney Osler had decided to support Trey's opponent. It had turned the mayoral campaign into a real race.

"I'm so tired I could cry," Diane said. "God, Jolie, I had no idea it would be like this."

Maria asked, "Just walking around is so terrible?"

"It's not the walking. It's the people," Diane said. "Oh, some are wonderful—they want you to come in and sit down; the old southern hospitality really comes out. But there are others!" She looked at me. "One woman said, 'If the Judge is backing Bill Tieman, so are we! How could you even consider going against a man as wonderful as that?' When I tried to explain she threw the pamphlet back at me and slammed the door. It's as if we're personally trying to insult him and it's not like that at all. Trey announced long before the Judge started backing Bill."

I patted her hand sympathetically. "Don't worry, it's almost over. The new radio commercials started today—maybe they'll help." I certainly hoped so. Trey and Diane had decided the campaign could use some extra clout, and I could use some extra money, so they'd hired me as campaign manager. It was the first time my copywriting talents had been useful in Purple Sage.

"I wonder why the Judge just didn't run for mayor himself?" Maria mused.

"I don't know," I said. "Maybe because he lost his last election; he's not even a judge anymore."

"Yeah, but that was a district vote. He carried Purple Sage by a landslide."

Diane began to knead her shoulders. "I just wish it were all over."

The door opened and June Ingram came in. "Hello, ladies." Her tone lacked enthusiasm.

As usual, June's compact, sixty-something body was clothed in faded jeans and a blue work shirt. On her feet were scuffed running shoes. The front of her short gray hair was standing up as if she'd been running her fingers through it.

"You don't sound happy," I said.

June placed her soft leather briefcase on the table and pulled out a chair. "Oh, I'm fine."

Maria leaned forward. "Let me guess; you just left the Judge and he wasn't in a good mood."

"No, I haven't seen the Judge at all today," June said, tiny frown lines appearing on the bridge of her nose. "I'm worried about Jupiter. He's cut his leg again and it's not healing properly. For a horse with his ability, he's the clumsiest oaf I've ever seen!" June trained horses on her ranch and Jupiter Fandango was her prize stud, as well as her favorite.

Maria looked at June. "That's weird. I was cleaning the Judge's house and he told me to hurry because he had a meeting with A Writer." She said the words as if they were in quotes. "I assumed he meant you."

It was a natural assumption; no matter how many books the rest of us cranked out we weren't published yet. Even if we had been, June was *the* writer in Purple Sage.

"It wasn't me," June said, as she dug manuscript pages out of her leather bag. "There are other writers in town; Rhonda writes for the paper, maybe he had an appointment with her. You know, spouting about one of his pet causes. I hope it's not this place, again." She looked around the museum. "I don't know why, but I have this feeling that he's looking for an excuse to kick us out of here. Oh well, Rhonda has better sense than to do a story on that. Where is Rhonda, by the way?"

"I saw her going in the opposite direction when I was driving over," I said and then let out a small groan. "If he got an exclusive interview with the paper about the campaign, I'll shoot myself." It didn't make me look very effective at PR.

"Don't worry about it," Diane said. "I heard a siren earlier—maybe she's tracking down some criminal."

"On her bike?" Maria said.

June plopped her neatly printed pages into the center of the table and pushed up the sleeves of her work shirt. "Well, I think we should get started."

"Great, let's read," Diane said, rearranging her elegant body into a more ladylike position. "I'd like to get out early and get some rest."

We took out pencils, then passed our manuscripts to the left, a weekly ritual that began the reading. Except for the clock, the room became silent. I noticed my heartbeat slowing to the rhythm of the soft ticking. Diane chuckled at something June had written and I lowered my eyes to the pages in front of me. It was Diane's spy novel. Jordon, the main character, was in a tube station in London with members of a PLO group in hot pursuit. It was fabulous, as always, and if Diane weren't my dearest friend I would hate her for it.

I had just finished reading about Jordon rigging a delayed bomb out of bullets and the inner workings of a toilet tank, when the door opened.

It was Rhonda, her blond ponytail fluffed to a *Vogue* perfection.

"Sorry I'm late," she said as an entrance line.

Heads moved to look at her.

"Big story?" I asked.

"Really big!" she said as she slid in between Diane and me.

Sometimes I thought Rhonda was a humanoid, devoid of the normal emotions that plagued the rest of us, but at that moment she was almost twitching in her need to talk. "You won't believe it," she went on, "you just won't believe it!"

"What is it?" Maria asked. "Can you tell us?"

Rhonda looked around, took a much-needed breath, and said, "The Judge is dead!"

TWO

"YOU'RE KIDDING!"

"How did it happen?"

"When?"

Rhonda leaned forward, her green eyes filled with an uncharacteristic excitement. "It's weird. I mean, really bizarre."

"Tell us," Diane said.

"Well, I don't know how it all started, but when I first heard the call on the police radio, they thought he was just some drunk."

"He doesn't drink," June said.

"I know. But at first they didn't even know it was the Judge."

Everyone was intently listening, as if it would hurry Rhonda.

"Start at the beginning," June said, "and tell us the whole thing."

Rhonda nodded, causing her white blond ponytail to bob. "Okay." She took a moment and gathered her thoughts. "Okay. I was at the *Trib* office, since no one had shown up for exercise class." She shot an accusatory look around at all of us, apparently decided it was no longer relevant, and went on. "Anyway, so I went back to finish up this one story and I had the police radio on. I heard a call that said they had some drunk over on Winchester. I didn't pay too much attention, but then the dispatcher came back on and said that this guy had driven up on a woman's lawn. And finally, he said it was the Judge. That's when I jumped on my bike and went over there."

It must have been happening while I was at the bakery talking with IdaMae Dorfman.

Rhonda took another breath and leaned forward. "When I got there, the car was right up on the grass, like he'd tried to park and had jumped the curb. It was wild; his great big old

Lincoln just plopped there under a tree! And this poor woman was ready to faint.''

Diane furrowed her patrician brow. ''But what happened?''

Oh, well, Andy Sawyer was the cop who showed up and the woman told him that she heard the car and all this honking so she went outside to see what was going on. When the Judge got out of the car, he was white and sweaty and shaking. He started yelling at her, only he wasn't making very much sense. The only word she understood was police, so she went inside to call them. That's all she knew.''

''When did he die? And what did he die of?'' I asked. ''Heart attack?''

''He died right there on her lawn, but I don't know what from, maybe a heart attack,'' Rhonda said. ''Andy thought that maybe the Judge started having some kind of pains and tried to drive himself to the hospital. Winchester is right on the way.''

''He must have been too sick to go on so he tried to get an ambulance.''

''You said 'police,''' June reminded her.

''Yeah, well, I don't really think he was coherent. And she was in shock at first; I mean, who wouldn't be? There he was, furious because she's not moving, so he's screaming for the police. Maybe he figured they could get him to the hospital.''

I leaned back in my chair. The Patron Saint of Purple Sage was dead. The man who'd given money, and lent his name to so many worthy undertakings: the museum, the United Way, the library, and a dozen more causes. It was like hearing that the president had been assassinated, only in my case, it was a president that I didn't like. My one and only conversation with him had been a public blowup that'd had half the town talking. Maybe he'd been getting senile.

It was June who broke the silence. ''It's like the end of an era.''

Diane sat up even straighter and turned to look at me. ''Now he can't back Bill Tieman.'' Her words seemed to surprise even her.

''Yes.'' But I didn't know how that would affect anything.

"Rhonda," Maria said, "shouldn't you be writing the story?"

"The paper doesn't go to press until tomorrow night; by that time I'll have the rest of the information. We don't really know very much yet, most of what I told you was just Andy's guessing. He'll piece the whole thing together and I'll get it from him later." She shrugged. "I did get a pretty good picture of the car up on the lawn. I think we'll run it on the front page."

Diane voiced my thought. "It seems such a melodramatic way for the Judge to die. Almost like he planned it."

June shook her head. "No, he would have planned something more dignified."

"The Patron Saint of Purple Sage." My sarcasm must have slipped out because I heard someone snort.

June seemed distant. "The whole town's going to be mourning his death. He's probably donated more money to charities than anyone. Whenever there was a need, he seemed to jump in to fill it."

"Not always," Rhonda said, placing her manuscript in front of her. "Well, shall we read?"

I wasn't in the mood anymore.

"Maybe we should skip tonight," Diane suggested. "I'm not sure I can concentrate. Besides, I need to get some rest."

June took off her reading glasses. "I'd be happy to wait until next week."

That settled it. June was our unofficial guru, and if she didn't want to read, then we wouldn't read.

"What about my punch?" Maria asked. "I spent all afternoon on this stuff and I have to know if it's okay before the political thing tomorrow."

June began packing papers. "Then bring it out and we'll try it."

Maria jumped up. "It will only take a second."

"I brought cookies," I said. "Shortbread, if anybody's hungry."

Nobody was, so we drank punch while we straightened the room, putting back chairs and making the museum look as if we'd never been there.

"This is really going to change things—I wonder how it will affect the political rally tomorrow?" Diane said.

June took a large swallow of Maria's green punch. "It probably won't—life in Purple Sage usually just keeps on going despite the funerals."

"Yeah," Rhonda said. "But this is the Judge's funeral." She looked around. "Funny, I didn't think he'd ever die."

WHEN I GOT HOME it was only a little after eight. I parked the Mazda in the garage and slipped inside the back door, my brain whirring with conflicting thoughts about the Judge. A cup of hot tea sounded good, so I headed for the kitchen. On the counter were the remains of Jeremy's dinner: a paper plate with a few broken potato chips, a glass with a film of milk, a dirty knife, and a scattering of crumbs. Automatically I cleaned them up, then I made myself a tuna sandwich, still wondering why the Judge had to die now, right after I'd had a fight with him. It made me feel guilty even though I hadn't done anything wrong. I put the sandwich on a plate, cut it carefully in two, and stared at it. I didn't want food.

I put it back in the fridge and gave some consideration to an open bottle of wine. Just the thought was revolting. Instead I headed for my room, but as I passed my son's closed door, I could hear computer-generated sounds coming from behind it. Cautiously I pushed open the door.

Jeremy was planted in front of the computer screen, his hands working the joystick with the familiar agility of a fighter pilot.

"Hi," I said. "I'm home early."

On the screen two planes blew up. Jeremy grunted.

I waited a few beats, then said, "You're still mad at me."

Nothing this time.

"Look, Jeremy, I'm doing the best I can. Can't you at least talk to me? Please?"

He tapped a key and on the screen a bomb froze in midexplosion, a plane hung in midair, and the bullets stopped halfway to their targets.

With infinite patience Jeremy turned in his chair. "Yes?"

It was a breakthrough; he was actually talking to me. I was seeing his face for the first time in weeks. It was a nice face and I had missed it, even if the scowl that was currently on it wasn't all that pleasant. "Jeremy, I'm sorry that things haven't worked out, I really am. I know you're not happy. The problem is, though, I've got to make a living, and the only place I can do that is in Austin."

"Sure."

Amazing how much sarcasm a teenager can put into a one-syllable word. "Hey," I said, "I don't have a choice. I'll have to go back into advertising; it's all I know; it's my life."

"Your former life."

He was right. I had given it all up three years before to marry Prince Charming and ride off into the sunset where we could live happily ever after. In my spare time I had planned to write the Great American Mystery Novel.

Unfortunately, the fairy tale didn't last as long as *happily ever after*. In just thirty-three short months I had realized that the sunset was merely a small town in central Texas and my first Great American Mystery Novel was dreck. My second was somewhat better and my third had finally gotten me an agent and, so far, two rejections.

Meanwhile, Prince Charming had transformed into a toad. Or maybe I had done the changing and he was exactly the same—that was the thing that had been bothering me the most.

Jeremy was still watching me. I smiled. "Everything will be fine. It always is."

"Mother," Jeremy said in that condescending tone that fifteen-year-olds reserve for their parents, "that's such a lie. What good could possibly happen?"

"I don't know," I said. "But it will be great."

At twelve Jeremy had been a willing participant in the move to Sage. He had thought it was wonderful, living on a ranch and having a stepfather who believed a boy should have a horse of his very own. When the marriage ended, I don't know which of us had been more disillusioned, Jeremy or me.

"Hey, maybe we can at least figure a way to keep Diablo," I said, as if his horse were the reason for his upset. "They have tables around Austin." Jeremy wasn't buying it for a second.

tried to sound even more optimistic—my pitch was nearing
he lunatic range. "Maybe I'll win the lottery. Maybe I'll sell a
ook."

One of Jeremy's eyebrows went up in a gesture that would
ave done Clark Gable proud. "I don't believe in fairy tales
nymore," he said.

Touché. "Well, I still believe in miracles."

"Give me a break."

"Break, hell," I said. "Why don't you give me one?"

"Like how?"

"Like picking up after yourself. You left a mess on the
ounter."

"You're such a perfectionist! Nothing is ever good enough
or you. I suppose you didn't notice that I took out the trash?"

Oh, hell, I hadn't. "No, I'm sorry. And thank you."

"You think you do everything by yourself, but there are lots
f people who help. Me, for one. And Matt, too."

Ah, yes. Matt. My very handsome but very ex husband.
Damn. I'd avoided saying his name, or hearing it, for almost
hree days, and I had thought it was working.

"No matter what Matt did," Jeremy went on, "it wasn't
nough for you. So now he's gone and I hope you're happy."

His words were causing a terrible pain somewhere near my
eart. Or maybe it had been there all along and I'd been ignor-
ng it. Either way, I couldn't just stand there and I couldn't
ight back because I knew that Jeremy was hurting every bit as
uch as I was. Worse, I knew that I had caused his pain. That's
hell of a realization for a mother to have to face. "I give up,
eremy," I said.

He stared at me for a moment, trying to take in that I wasn't
oing to fight with him. Maybe that's when he recognized that
he battle didn't matter because we'd already lost the war. He
hook his head sadly and carefully turned back to the com-
uter screen. All I had now was a view of the back of his head
nd his hair, which was a light brown, same as mine. It needed
utting.

He gave another small grunt, touched a key, and the screen sprang back to life.

Luckily, I have my own personal world where I can hide out anytime I want to. There are people there who do exactly what I say or else I delete them. I decided to spend the evening with them; I closed the door and headed for my computer.

THREE

PURPLE SAGE, or just Sage, as it's called by the old-timers, has always seemed to me a unique mixture of the pioneer West, the Old South, and a small town struggling to survive. Just in the three years since I'd moved to Purple Sage, tourists were beginning to discover it: there were deer and dove hunters in the fall and antique hunters in the spring and summer. It helped the economy some, but not enough. On the west, just outside the city limits, there were cheap tin buildings that housed farm-implement dealers. Half a mile away to the south, on tree-lined residential streets, were antebellum mansions. Like I said, a unique mixture.

Some things, however, were universal.

News is one of those things, and the Judge's death was big news. I suppose I shouldn't have been surprised. After all, the man had been a huge frog in a pond where everyone knew everyone else, and everyone else's business. Still, news bulletins on the local radio station? And then when I went to the grocery store about every third person stopped me to talk about the Judge.

"Imagine him up and dying like that—and right after you had that big fight with him, Jolie!"

I gave up after two aisles, bought some bread and milk, and went home.

Foolish me, I assumed the political rally that afternoon would be different, that people would be there to talk politics. Ha! I hardly had my car in one of the few remaining parking spaces before I overheard Jennifer, the town librarian, and another woman talking about the Judge. I rolled up my window and waited until they were inside before I got out of my car. Another figure was lurking near the bushes at the side of the building, but I wasn't worried about what he'd say.

"Hello, Captain," I called.

His loose white cotton pants and V-neck cotton T-shirt perfectly matched the bristle of white hair on his head.

He stared at me, a scowl crossing his deeply tanned face.

"Big turnout," I said.

He merely grunted and strode inside, holding his thin body rigidly erect.

The Captain, as he was known to one and all, didn't like to talk, and hadn't, so I'd been told, since his ship sank at Pearl Harbor. He stayed to himself and walked downtown when he needed to shop for food. Usually I only saw him in midflight.

I followed him inside where the candidates were scurrying into something that resembled a receiving line while the citizens poured in, ignoring the table where they were supposed to make out name tags. Most were in their "Sunday-go-to-meetin'" clothes.

Diane saw me from a distance, and winked. I waved back, and Trey, standing beside her, smiled.

"So what do you think?" Maria whispered as she sidled up to me, all the while watching people coming in.

"Big crowd," I responded.

"No, I meant about Trey's chances. You think he'll beat Bill Tieman?"

"I think he would have beaten Bill if the Judge hadn't died. This is going to throw everything off."

"Sympathy vote?"

"Something like that," I said. "But Trey looks better than Bill. Of course, almost anyone looks better than Bill."

We both turned for a better view of the candidates. Bill Tieman had made the unfortunate mistake of taking his coat off so that his shirt bulged open slightly over his beer belly. Coarse black hair poked out near his navel. Not a pretty sight. His face was ruddy with puffy jowls that made me think of a bullfrog.

Beside him Trey stood tall and slender. Trey was just over six feet with brown hair that was both thinning and graying; he wasn't a terribly attractive man physically, but he had charisma and a way of looking at people as if he were really pleased to see them. I'd even seen old ladies flirt with him. Diane joked that Trey was born, not only with a silver spoon in his mouth, but also with a magic amulet around his neck. I think he was just one of those deep-down nice guys.

Maria's voice was just this side of snide as she said, "Sometimes I think Trey and Diane are too slick. You know, a little too good to be true. They aren't royalty."

"They're the closest thing we've got," I said. "Besides, I've always thought Bill Tieman didn't have enough backbone or brains for the job of mayor. Come to think of it, he doesn't have enough for chief of police, either." Which was the position he currently occupied.

"Yeah, maybe you're right. Oh, hell! Captain is over there at the buffet table eating the hors d'oeuvres."

"So is everyone else," I said.

"He's just here freeloading."

"So is everyone else."

Maria shot me a disgusted look. "Excuse me," she said, hurrying away through the crowd.

I followed her more slowly and got a glass of her famous green punch. It wasn't bad. I checked out the buffet table, which held a little more than the usual cookies and punch. There were two huge rounds of cheese, one was actually a brie; the other was the ubiquitous cheddar. Baskets were filled with a variety of crackers and hunks of French bread. The only thing that really showed any flair was the centerpiece, a wicker tray with a mound of fruit interwoven with white paper flowers and small U.S. flags. It didn't appear that Maria had spent much time on the food, or else she'd been on a tight budget. Knowing what I did about committees in Purple Sage, I assumed money had been the problem.

I nibbled at a cracker topped with brie, and then wandered around a bit, frankly eavesdropping, hoping to hear something useful about the campaign. No such luck. Politics was not the topic of the day. I overheard bits and pieces of the story of the Judge's car jumping the curb at least twice, the heart-attack theory three times, and I heard my own name mentioned more than once. Of course people rapidly changed the subject when they saw I was right beside them.

I was about to call it quits and go home when a hand lightly touched my arm.

"Jolie?"

I'd recognize that voice anytime, anyplace, anyway. It belonged to my ex-husband, and I'll admit it created a ripple along my spine that was more pleasant than anything I'd felt in a while. Then I got nervous. I was too new at being divorced to know what to expect from Matt now that our marriage was officially over. I kept anticipating the kind of rude remarks that ex-husbands were supposed to make. Instead I got Matt, seemingly the same as ever. I didn't know if that was good or bad.

I met his glance squarely and smiled. "Matt, how are you?"

"Just fine," he said.

It was obvious. He must have been playing more tennis because his skin glowed with a healthy tan, and his hair had lightened from the sun. His dark eyes, striking in comparison to the light hair, glanced down at my name tag. He frowned slightly. "Jolie *Berenski?*"

"I thought I'd go back to that name, since that's the name everyone in Austin knows." I didn't know why I was defensive about it, but I was. "Less confusing."

His eyes traveled up to meet mine. "I always thought Jolie Wyatt had a nice ring to it."

"Fair," I said. "Matt Wyatt has a very nice ring, but your mother planned it that way."

I was trying to keep it light, and I thought I was doing pretty well.

When I had first met Matt, he had been the one who was instantly smitten. He had sent me flowers, and spent time finding new restaurants in Austin where he could take me. We ended most evenings sipping wine at some quiet spot with Matt listening to me talk. Then I had taken him home and he sat and listened to both Jeremy and me talk. I had to pull out of him that he was a graduate of Harvard, had a huge ranch outside Purple Sage, as well as business interests that took him often to Dallas, Houston, and Austin.

None of it had seemed important. What had caught me was simply Matt. And maybe I was swayed a little by his physical appearance; I've always been a sucker for a handsome face.

But things change, and marriage certainly changes things. Maybe I'd been single too long to have another person in the house besides Jeremy. Or maybe I couldn't live in someone else's house. Or maybe it was because you can't have real communication with a man who never talks. Matt would be gone for three or four days before I would realize that I didn't know why he was doing anything wrong, it's just that I didn't know what he was doing.

The main thing was, though, that I'd always thought our marriage could be fixed. It probably could have been, but I had blown my one big shot at it. And from then on, there had been no going back. I still couldn't think about that night without turning red and wanting to run and hide.

I realized I was staring. "So, how are you?" I asked. "Oh, wait, I already asked you that, didn't I?"

"And I'm still fine. How's Jeremy?"

"He's great. You know Jeremy." I cleared my throat. "Fine."

"He's got a baseball tournament this weekend, doesn't he? Is it here in town? I'd like to watch him play."

I had no idea if there was a tournament in town or otherwise. For all I knew Jeremy could have dropped out of baseball and taken up robbing banks as a new form of exercise and recreation. "I'm not sure where the tournament is, but I know he'd like you to be there," I said. "He hasn't mentioned anything to me. Jeremy's been busy lately, you know how uncommunicative he can be when he's busy."

Matt raised one eyebrow, maybe because he remembered that I used to level the same accusation at him. When he spoke, though, his voice was mild. "I'll give him a call this evening and find out."

"Good idea."

"I've been trying to get a hold of him for a couple of days. You must have been out a lot." There was a suspicion of a question in the statement; the kind of question that Matt would never ask. "No one's been home much."

"Exercise class, writers' group, meetings..." My voice trailed off. "Just life."

"I see. I didn't ask you how you're doing. You look a little tired. Are you okay?"

I wanted to deny that I was less than at my peak, but I didn't. If Matt said I looked tired, I probably did.

"I'm fine," I said. "Just fine. Really burning the midnight oil on my book." Now I wasn't just writing clichés, I was saying them out loud. "I guess I need a little rest."

"If things aren't going well—"

"No, they're fine."

"Well, if you do need anything..."

I flashed him what I hoped was a winsome smile, thinking that maybe the dimples would convince him. "Just a few more hours of beauty sleep."

Matt continued to watch me, waiting for something more. When I just stared back, he said, "Well, I guess I'd better get my hellos said so I can get out to the ranch to see Bart."

Bart was the foreman who ran the place. "Tell him I said hi."

"I'll do it." And with that he left me standing alone and feeling a sense of loss all over again. That was the major reason I couldn't stay in Purple Sage. I couldn't keep running into Matt every five minutes. Wounds don't heal that way, even self-inflicted ones.

The temptation to scurry home and hide for another month or so was strong, but I wasn't about to give in. I was a big girl and I was perfectly capable of making my own life without Matt Wyatt. I'd had a fascinating life before I'd met him. Well, maybe not fascinating, but at least I'd had a job and some friends and I'd spent plenty of time at Little League games. Once a month or so I'd gone to a movie....

I looked around for a friendly face to divert my attention and spotted Liz Street. If anyone could be a diversion it was Liz. Maria called her psychedelic and she was right. Liz's hair was like a wild mane of dark brown and gray that sort of frizzed its way to her waist. Sometimes she braided it and wrapped it around her head, at other times she hid it in a turban. That afternoon it was flowing free and she was wearing black workout clothes under something that resembled a fuchsia shroud. It was belted at the waist with a chartreuse scarf, and accessorized with clunky earrings and children's building blocks painted turquoise and strung on a chain around her neck.

Psychedelic.

She swept toward me, leaving a trail of staring Purple Sageites in her wake.

"Jolie! Isn't this dreary? I hate politics, but I felt I had to come to support Trey and Diane."

"Well, that's nice," I said. With Liz I usually felt left out of the conversation, even when it was only the two of us. "How have you been? We haven't seen you lately."

Liz was an on-again, off-again member of our writing group. She showed up about once a month and brought with her an obscure literary piece that made me glad she wasn't a regular attendee. It's tough critiquing something you don't understand.

"I've been busy," she said. "Albert is working on a book, and it requires my full-time editing."

Liz had once been the fashion editor for a New York newspaper and Albert was her husband. A genius, some said, although I couldn't venture an opinion because the man had never uttered a word in my presence.

"I'm sure your help is invaluable," I said.

"Well, it's cutting into my writing time. Lord, aren't men just too demanding?" Before I could think of anything to say in response she leaned toward me and lowered her voice. "What did you think of the Judge dying?"

I was surprised Liz had touched Earth long enough to hear about it. "I really don't think much of it at all," I said. "My main concern is for Diane and Trey and how it will affect his campaign."

Liz looked sly. "Now, Jolie, everyone's heard about your little contretemps with the man, you don't have to be so cautious. Not with me, at least. I certainly won't miss him." She leaned closer. "He was a hateful man, and I can't think of anyone who deserved to die more! I almost wish I believed in hell, so I'd know he was burning in eternal damnation."

My mouth dropped open; I'd never heard Liz express that strong an opinion on anything except some unpronounceable tribe that lived in a rain forest. Besides, the Judge had been universally loved, and Liz was a self-proclaimed lover of all mankind. I rearranged my face into some kind of more sociable expression and said. "Did you have a run-in with him, too?"

"It's over and done with."

From across the room I noticed Rhonda waving at me, her ponytail bobbing frantically. Liz saw her, too. "It seems you're needed," Liz said. "I won't keep you."

She sailed into the crowd before I could say anything more. I turned back to look for Rhonda and discovered she was already at my side.

"Hi," I said. "What's up?"

She was searching the crowd around us. "What?" For being in such a hurry to get to me, she was easily distracted.

"Are you here in some official capacity?" I asked.

"What? Oh, yeah, I'm supposed to be, but to hell with it. Morris will cover for me." Morris Pratt owned the Purple Sage *Tribune*.

Rhonda continued to shift around uneasily.

"What's the problem?" I asked.

"Shh, someone might be listening to us."

Since Purple Sage has more eavesdroppers per square inch than *Days of Our Lives,* I didn't doubt it, but I didn't see that it mattered since we hadn't said anything.

"Is something wrong?" I asked.

Rhonda grabbed me by the arm and practically dragged me into the corner. "Listen," she finally said. "We've got to have an emergency meeting. In half an hour."

"Meeting? What are you talking about?"

"We've got to meet. All of us. The writers. It's urgent."

"Can't you just tell me what's going on?"

"No! Not here; not now. Half an hour." She looked out over the room. "The museum. Don't be late!"

She whirled around, almost knocking a plate of food out of IdaMae Dorfman's hands.

"Rhonda Hargis, you watch where you're goin'!" IdaMae snapped.

"Sorry." And then she disappeared into the crowd.

IdaMae was still frowning as she looked at me. "I'd sure like to know what's come over that girl."

My thought exactly, but I didn't say it. "Oh, you know Rhonda. She's always in a hurry."

"Maybe. Lately though, she's been so crazy she's goin' to fizz up and explode." IdaMae leaned closer. "You think she's up to somethin'?"

"Like what?"

IdaMae looked coy. "I don't know, but it makes me wonder."

"I'm sure she's just busy," I said. "So how are you this evening?"

"I'd be a damn sight better if they served some decent food. But forget the food, what do you know about the Judge up and dyin' like that?"

The question of the hour, and I didn't have any kind of an answer.

FOUR

"WHAT IN THE WORLD is going on?" June asked as she got out of her car.

"No idea," I said. I was unlocking the door to the old jail. "Maybe Rhonda is having a breakdown; or maybe I mean a breakthrough. She's actually behaving like a human being. A crazy one, but that's an improvement."

June nodded as she followed me through the door. "You think it's because she's been waiting so long to hear from that editor?"

"Who knows?" It made as much sense as anything I could think of. "Waiting makes people a little nuts; at least it's been making Maria a little wilder than usual. And I'm ready to join the lunatic fringe."

"How long has your book been out this last time?"

"Two months, two weeks and, ah" —I did some quick counting— "four days."

June nodded. "The first one's always tough." A concise, no-nonsense response; I always wanted more from June. I wanted her to help us find an editor or an agent, and it sometimes pissed me off that she didn't. I guess she figured that since she made it on her own, we could too, which was certainly her right. It just wasn't much consolation.

"At least you're not behaving like Rhonda," she said.

She obviously hadn't been spending much time with me. "Should we get the table out?" I asked.

"No, let's just use the chairs. I don't think we'll be here that long. At least I hope not."

Maria and Diane came in together.

"What is the deal with Rhonda?" Maria asked. "I'm supposed to be supervising my crew at the Community Center, so this had better be good."

"And I should be there, too," Diane said, although she almost sounded relieved to be away from the politics for a while. "Rhonda isn't here yet?" she asked as she sat down.

"Not yet," June said.

"I'm going to make some popcorn," Maria said, but she'd only taken a step or two toward the kitchen when Rhonda blew in the door.

"Thank God you're all here! We have to talk. Wait a minute, where's Liz?"

"Did you ask her to come?" Diane asked.

Rhonda nodded as she perched on the edge of a chair. "I told her, but she's so flighty she probably won't show. Oh, hell, this is important, too."

June reached over and patted Rhonda none too delicately on the arm. "If it's all that important it will bear repeating when she gets here. I think you'd better tell us what's going on."

"And make it quick," Maria said as she sat down.

"All right." Rhonda took a big breath and eyed each one of us before she spoke. "I just found out some news that affects all of us." She paused before she said, "The Judge was murdered."

No one spoke. I had the uneasy feeling that there was more.

Rhonda leaned forward, then looked directly at me. "It was your murder, Jolie."

"My murder? What are you talking about?"

"Your murder. Just like the one in your book."

Now everyone was staring at me. "Nicotine poisoning?" I asked.

"Exactly. And he got the poison through a wound on the back of his neck; a pinprick just like you described in *Murder for Fun and Profit*." She leaned toward me. "And right after you had that big fight with the Judge last week, too!"

My stomach started a slow churn and my fingertips began to numb. "But that's crazy! Who would use my murder? No one knew about it . . ."

"But us," Rhonda said.

There was a nervous silence.

"Are you positive about this?" Diane asked.

"Yes."

"How do you know?" she pushed. "Who told you?"

"I found out from the police report, that's how I know. Christ, Diane, I'm a reporter; it's my job to find things out."

"Were they sure?"

"Diane, it was on the report; they must be sure."

June frowned. "They told you all this, Rhonda?"

"Well, not exactly. They always hide things when it comes to the big stories, so I just took the initiative and sneaked into Andy's office and read the report. Not the whole thing, because someone came in and I had to put it away." She became slightly defensive. "It's not like I'm going to write a story until they corroborate what I read. And please, don't any of you say a word or they'll start locking things up all the time. Promise me."

We all mumbled words that sounded like promises, although personally I didn't give a damn how Rhonda got her information.

"This is ridiculous," June said. "None of us killed the Judge."

"Exactly," Maria agreed. "So obviously someone else read your manuscript, Jolie."

I thought about it for a long time, wishing I could give us all an easy out. "No one," I said.

"But someone must have," Maria said. "Think. Who?"

"I told you, no one."

"What about Matt? He must have read it."

"No, he didn't."

"You were still married when you worked out the murder. You must have told him about it, didn't you?"

"No."

"But your manuscript was in the house," Maria pushed. "He could have seen it."

"Never! That was during the time when things weren't going well, and I wasn't telling him anything," I said. "Besides, my ex-husband is not a murderer."

Rhonda was tapping her foot. "Okay, if Matt didn't read your book, then who did? What about Jeremy?"

"Jeremy? You're talking about my son, Rhonda! Jeremy is a wonderful kid and he doesn't kill people!"

"Of course not," Diane soothed. She shot an annoyed look at Rhonda. "Relax, Jolie. Rhonda just meant that Jeremy could have read it and told someone else."

"Oh, right," Rhonda said. "I didn't mean that Jeremy murdered the Judge, but someone saw this whole perfect plan that you had worked out and then followed it to a tee."

"Bullshit!" I snapped. "Someone got a very dangerous pesticide and distilled it into a substance that can kill. It isn't like it was an original idea. Bow hunters use that poison, remember? That's how we came up with it. We've got a few bow hunters in town and any one of them knows about that method."

"Except," Rhonda said, "it wasn't just the same poison. I mean, the wound was on the back of the neck, there was this little pinhole—sound familiar? Now, doesn't it seem a little odd to you? A little coincidental?"

"Maybe."

It did seem too coincidental, and their badgering was making me feel like a Nazi being interrogated for war crimes. Worse, having written the murder, I knew exactly what effects the nicotine would have on the victim. The Judge. God, what he had gone through. It was not a pleasant death; just thinking about it was making me feel those same symptoms myself. My stomach was starting to cramp and my fingers felt like they were going numb. Even my brain felt heavy.

"There has to be another explanation," I said, hearing the tiny slur to my words.

"Are you okay?" Diane asked.

My head rolled as I nodded. "Fine."

"Let me get you some water." She jumped up and Rhonda took the moment to lean even closer to me.

"Somebody knew about your manuscript, Jolie. Now think, who could it be?"

"That's enough, Rhonda," June said.

Diane handed me water and I sipped it carefully. The slick coolness of the glass felt good in my hands and I raised it and pressed it against my forehead. "I'm okay," I said. "I just keep imagining what the Judge was feeling. It must have been so awful." I shook my head.

"A Method writer," Maria said.

"Well, I think you need to forget about it entirely," June said. "The Judge's death has nothing to do with you."

"The murder is in her book!" Rhonda corrected.

"That is ridiculous," June said. "If some deranged person is intent on killing another human being they'll find some means; they certainly don't need any help. Just forget that kind of thinking. It isn't accurate and it's certainly not productive."

"I didn't mean it was Jolie's fault," Rhonda said. "I mean, all of us in this room..."

"We know what you mean," June said. "We are the obvious choices."

Maria sat up straighter. "There have to be others. What do the police think?"

"That's it! The police!" Rhonda said. "Jolie, it could have been your friend Andy!"

I had started to say that he was hardly a friend when I realized what she was saying. It must have hit us all at the same time because I heard a small sigh of relief and a tiny giggle. There was someone outside this room who knew all about my murder.

Andy Sawyer, assistant chief of police, knew about my book because I'd told him. I'd needed to know police procedure on a murder case like I'd concocted, and Andy had obliged.

"Jolie, do you think he'd do something like that?" Rhonda asked me.

"How should I know? I hardly know the man, we've only had coffee twice, and that was only because I needed more information." Actually, I'd thought at the time that Andy was interested in me. Attracted even, but I was in the midst of a divorce in Purple Sage, Texas. Not a good time or place to start investigating a new relationship.

"Andy Sawyer," Rhonda said softly. "My, my..."

"You can't really think that Andy killed the Judge...." I said. Everyone turned to look at me. "You do?"

Rhonda was nodding. "It's a possibility.

And we'd all have preferred it to be him instead of one of us.

"There's someone else, too," Maria said. "Liz read your manuscript."

"And she didn't show up tonight," Rhonda added.

Diane shook her head. "Liz lives in another world; she probably just started talking to someone and forgot all about Rhonda asking her to come. For that matter, she's probably forgotten all about Jolie's murder, too."

"Not my murder," I said, finally realizing that I'd been taking the rap for something that wasn't only my fault. "The method we all worked out. Together."

There was a long silence.

Finally Maria stood up. "Look, if that's everything, I need to get back."

"Oh, hell, I do, too," Diane said. "Unless there's something you think we ought to do?" She looked at June, our unofficial den mother, who was deep in thought.

"I don't think we have to do anything," June said slowly. "Rhonda, is Andy handling the investigation?"

"Yeah, he's the one."

"What are you thinking?" I asked June.

She shook her head firmly. "Nothing, nothing important. I think we should forget about this; the whole thing is probably solved and done by now, anyway."

"I don't think so," Rhonda said. "If the killer followed Jolie's plan all the way, there might not be any evidence."

My plan. My method. Jolie's murder.

"Listen, if anyone hears anything, call me, okay?" Diane said as she put her chair back under the antique oak table.

"Me, too," Maria said. "Rhonda, you'll keep in touch, won't you?"

Rhonda stood up. "Sure."

"Okay, then. 'Night," Maria said as she left.

Diane went out with her, calling a good-bye over her shoulder.

I stood up slowly and watched while June and Rhonda put away the last of the chairs. "I still can't believe it."

June came over and slipped an arm around my shoulder. "Maybe this has nothing to do with you. Or any of us, for that matter. Why don't you go home and have a good stiff drink and get some sleep? I think that's the best thing for you. I'll follow you home to make sure you get there."

"No thanks. I can make it." It was only a four-minute drive if both stoplights were red.

I waved one last time as I pulled out of the parking lot, and then headed south toward the square. June turned in the other direction.

It was a dark and quiet night without any traffic, so I spotted the car that was following me as soon as I turned off the square. Damn, there had been nothing on my calendar to warn me that it was going to be one of those nights.

FIVE

I THOUGHT ABOUT trying to lose my tail, but I didn't want to risk getting a ticket. You see, despite a murder, Purple Sage wasn't rampant with crime, so I knew who was behind me. A cop. Probably Andy Sawyer, our assistant chief of police, and thanks to Rhonda's underhanded methods of gathering information it was going to be pretty tough for me to look surprised when Andy told me that the Judge had been murdered.

The lights stayed with me when I turned on Winchester and then as I drove the four blocks to Pine. I pulled into my driveway slowly, and waited with the motor still running. The headlights behind me slowed, then the car slid past. Sure enough, it was a police car.

My front door was unlocked, and inside I found the kind of quiet that means no one is home. I called Jeremy's name, but got no response. I opened his door, just as a final check, and found only the blank computer screen staring back at me.

With a sigh I headed for the kitchen. Jeremy had left a note: *Mom, I went out. —J.*

So, what do you do when you know the cops are coming? Act natural? When the doorbell rang less than five minutes later, I sauntered to the door casually like I didn't know who was there. I wasn't fooled.

Andy was in his khaki uniform, a Stetson on his head, his face impassive. His cheekbones, always prominent, stood out even more than usual in the yellow glare of the porch light. Andy's eyes were dark and flat, without their usual animation.

"Good evening, Jolie. May I come in and talk with you?"

Like I was going to say no. "Sure."

He followed me back to the living room, and, at my gesture, sat on the couch.

I stood. "Would you like something to drink? I've got some soft drinks."

"No, thanks."

I couldn't seem to find my balance. I felt guilty, as if I were somehow responsible for the Judge's murder, and for Rhonda's snooping.

Finally Andy glanced significantly at a chair; I took the hint and perched on the edge of it.

He removed his hat and placed it on the couch beside him. There was just the tiniest crease where it had rested against his forehead. He ran his fingers through his dark hair to put it in place.

"Jolie, this is official business, but I imagine you already figured that out. I'm sorry if it makes you uncomfortable. It isn't comfortable for me, either. I want you to know that right off."

I nodded. Nodding was good, it didn't require any admission of guilt.

He took a long breath of air. "We now suspect that the Judge's death was murder, and I need to talk to a number of people about it. You're one of them."

I nodded again, wondering if I seemed wise or like a mute.

He looked me over. "I understand you had a run-in with the Judge last week. Is that so?"

I finally got out a word. "Yes."

"You up to telling me about it?"

I was still nodding, mesmerized, following his eyes. "Sure."

"Go right ahead."

"Oh," I said, swallowing. "Ah, well, where do I start? You probably already know the story. You must have or you wouldn't be asking about it." Like this was a Mensa test or something.

"I have, but I need to get to the whole truth."

Right. And I was going to tell the truth and those others had lied. Good tactic, but it didn't relax me any. "It happened at the courthouse, last Friday," I said. "It was the first time I'd ever had any dealings with the Judge, except to say hello at a reception or something."

He referred to a notebook. "You went up to the county clerk's office."

"That's right. To file the campaign spending report for Trey. Trey Atwood." Andy had begun to take notes, and I became more precise. "One of my legal duties as Trey's campaign manager was to file that report. I didn't have to do it then, I still had a couple of weeks, but we had completed our expenditures, so I thought I might as well get it out of the way. I've got a lot of other things to think about right now."

"I know about campaign spending." He had once run for sheriff. "Just tell me exactly what happened."

"Well, I went up to the office and Cynthia was there. You know, Jim Moody's secretary." Jim Moody was the county clerk. "Cynthia and I started chatting, and I had the report on the counter in front of me. That's when the Judge came in. He asked for Jim, and when Cynthia said he was out, the Judge turned around and looked at me. I think that's the first time he'd noticed me.

"Then he had spotted the report, and his expression had turned sly as he recognized what it was. He'd let out a cackle of absolute glee. 'Well, now lookee here. This looks like something I'd have to have.' Without another word he had snatched up those three pages, pages that represented hours of work on my part, and had folded them in half, like they belonged to him. I was totally outraged, and when he saw my face, he'd put the report behind his back, saying, 'Come on, girlee!' Daring me, as if it were some kind of kids' game.

"Without thinking, I'd reached out toward him, but that was a mistake. The Judge had jerked away and somehow tripped, his frail old body hitting the floor. When I'd tried to help him up, he'd howled like a demented banshee. 'Don't touch me! Get away! No more, no more.'

"Practically everyone in the courthouse had responded, dropping whatever they were doing to rush to his aid. And there I'd stood, mute and frozen, while he continued to point an accusatory finger at me.

"I couldn't believe it, Andy," I said, after I'd told him the story. "First he took the report, and then when he fell, he acted like I'd attacked him. It was a nightmare!"

"I heard you were pretty fired up when you left the court-house, is that true?"

I'd thought very seriously about letting the air out of the Judge's tires, or papering his house or something equally adult, but I didn't think it was necessary to mention that part to Andy. "I filed a formal complaint with Jim Moody," I said.

"How important was that spending report to Trey's campaign?" Andy asked.

"Not very," I said. "We didn't spend any more money than Bill Tieman did, at least, not much, so I wasn't worried about him making it public." I took a breath. "Look, Andy, it was over and done with a week ago."

"You still got pretty hot when you told me about it just now."

"Wouldn't you?"

Andy didn't answer the question. Instead he asked one. "Did you talk to the Judge after that?"

I shook my head firmly. "No. Never."

"Everybody at the courthouse knew about it?"

"Of course they did! I'm surprised it wasn't on the front page of the *Trib*. The Judge probably told everyone." I stopped talking; the Judge had not been a gossip, and my anger at the old man was showing, again. Somehow I'd always thought I'd do better if I were ever interviewed by the police. "Look, Andy, I didn't like the man, but so what? If you went around town asking I'm sure you'd find at least a few other people who didn't like him; there has to be one or two."

"You'd think so, wouldn't you? Even with the Patron Saint of Purple Sage..." He let the sentence trail off, then said, "So, how'd you find out the Judge had been murdered?"

I almost jumped. "Why do you think I knew?"

"Because you weren't a bit surprised when you saw me at the front door. You were expecting me, and you knew why I'd come, too."

"Someone told me."

"At the political reception? You didn't stay long."

"No, I didn't."

"Had to meet with your writers' group."

"Yes." The man knew everything.

"Have you heard *how* the Judge was murdered?"

I glanced at him, looking for a hint as to how to respond. I got nothing, so I shifted my attention to the coffee table, the lamp, and finally, Andy's hat. "I heard a rumor."

"And what rumor was that?"

"I heard that it was poison; nicotine. Pest Out."

"And how did you hear how he got the poison?"

I waited. "Pinprick," I finally said.

"Your informant's done real well, so far. Anybody I know?"

"Uh, I don't think I have to tell you that."

"I've got a pretty good idea." He laid his pencil and pad beside his hat. "Jolie, we both know that you created a murder just like this one. I have to tell you that when I first read that part of your manuscript, I was impressed. Especially how carefully you worked it out. That's one clever mind you've got."

I'd passed the Mensa test—which didn't mean I got a 'Get Out of Jail Free' card. "Thanks."

Andy was still watching my face with his very serious *this is business* look. "You knew exactly what official steps would be taken after the murder was committed. You knew where we'd find fingerprints, and where we couldn't."

There was no use denying it. "So?"

"So, now, I've got to find out where you were when the Judge was killed." He picked up his pencil and pad.

"Wait a minute, Andy," I said. "This is ridiculous. First of all, I don't kill people. Secondly, if I had wanted to kill someone, do you think I'd have shown you my manuscript? That's just plain stupid."

"Or very smart."

I made a sound of disgust. "How do you figure?"

"Because in a small town someone was bound to tell me about your book."

We were back to my book, my method for murder, my fault.

"Jolie?"

"I'm sorry; what did you say?"

"Why don't you tell me where you were from five to six-thirty last Tuesday."

"I was here."

"Alone?"

"Jeremy was here."

"I thought he was on a Pony League team," Andy said. "They usually practice until six or six-thirty."

"Oh." I thought about it. "I didn't actually talk to him. I heard him in his room on the computer when I left. After that I went to the bakery on my way to my writers' meeting. I was at the bakery when I heard the siren."

"I see." He waited for me to say something more, but there was nothing to add. Basically I had been alone when the Judge was killed, so I didn't have an alibi. If only someone had told me they were going to kill the Judge with my murder method, I would have arranged something better.

Andy put his notepad away and reached for his hat. "That's about all for now, I guess. Thanks for your time." He gave me one of those all-purpose nods, then started for the door. I followed.

"Wait a minute, Andy. What about the cases the Judge presided over? There could be dozens of criminals who wanted to kill him."

"Yes, ma'am, we're already checking," he said as he stopped at the front door. "But I'm not holding out much hope for that. The Judge left the bench over a year ago, and I usually hear if some hard-core type makes parole. Besides, he was soft on most people. Those he wasn't soft on are in jail, so none of them could have read your book."

I thought about saying something smart, but the front door opened. Jeremy came in, saw Andy, and grunted a hello.

"Jeremy," Andy said formally, then turned to me with a brisk "Good night, Jolie" as he left.

I closed the door behind him.

"I don't like that guy," Jeremy said as he went past me.

"He's only doing his job."

Jeremy stopped halfway down the hall to turn around and stare at me. "What do you mean, his job?"

I realized that Jeremy's hostility toward Andy was some primitive male territorial thing. Jeremy saw Andy as Matt's rival. He'd had no idea that Andy had been there for official reasons.

"I guess you haven't heard about the Judge," I said.

"He died of a heart attack."

The story of the Judge's murder was going to be public knowledge soon; there was no point in trying to hide it from Jeremy. "I think we'd better talk," I said, starting to slide an arm around his shoulders.

He twitched away. "Did you do something to the car? Have a wreck?" With his sixteenth birthday only a few months away, Jeremy was becoming possessive about my car.

"No, it's not the car. Let's go sit down."

Jeremy's expression changed from belligerence to wariness. "What's going on?"

I waited until we were seated in the kitchen, our standard talking place.

"Well?" he said, still wary.

"It's like this," I began. "It seems that the Judge didn't die of natural causes. The police think he was murdered. Andy is investigating the murder, and he needed to ask me some questions."

"Because of your fight with the Judge?"

"It wasn't a fight, but, yes, partly because I'd been angry with the Judge."

Jeremy shrugged it off and started to rise. "So, big deal. That's not much."

"There's more."

He sat, a touch of worry crossing his face. "Like what?"

I leaned forward. "Jeremy, the Judge was murdered the same way that I described in my book. The exact same way."

Silence, long and protracted. I saw the child in Jeremy, the little boy I adored and tried so hard to make happy.

"But that's crazy," he said, "you didn't kill him."

"Of course not. And this police thing is probably just routine, so please don't worry, okay? Still, I guess I do feel a little guilty; I mean, if I hadn't come up with such a good idea for a murder..."

Jeremy stood up.

"Where are you going?" I asked.

"I'm going to call Matt."

"Wait a minute. It's none of his business."

"He'll know what to do," Jeremy said, starting for the phone.

"Forget it." I stood, too. "This isn't a broken bicycle or a flat tire!"

"He can still fix it."

"Just because he's got hair on his chest you think he knows how to fix everything."

Jeremy threw me a look of disgust. Damn male bonding, anyway.

"Look, Mom, Matt knows everyone in town. He's got connections; he can help. Why don't you let him?"

"This is a police investigation, and as a citizen it's my duty to help as much as I can." It sounded weak even to me.

"Right, Mom." He started for his room and I let him go. If he wanted to call Matt, that was his prerogative. Maybe it would do him some good; maybe he needed some male reassurance. He certainly wasn't listening to me.

SIX

THE NEXT MORNING I was whipping through my "To Do" list like some kind of time-management freak. Beside the computer sat four neatly printed envelopes addressed to advertising agencies in Austin. Inside each envelope was a copy of my resume and a letter asking if I might make an appointment to discuss any job openings. Begging letters.

I made a thick black line through the *send resumes* entry on my list, and started looking for something else that I could accomplish quickly. The items carried over from the previous day, or week, were highlighted in hot pink, and they demanded attention. The first said *rewrite chapter twenty-four and twenty-five.* Fat chance. I wasn't up to syntax problems, not when I felt like I was operating on a borrowed substandard brain.

Next: *write a letter to Mom.*

In all fairness to me, I'd written my mother several letters; I simply hadn't had the courage to mail any of them. My mother, happily married for twenty-seven years before my dad died, didn't believe in divorce. Sometimes I felt like she didn't believe in me very much, either. Especially after Jeremy's father skipped out on us when Jeremy was just a baby. That event had affected all of us; it was probably why Jeremy had jumped so readily at the chance to have Matt for a father.

I pulled up the file that contained the last abortive missive addressed to my mother. It was the "let's lay it all on the line" version.

Dear Mom,

I know you're not happy with me, and I'm sorry, but there are times when you just have to accept who I am and the things that I do. I know you think I made a big mistake, so does Jeremy, but it's my life. Mom, you have to understand that things changed. Matt's business became more important than me. He was gone too often, and I felt abandoned in a small town where I didn't even have an identity. I was just Mrs. Matt Wyatt, except that Matt was never around....

That was as far as I had gotten.

Rereading it from my mother's point of view, it made me sound shallow and whiny. I didn't seem able to justify my actions, which was an absurd thing for a thirty-eight-year-old woman to be doing, anyway.

Actually I didn't want to tell her the whole story; swallowing my pride was not something I did well with my mother. How could I admit that while I'd said I wanted a divorce, I hadn't really meant it? It had been more of a plea for help than anything else, and if Matt had said even one word to dissuade me, I'd still have been married. Unfortunately, Matt hadn't. He'd merely stared at me. Finally, he'd nodded solemnly. "Whatever you want, Jolie."

Being a compulsive idiot, I'd turned and fled, packing that very night. I'd justified it to myself by saying that it was best. After all, I'd felt that my identity was slipping away in Purple Sage. I was no longer Jolie Berenski, award-winning advertising writer and humorous woman-about-town who was the sole support of her delightful young son. I had become Jolie Wyatt. Matt Wyatt's wife. A woman who lived in her husband's ancestral home, and as a hobby wrote mysteries. But she wasn't a real writer, not to the people of Purple Sage, because she wasn't published.

And I refused to wind up with something disgusting like that on my tombstone.

There were other reasons, too, but I didn't really understand them myself, and I knew I might not ever be able to explain them to my mother, but as soon as Jeremy finished the school year, and maybe sooner, I'd make the break complete. Some people just aren't meant to be married and apparently I was one of them. I could close off the memories of the past few years and never torture myself with them again.

I deleted the letter and retrieved chapter twenty-four, then spent some time going over it, carefully trying to find the elusive flaws that kept it from working. It read like something from a third-grade primer.

Eventually, though, I began slipping into the world that I'd created. I lost myself completely, forgetting to worry about my problems and even that they existed.

The doorbell rang.

I stored the file, turned off the computer, and went to answer the door, feeling as if I'd been wrenched away from the only bright spot in my life. My annoyance grew when I saw who was there. On the porch stood Andy Sawyer, his solemn expression firmly in place.

"I have a few more questions, if you have time, Jolie," he said as I opened the door.

I glanced at his police car parked in my driveway. "The neighbors are going to start talking," I said.

"It's official business."

I led him back to the sunroom, where I'd been writing. Jeremy called it *my room,* and it was my favorite, with white wicker furniture and hanging baskets of plants. The back wall was solid with jalousie windows that opened onto the patio.

For some perverse reason I wanted to make Andy uncomfortable, so I took the love seat and left him the small wicker rocker.

"What did you want to know?" I asked as I sat.

Andy looked at the rocker, sat, and tried to get comfortable. It wasn't possible with his over-six-foot body.

"I made an assumption last night," Andy said, still shifting awkwardly. "I need to know exactly who in your writers' group helped you concoct that murder."

His no-nonsense request annoyed me even further.

"I don't remember."

"Could you think about it?"

I took my time. "June was there that night. So were Maria, Rhonda, and Diane. I can't remember if Liz Street was there or not. Probably."

"Whose idea was it to use Pest Out?"

"It was a brainstorming session, Andy, so everyone was throwing out suggestions; I don't remember who came up with the original idea."

It suddenly struck me that I'd written a scene for my book that was just like the one we were playing out. The tall, dark, and handsome detective had come to the house of the heroine hoping to get some additional information. Only in my book there had been some fireworks; some sexual tension.

I looked over at Andy. He might be tall, dark, and handsome, but at the moment he reminded me of a stone statue, and exuded about the same amount of charm. As for the tension in the room, it had nothing to do with sex.

"Who helped you perfect the method for killing?" Andy persisted.

"Why don't I get my notes from that night and see if they jog my memory?" I was stalling, purposely trying not to think about the answer to his question. The women in my writers' group were friends, and incriminating them didn't make me feel any better about my own position.

"Good idea," Andy said. "If you have any notes about what you did on Tuesday, you might bring those along, too."

So, he did still have his sense of humor. "Would you like something to drink while I'm up?"

"No, thanks."

Andy had refused my offer of something to drink on both of his official visits. I wondered if he thought acceptance might in some way compromise him, or if he thought I'd put poison in his glass. Perversely, that made me feel a little better.

I went to the corner and there, next to my computer, were two notebooks. Green for ideas on future projects, yellow for notes and the outline of *Murder for Fun and Profit*. I picked up the yellow notebook. "This is it." I went and sat back down.

Andy leaned closer, saw the title, and raised an eyebrow. I flipped open the notebook. The title had seemed funny just a few weeks ago. I scanned pages until I came across my carefully taken notes. My writers' group had discussed the method for murder thoroughly. Someone had told me you had to boil the liquid pesticide in a glass container until the volume was half the original portion. It made the nicotine more potent. Someone else had said that even touching the distilled liquid would make you violently ill. I hadn't written any names, and at first none came to me.

"I don't think this is going to be much help," I said, staring down at the carefully filled page.

"Who told you about boiling the poison?"

I heard June's voice explaining it. I shrugged to make my answer seem less important. "June Ingram."

Andy took some notes of his own. "Who came up with the idea of putting it on a pin?"

I hesitated and Andy looked up at me, waiting patiently.

"Diane suggested it," I said. "Her dad used to bow hunt." I wondered if Judas had felt like I did. "Everyone who knew about bow hunting helped," I said. "We didn't intend for anyone to carry out the murder."

Andy ignored the editorial comment and went on. "And after this brainstorming session you went out and bought some of the poison."

The man was doing a very thorough job. "Yes, I did. I had to make sure I knew what I was talking about."

"You must have had some left over. Where's the rest of that can?"

"In the garage. I bought it right after Jeremy and I rented this house."

"Mind if we go look at it?"

"Sure, I mean, no, I don't mind."

He followed me out the back way to the garage. It was hot in there, a steamy kind of heat that made little beads of sweat pop out on my upper lip. I turned on the overhead light and opened the big door. Along the back wall were shelves still filled with boxes from the move away from Matt's sprawling ranch house. On the end of one of them were the things I'd used since our arrival: Yard Guard, fertilizer, pruning shears, gardening gloves, and a few rags. All the paraphernalia I seem to collect for keeping the yard well tended.

"It's here," I said, moving some things.

Andy stepped in close. "Let me." He moved cans and bottles aside. It wasn't there. "It seems to be missing. Where else could it be?" he asked.

I shook my head, suddenly worried. "I don't know. I put it here when I was finished with it. I thought I might need it for the yard."

"Could you have forgotten and left it in the kitchen? Under the sink, maybe?"

"No, I put it on a shelf." I tried to remember. "I'm very careful about things like that. When Jeremy was little he was into everything, and I forget that he's grown up. I'm positive I put it here."

"Could it be in one of the boxes?"

"No. They're still sealed from the move."

He began to walk around my car and I followed. In one corner was a plastic sack of trash. Beside it on the cement floor was the can of Pest Out. "This it?" Andy asked, pointing.

"I guess so." My mouth went dry. It's from the heat, I told myself, just the heat.

"You have a rag or something?"

I got one and handed it to him. He pulled a large plastic bag from his pocket and carefully put the can in it. "We'll be dusting this for fingerprints."

"Wait a minute, Andy, you can't really think that this is the same can that was used . . . I mean, other people must have bought this stuff. It's common, isn't it?" I needed some reassurance, and I needed it fast.

I didn't get any. "You'd think so, wouldn't you? But no one in town remembers selling any since you bought yours. Seems it's not the season yet."

"Oh."

Without a word Andy helped me close the garage door, and then slowly followed me back to the house. Everything felt wrong. The can had been moved. I hadn't put it on the floor, and Jeremy certainly didn't need it. I couldn't make sense of it and that worried me.

"By the way, how much of this did you use?" Andy asked as I held the door for him.

I knew the answer to that, but what if more was missing? "Half a cup," I said, almost forcefully. "I put it in a glass measuring cup and boiled it in the microwave. Afterward I broke the cup and threw it away." And I'd cleaned the microwave and practically scoured the entire kitchen with disinfectant, just to be safe.

Andy sat on the couch this time and laid the plastic bag on the floor.

"Andy, why am I feeling so anxious about all this?"

"I don't know." His wide shoulders shifted, but his tone remained noncommittal. "Should you be?"

"Of course not. I didn't kill the Judge. There must be dozens of cans of this stuff in other people's garages."

"Might be," he said.

I stood up. "And what about someone who might have bought it out of town? People shop outside of Purple Sage. They could have bought it anywhere."

"Could have," he said. "Is it okay if I look at this notebook?"

"Go ahead." The air in the house was suddenly cloying, making breathing difficult. I went and turned on the air conditioner.

"You always take such nice neat notes?" Andy asked.

"I try."

"Very precise."

I didn't know whether to thank him for the compliment or feel insulted. I didn't say anything.

Andy flipped through several more pages. "Is this how you write a book? With all this outlining?"

I sucked in air before I tried to talk. "It's how I write a book. Diane just writes an opening scene and then wings it."

"She any good?"

"Very good." If I couldn't protect her from Andy's questions, I could at least defend her writing. "When she gets pub-

lished she's going to be right up there with Ludlum and
Clancy."

Andy nodded, read a few more pages, then set the notebook
aside. "You're looking for a job in Austin, aren't you?"

"Yes."

"Not planning on moving anytime soon, are you?"

I'd read enough mysteries to know what was coming. "No.
I haven't found a job yet."

"I wouldn't advise getting in any hurry, if I were you." His
voice was almost conversational.

"I might have some interviews next week...."

"Let me know if you do. I may need to talk with you some
more," he said as he stood up. "Oh, by the way, I like your
perfume. What is it?"

"My perfume?" Now what the hell did that have to do with
anything? "It's My Sin."

"You wear it all the time?"

"No. Just in the winter. I haven't switched to my summer
perfume yet."

"And what is that?"

This wasn't idle interest—Andy had never mentioned perfume before. "Why are you asking? Wait, let me guess, there
was perfume on the Judge. Or in his house or car." Andy didn't
move an inch, nor did his expression change. I had it. "There
was perfume on the straight pin."

His right eye twitched. I'd guessed it.

"You didn't tell me what your summer perfume was," he
said mildly.

"Muguet. Lily of the valley," I said. "What perfume did you
find?"

"Mind if I look in your bathroom?"

For just a moment I was struck by his gall, and I had the
sudden urge to tell him to get a search warrant. Or just get the
hell out of my house. Then I realized that if I said no, Andy
would get a search warrant. Within a day or so half the town
would know about it. I tried to sound gracious. "Go ahead and
look. This way."

He followed me into the bedroom, and through it to the master bath. I pointed at the counter. "Enjoy yourself."

I left the room so he could poke around in private. I hoped it made him uncomfortable—it certainly made me uncomfortable.

From the hall I could hear cabinet doors and drawers being opened and closed. I wouldn't have any secrets from him now. He'd find every medicine I'd ever taken, my makeup, the creams and lotions I used to hold age at bay. He'd find the depilatory I used for my bikini line, and the false eyelashes left over from a Halloween party. And there was a box of tampons, not to mention a few of those handy birth-control sponges.

I waited for him, my arms folded across my chest, trying to look nonchalant.

Andy reappeared. "Mind if I look around your bedroom?"

I decided to bite the bullet and get it over with. "Go ahead." I did my best to make the two words sound rude.

He did a pretty thorough job of it. He looked under my clothes in the dresser drawers, and I thanked the gods that I hadn't unpacked any of my sexy lingerie.

Andy didn't comment on anything he saw, but moved over to the nightstand and took everything out of the drawer. I couldn't watch anymore. I went to the kitchen and waited.

He took his sweet time, and when he appeared his face was as noncommittal as before. "Thank you."

"You obviously didn't find the perfume you were looking for."

"Nope."

"What was it?"

He paused for a moment, then asked, "Who do you know that wears Youth Dew by Estée Lauder? Or a clone of it?"

I shook my head. "No one. It's an old perfume."

"What do you mean? Only old people wear it?"

"No. It's just been around a long time. It's pretty distinctive and I'd recognize it if anyone had it on."

"Well, if you do smell it on anyone, let me know." He reached for the can of poison. "I appreciate your time, Jolie. Don't bother to see me out."

I stopped him. "Andy, you know you're really pushing this, don't you?"

The light reflected off his dark eyes, glinting with what might have been humor. "And I do it very well."

WHEN JEREMY GOT HOME from school I followed him to his room. "Jeremy, I need to ask you about something."

"Whatever it is, I didn't do it," he said, tossing his knapsack on the bed and pulling the chair out from under his computer table. The computer had been his Christmas present from Matt.

"Look, this is serious," I said. "When you put that sack of trash out in the garage, do you remember seeing a can of insecticide?"

"Yeah, I saw it." He turned to face me.

"Where? Where did you see it?"

"On the floor, in the corner. Why? What's the big deal?"

I plopped down on the bed. "Oh, it's probably nothing, but it just seems weird. Andy was here, and wanted to see it, and then I couldn't find it," I said.

"What do you mean you couldn't find it? You just said it was by the trash."

"But I left it on a shelf," I said. "At least, I think I did. Damn, I'm just not positive anymore."

For a moment he was bewildered, then he became still, his voice turning flat and soft. "That's the stuff you used for the murder in your book, isn't it? The stuff that killed the Judge."

"That's the stuff," I said.

"Mom, I think…" His voice trailed off and he continued to stare at me.

"What?"

For a moment he didn't move. I waited. Finally he shrugged. "Oh, nothing."

"Something. You were going to say something."

He shrugged again. "I was just going to say that I think I'm going to invite Matt to the game."

"That's a good idea," I said. He began to fidget and I went on. "Listen, I know how you're feeling, because I'm feeling that way, too. A little crazy. It almost seems surreal—"

"Mom, look, I have a bunch of homework, okay?"

Homework, what a marvelous device for getting rid of a mother you weren't ready to let back into your world.

I nodded and left the room.

SEVEN

FRIDAYS IN AUSTIN had been hectic; at the agency we were always trying to tie up loose ends so we could enjoy the weekend and start fresh on Monday. It never seemed to work, though. I always left the building late and began a rush through the maze of traffic to get to the cleaners, the grocery store, the bank. Then home to straighten up the house and do some laundry. Life was never leisurely.

It was a world away from Purple Sage, where Fridays were like all the other days, and they crawled by as slowly as the traffic. Jeremy and I sat in the Mazda behind the only two other cars at the light on Main. The light changed and we all moved lazily forward. I followed until we turned down the quiet dirt road that led to the baseball park. Ancient pecan trees afforded the only shade, and a few early bluebonnets had sprung up, making patches of soft color on the ground.

I became aware of a rhythmic pounding and turned to glance at Jeremy. With distracted precision, he was punching his fist into the center of his baseball mitt.

"Is there something on your mind?" I asked.

He looked up, surprised and vulnerable. For a moment I thought he was going to really talk to me. Then a sweep of lashes closed over his hazel eyes, and his face shuttered. "Nothing," he said.

"Did you call Matt last night?"

"Yeah." Jeremy gazed out the window as I turned into the cleared area behind the baseball field that served as a parking lot.

"Are you worried about the game?"

Jeremy shrugged and I remained outside his thoughts.

I pulled the car into an empty space and turned off the engine. Before I could get out of the car, Jeremy said, "Mom, listen . . ."

I turned to look at him. "What, honey?"

"Mom, I just want you to..." He paused.

"What?"

A longer pause. He reached for the door handle. "Nothing. I'd better go." And then he was gone, loping off toward the field, where his coach was unloading equipment.

Damn. Every time he started to talk to me, he changed his mind. I decided the break in our relationship was hard on him, too. Harder because he didn't know how to end it without losing face.

I got out of the car and walked across the hard-packed dirt toward the small cinder-block building that served as the concession stand. It occurred to me that my own worries might be taking their toll on Jeremy, too. And what was I supposed to do about that?

I went around the far side of the tiny building and found that the back door was open to catch what faint breeze was drifting by. I looked inside and saw that two women were already bustling around, popping popcorn, cooking hot dogs, and putting bags of ice in the old tin sinks.

"Can I help?" I asked, poking my head in the door.

Without looking up, Linda Beaman wiped her sleeve across her plump face to remove the sweat. "An answer to a prayer!" She hoisted a final bag of ice, then turned to look at me. "Oh. It's you, Jolie."

Beside her Sharon Colburn froze, like in the child's game of statues.

"Actually," Sharon said, carefully turning her thin, lined face away from me and averting her eyes, "we've got everything handled for now." She started bagging popcorn rapidly.

"Guess I spoke too soon," Linda said, now taking long stacks of cups from their plastic wrappers with her plump hands. "Thanks anyway."

Neither one would look at me.

"Are you sure?" I asked.

"We've got Sue coming," Sharon said, "and there just isn't room for that many people in this little space. We run into each other." She paused, and faced me with something that was almost a challenge. "You know."

Linda remained with her broad back to me.

They were always begging for help in the concession stand. Just a few days before Sharon had called, asking if I couldn't spare at least an hour or two "for the sake of the boys." At the time, I hadn't been sure of my schedule with Trey's campaign so I had demurred. Now I was unwelcome.

"Another time," I said, stepping back out into the sunlight.

I decided their coolness was my punishment for saying no earlier in the week. I glanced around at the ballpark to see if I could spot Diane. Her car wasn't in sight, and as I looked out on the field, I didn't see her son Randy, either.

For some reason, I was feeling guilty about what Linda and Sharon must have considered my lack of dedication to the Little League. Well, there were other jobs; I might be able to fill in somewhere else. I started for the tiny metal platform set directly behind home plate, where the game announcer and the statistician sat.

"Hi, Roland. Where's your sidekick, Buddy Wayne?"

Rhonda's husband was usually there.

Roland Marshall peered down from his metal throne. "Oh." He paused. "Buddy Wayne's not going to make it tonight."

"Do you need a spotter?"

The stiffening of his back told me that even if he did, I wasn't going to be the one. "Thank you, no. Excuse me, I've got to get the lineup."

Male chauvinism? I didn't think so.

Slowly I made my way back to the concession stand, only this time I went to the window.

"Guess I'll be your first customer," I said.

Sharon stood unmoving on her pole-thin legs. Her face was guarded. "Be with you in a minute."

"Look, Sharon, I'm sorry if I annoyed you when you called, but I really didn't know if I'd be free tonight."

Sharon looked to Linda but Linda's broad face was bland as she shrugged her heavy shoulders. Sharon slapped a roll of coins against the edge of the till to break it open. "I don't know what you're talking about. I just don't have the change sorted out yet. Why don't you come back in a little bit. . . ."

I heard soft footfalls in the dirt and turned to find Diane.

"Hi, Jolie," she said. "Hot today, isn't it?"

"Very," I said.

Diane stepped up to the counter. "Hi, Sharon. I'd like a large Coke."

With a shrug, Sharon reached for cups; she was suddenly ready for customers. "Anything else?"

"I'll take one, too," I said. "With lots of ice."

"Make it two," Diane said. "Randy thinks the Tigers should win the tournament; what does Lucas say, Sharon?"

"Same thing," she said without enthusiasm as she handed over our drinks.

We paid for them and then Diane and I started off toward the bleachers.

Diane leaned closer to me. "What the hell was that all about? Did Sharon seem rude? What did you do? Insult her kid's fielding? Which, by the way, is terrible."

Diane, for all her elegance, grew up on a goat ranch outside of Menard, and she's a scrapper at heart. With a little motivation she can out-tough almost anyone, but I didn't want her taking on the Pony League mothers on my behalf.

"I'm not sure what her problem is," I said. "Maybe just a bad day."

"You don't look like yours was so good, either. Where have you been, anyway? I tried calling you all day and you never answered your phone."

"I unplugged it," I said. "The police."

"They visited me, too."

"Andy's been at my house twice. I wasn't up to any more."

Diane heard the snap in my voice and stopped. "Do you want to go somewhere and talk?"

The boys were already on the field, in the midst of their pre-game practice, and the parents were filling up the bleachers. I shook my head. "No, we'd miss the game and I need to be here. Maybe it will convince Jeremy that I'm not quite the worst mother in the world," I said. "Where's Trey?"

"His meeting ran late. He'll be here later."

We were at the bleachers. "Where do you want to sit?" I asked.

"Anywhere. Oh, wait," she said. "I've got to get my camera. I finally got that zoom lens and I promised Randy I'd take some pictures during the game. As if I'm really going to know how to work it!" She held out her drink. "Would you take this for me, Jolie, and get us some seats? I'll join you in a minute."

I took the cup. "Sure."

I looked up at the splintery old wooden structure. Already it was half filled with the players' parents, grandparents, brothers and sisters. I smiled at the group in general but they all seemed intent on the playing field. I moved toward the center of the bleachers, then started climbing. I halted at the third row beside a young girl.

"Hi, there," I said.

"Rosalie!" The girl's mother snatched up the tiny girl and yanked her away. "You stay beside me! Do you understand?"

The little girl began to cry.

I looked around at all the faces now turned to me; they were closed and angry. My adrenaline was flowing as if I were facing some impending physical danger. Ridiculous, I told myself. I know these people. Our kids play on the same baseball team; we say hello at PTA and nod to each other in the grocery store. These were moral and upstanding citizens.

The kind who stone outsiders.

The thought came out of nowhere and frightened me more than the hard faces staring at me. I turned my back on them and made my way carefully to the empty uppermost corner. People cautiously slid even farther away.

I wasn't imagining it. I was a pariah and there was only one reason for it that I could imagine. Even with the sun beating down on me, a prickle of goose bumps broke out on my body. *These people think I killed the Judge.*

I focused on the field. The coach was calling the boys to the dugout for a final pep talk before the game. The little batboy was struggling under the load of a heavy water jug. A dust devil whirled across the outfield, spinning a wisp of dirt before it blew itself out.

I wanted to cry.

"Is this where you want to sit?" Diane asked as she carefully picked her way to the corner of the bleachers where I was huddled. "Not exactly the best seats in the house."

"Not exactly," I said. I sipped my drink, a few drops of sweat rolling off the cup and making dark spots on my green blouse.

Diane sat down beside me, holding the camera gingerly on her lap. She saw my face. "Jolie, you look like you're going to faint. Can I get you something?"

I shook my head, trying to keep my expression neutral. "I'm all right."

Diane spoke softly. "What is it?"

"Later, okay?"

She nodded, but I felt her continue to watch me. If what I was sensing were real, eventually she'd recognize it, too. Maybe it was just my imagination. I waited for the game to start.

THE SCORE WAS three to two and we were winning as the side retired and our boys scuffled off the field. Jeremy put on a batter's helmet and picked up two bats, swinging them fiercely in the practice box. Randy, Diane's son, was standing off to the side, ready for his turn at the plate after Jeremy.

A small group of boys on bikes had gathered behind the bleachers, all too young to be playing in this league. Their voices had been getting louder, and now it was impossible to ignore them.

"I am *too* sure," I heard one of them say.

Diane shifted beside me, apparently annoyed by the kids.

"Who told you?" another of the boys asked.

The response was brazen. "Everyone knows!"

Diane turned around. "Would you kids mind playing somewhere else?"

One of the boys pointed at me. "See, right up there in the green shirt. She's the one that killed the Judge."

"You apologize, you little trash-mouth liar!" Diane yelled.

The boys pedaled away furiously, some laughing, some frightened.

Diane's eyes radiated fury. She grabbed my arm. "Don't pay any attention to those rotten little bastards."

A breeze was sweeping over the grandstand. Diane clutched at my damp hand and I realized we were both shaking.

Shouts from the field distracted us. Two kids were fighting at first base. There was a flurry of dust and bodies, arms and legs thrashing out. The coaches were racing toward them, yelling, but the fight continued with a vengeance; two more boys jumped into the fray.

Automatically I looked for Jeremy. He wasn't in the dugout or near the plate. Neither was Randy. My heart began to pound furiously. The coaches reached the fight, and began pulling boys off the brawling pile. The first was Randy, his face red, his arms still swinging. Next were two boys I didn't recognize. The last to be yanked up was Jeremy.

"Oh, God." I leaped up.

Diane pulled me back down. "They're okay, let the coaches handle it."

I tried to stand again but my knees didn't hold me. I sat down hard. She was right; I couldn't do anything that would help. And Jeremy and Randy would hate it if we went toward the field. Mothers weren't welcome.

"Damn kids!" Diane said, then pointed toward the visitors' bleachers. "Look."

I looked down along the fence just below the visitors' stands and spotted Matt's light hair, glinting in the last of the afternoon sun. He was moving purposefully toward the back of the dugout, where the coach was lecturing the boys.

"Matt will find out what's going on," she said.

An official joined the conference on the field and someone tilted Jeremy's head up to look at it. Even from that distance I could see a cut below his eye that was starting to bleed. The coach looked at the cut more closely, then dismissed it to examine Randy. The official said something, the coach argued, and in the end, Randy and Jeremy both stalked off toward the dugout. The difference was that Randy sat down on the bench, while Jeremy retrieved his glove and slammed off the field.

Matt was waiting for him. The two moved behind the bleachers and I stood up.

"Looks like the game is over for us," I said.

Diane was sympathetic. "I hope he's okay."

"I think he got thrown out of the game, which means he instigated that fight." It wasn't Jeremy's style. He was passive in all but the most extreme situations.

"You want me to come with you?"

"No, thanks. He'd just be even more embarrassed. I'll call you tonight."

I ignored the crowds as I made my way carefully to the ground and then hurried to find Jeremy and Matt. They were standing beside Matt's Bronco.

"Are you okay?" I asked Jeremy.

He shrugged and tried to look tough, but he was shaken. I touched his cheek. "That's a nasty cut. You want to tell me what happened out there?"

He shook his head and I could see the beginnings of tears in his eyes. It rattled me. "Come on, honey, I'll take you home."

Matt stepped forward. "Jolie, I think Jeremy should sit in the truck and get cooled off." He looked at Jeremy, who was nodding furiously. Matt tossed the car keys to Jeremy. "Go ahead and turn on the engine."

I waited until Jeremy was insulated in the air-conditioned Bronco. "That's pretty high-handed of you. Aren't you even going to tell me what happened out there?"

Matt took a few steps away from his vehicle and took my elbow to move me with him. I shrugged off his hand, but followed.

"Jolie, I don't know the whole story yet, but I think it had something to do with you."

"Me? The fight? What the hell..." And then I knew. Someone had made a crack about me. Probably the same kind of things the kids under the bleachers had said: I had murdered the Judge. I felt my chest heaving with my anger.

Matt was nodding slowly. "Jeremy told me on the phone last night that it happened at school, too."

"Goddamn small towns! Damn small-minded people!" I clamped my jaws together hard. "Matt, I can't even take Jeremy out of town. I can't leave because of the police. Oh, God!" The last sounded almost like a whimper.

Matt touched my shoulder. "You need some time," he said. "Why don't you let me take Jeremy out to the ranch? He can ride Diablo, wander around and get some of the anger out of his system."

I dropped my head and studied the ground. My thoughts were too fast and fragmented to catch. I could feel my chin beginning to tremble and I stuck it out, trying to look tough as I raised my eyes to meet Matt's. "Let me think a minute."

I turned away and caught the hint of a breeze against my flushed face. I kept swallowing. Maybe it would be best for Jeremy to go out to the ranch. "Okay," I said. "Then Jeremy won't be subjected to any more of this monstrous treatment."

"People are the same everywhere, Jolie. They're no worse in a small town, you just see them a little more closely."

"Miss Marple said that."

He gave me a half-smile. "You're welcome to come out and stay, too. There's plenty of room."

Five bedrooms. Places to hide, but not for me. I couldn't find comfort in that house. It was my ex-husband's family home.

I shook my head. "We can protect Jeremy, but I'm afraid that I have to face this, Matt." And then I wondered how much Matt knew of the story. He hadn't heard what had gone on at the concession stand, nor had he heard the kids under the bleachers. Neither had Jeremy, thank God. "Who told you about the Judge's murder?"

"Trey and Diane. We had dinner last night," he said. How easily I forgot that he knew my friends, had known them longer and probably better than I did. "Trey was telling me how the police had everyone in your writers' group under pretty close surveillance."

Small towns. Too small a town.

"You'll take care of Jeremy's cut, won't you, Matt?" I asked. "He should probably see a doctor."

"I thought I'd run him by the hospital and let Doc Baxter look at it."

I nodded and realized that a steady stream of people were eyeing us as they shuffled back and forth to and from the concession stand.

"We've got to get out of here," I said. "Let me say goodbye to Jeremy." I walked over and opened the door to the Bronco. Jeremy pretended to be surprised, but I knew he'd been watching us. "How are you doing?" I asked.

"I'm okay."

"Do you want to spend the weekend out at the ranch?"

"Am I kicked out of the whole tournament?"

"I don't know," I said, turning to look at Matt, who had remained some distance from us. "Is Jeremy out of the whole tournament?" I asked.

Matt shook his head. "Just this game. You can come back and play tomorrow if you want, Jeremy."

Jeremy shrugged, pretending it didn't matter. "Maybe. Maybe not."

I leaned closer. "Jeremy, I know what started the fight. I know what people are saying about me, and I'm sorry about what it's doing to you."

He covered his hurt with a flash of anger. "Why'd you have to write that book anyway?"

I let his words bounce off me. "Because I'm a writer. I write mysteries. It's not my fault that someone used my method to kill the Judge."

Matt moved back into the conversation. "Jeremy, someday you're going to be proud of your mother's writing."

I was surprised. I hadn't expected vocal support from Matt since we were divorced.

"Jeremy," Matt continued, "if you want to come with me, we'd better get moving. I'd like to catch the doctor before it gets too late."

Jeremy looked back and forth at both of us. "Thanks, Matt, but I think I'd better stay with Mom."

"Don't worry about me," I said, smiling at Jeremy, trying to look more nonchalant than I felt. "I'll play hermit and get a lot of writing done; nobody is going to bother me. But I want you to call me after you get your face fixed up." The cut wasn't deep; I doubted that it would need stitches, and even if it did, Jeremy wouldn't care. He collected scars on his smooth skin, and the stories that matched each one, like some kids collected baseball cards. I was more worried about the emotional wounds that were being inflicted on him. Maybe someday those would turn into hero's tales, too. I hoped so, and I hoped it would be soon.

"I don't know, Mom—"

"I do," I said. "Go. It will be fun for you and it will give me a little time to myself."

Jeremy tossed his mitt on the floor. "Yeah, okay, I'll go. I need to see Diablo, anyway."

I leaned forward to give him a hug and was surprised when he jumped out of the truck and wrapped his arms around me. He dropped them quickly, but said, "Mom, pretty soon we've got to do something about this."

"I know."

He looked me over. "Be careful, okay? If you need me tonight, just call."

"I promise," I said, solemnly. "I love you."

"I love you, too." He jumped back in the truck.

I stood there watching as Matt got in, started the engine, and they both waved a final good-bye before they pulled away in the deepening twilight.

EIGHT

BEING A LIST MAKER, the first thing I did was make a list. I put down Diane, June, Maria, Liz, Rhonda, and myself. Then I added Andy's name. Everyone who had read my manuscript. Obviously I didn't think all of those people were actual suspects; I knew for sure that I hadn't killed the Judge. Those were the people I wanted to talk to.

I called Diane first and listened while her answering machine told me that she and Trey were out and if I wanted them to call me back I should leave a message. I did. They were probably still at the baseball field but the game would be over soon. In the meantime I fixed myself a caesar salad (without anchovies), heated up a slice of IdaMae's bread, and paced around the kitchen while I ate it. Just as I was finishing, Diane called and said to come over. She didn't have to say it twice.

Their home is about a mile from the little house that Jeremy and I were renting, and it's about four times as big. They had just finished building it when I moved to Purple Sage. In fact, my first view of their house was also the day I had my first view of them. They were having a fund-raiser for some state representative and Matt, along with his new bride, had naturally been on the guest list. As Matt and I had driven up to the house, I had taken one look at the two-story portico and the sweeping circular drive and my post-honeymoon glow had turned a whiter shade of pale. The house and the party were much grander than I was comfortable with, and I was terrified I would say or do something totally inappropriate.

Actually, at first I was fine. I had a glass of wine and mingled. Then I had another glass of wine and mingled some more. Then I had a third glass and decided to give myself an unguided tour of the house. That sounds brash, but we had all been urged to look around and "enjoy" the place. Lots of other people were gawking as openly as I was.

I *ooh*ed and *ahh*ed with everyone else over the central atrium and the veranda off the master bedroom. I goggled at the walk-in refrigerator, and grew lustful when I saw all the spectacularly blooming flowers in their garden. The only thing I didn't like was the dining room. It was formal with white walls, white carpet, and white drapes. In the center of all this stark white was a ten-foot table of some dark, heavy wood with ornate carvings all over it. There were sixteen matching high-backed chairs. I took one look and said, "Who are they expecting for dinner? The pope?"

Diane was right behind me.

She burst out laughing. "No wonder I don't like this room," she said, "it's too damn ecumenical!"

From that moment on Diane and I became friends. And I still love her house, except for that dining room. I spent most of my time in her office/den, which is where she led me as soon as I arrived that Friday evening. It has floor-to-ceiling bookshelves on one wall filled with everything from the classics to the latest paperback mysteries. There are also some leaded-glass windows, wide french doors, a used-brick fireplace, and a computer system that could guide the space shuttle. I covet that room.

"What's your pleasure?" Diane asked as she slid back an oak panel to reveal a wet bar complete with refrigerator and microwave.

"Diet Pepsi," I said, curling up in a wing-backed chair. "Well, leaving Purple Sage won't be so hard now. At least I'll be able to protect Jeremy from this small-town viciousness."

She opened a Pepsi, then seemed to forget it as she turned around to face me. "Jolie, think about what happened today rationally for a minute. It's only been two days since we found out how the Judge was murdered, and we're the only ones who know you used the same murder method in your book."

I met her intent stare. "So?"

"So, how did those rumors get started?"

"I don't know. How does any rumor get started?"

"By someone talking. And in this case it had to have been one of us, or Andy, who did it."

I closed my eyes to think. I kept seeing the members of our writers' group seated around our battered card table. Admittedly June could be rather succinct if she didn't like something, but I couldn't see her going out and starting rumors. It was much too frivolous for her. And too frivolous for Rhonda. Maria would say things to your face and maybe with a lot of fire, but she didn't seem like the sneaky type. As for Liz—too ditsy.

I opened my eyes and shook my head. "I can't make myself believe that anyone in our group would tell people. They know what kind of gossip it would start. And why? What would they gain from it?"

"That's what I wanted to tell you; I think I have an answer." She finished pouring our drinks and handed me a tall, heavily bubbled glass, then sat across from me. "Now, just hear me out, okay, even if it sounds a little wacko. Promise?" I nodded and she went on. "Now, just suppose that one of them killed the Judge . . . don't interrupt, just humor me for a minute. So one of them murders the Judge, and then has to figure out the best way to keep the focus off them. It's easy—they put it on you. In fact, they get the whole town talking about you. And by doing that, they also put pressure on the police to go after you. Andy's only human, and right now he's so stressed he can barely think. Bill Tieman is probably pushing him to get evidence against you, too."

I sat back in the chair, thinking. "That would work."

"Look, Jolie, I'm not trying to frighten you, but damn it, I'm half out of my mind! Andy's not even considering an outsider; he's positive it's one of us."

"Say what you mean—he's positive it's me."

"You know what really worries me? What if Andy killed the Judge? It will never be proved."

"Which means everyone will always wonder if I did it, even if they don't bring charges." What I didn't say was that the rumors could follow me forever. And follow Jeremy.

"Wait a minute," Diane said. "I just realized something: there are three other cops in this town and they've all probably heard about your manuscript by now—"

"Of course! And there's the dispatcher at the station. And some high school girl does clerical work for Bill Tieman after school—any of them could have said something." I felt a huge sense of relief. My friends weren't the only ones who could have started the horrible rumors about me. I leaned back and sipped my drink in silence. It felt good to let go of that one small part of my worries.

"I'm sorry I dragged you over here," Diane finally said.

I sat up straight and opened my notebook with resolve. "You didn't; I'm the one who wanted to talk to you. I want to get some things cleared up on the Judge's murder and I want your help. I've made a list of everyone who knew about my manuscript, and therefore knew about the murder method. Will you help me talk to them?"

Diane stood up. "Are you serious? Jolie, you're being too naive about this whole thing."

"Why?"

"Someone murdered a man and it's probably one of the people on your list. You can't just bumble up to them and expect truthful answers. Besides, it could be dangerous."

"Then what would you do, if you were me?"

Diane had the kind of mind that might conceive some flight of fancy, but would follow that thread of imagination all the way to the end before acting on it. It's what made her plots work so well. "I'd look at it like a book. Work it like a book."

"Like a mystery? That's good, except, when we start writing a book we already know who did it, remember? Unless, of course, you know something about the Judge's death that you're not telling me."

"No, no, nothing like that," Diane said. "I meant, we start with character."

"The Judge's character!"

"Exactly. Who hated him; who might have wanted him dead. Who profits from his death."

"Oh, shit. The profit angle; that's something I hadn't even thought of." I got up and held out my notebook so she could read it. "Any names on the list jump out at you?"

She leaned forward and looked it over. "Mine."

"Sorry. This isn't actually a suspect list, it's more like the people to talk with."

"But, Jolie, we didn't know the Judge. Not well. No one on this list did. Well, maybe someone did, but to find out, we have to start with people who knew his business dealings. We have to talk to his friends."

"His enemies," I corrected, as I sat down. "His friends wouldn't tell us the dirt, and that's what I want. People aren't killed for their good deeds. Do you know anyone who knew him well and hated him?"

"Who hated the Patron Saint of Purple Sage?" She took a sip of her drink as she thought about it. "The problem is that this could be an old grudge, one that goes back years. God, I wish Trey's dad were still alive. The stories he could tell! Actually, though, Trey might be able to help."

"Would you ask him?"

"Sure. As soon as he gets home," Diane offered.

I hadn't been completely comfortable with Trey since the divorce. In part because he was one of Matt's best friends, although I must admit he never acted like he was taking sides. When I stopped and thought about it, though, I'd never been completely comfortable with Trey even before the divorce. It's probably because I've never heard Trey say anything bad about anyone. It was unnerving. Talk about the saint of Purple Sage—maybe Trey was it.

"Where is Trey?" I asked.

"He took Randy and some of the boys out for pizza."

"Is it a victory celebration or a consolation meal?"

"We lost," she said. "How's Jeremy?"

"He's fine. They put a butterfly bandage on his cut, but that's about all he said when he called. It wasn't what I consider real communication. I ended up telling him to take care of himself, and not to worry. You know, all those meaningless things that mothers say and teenagers ignore."

"I know about those."

"Are we out of the tournament?"

"No, it's double elimination," she said, rising and going to the bar. "Are you ready for some more?"

"No, thanks."

"Want something else?"

"No, I'm fine."

She poured out her drink, rinsed the glass, and filled it halfway with white wine. "The coach was so mad at Randy he kept him on the bench the whole game. Between that and not having Jeremy we didn't have a prayer."

"Jeremy might not be back this weekend."

"Which would be the best thing for him." She went to her chair and sat back, her voice softening as she thought aloud. "We've got to protect him, Jolie, and the only way we can do that is by getting this thing done and over with. I'll pump Trey."

"And I'll talk to people."

"Actually, I have a better idea. You might take a look at some old *Tribunes;* I once heard Trey's dad make some crack about the Judge being an opportunist. I can't remember much else, but it seems like it had something to do with the lake and the building of it. Maybe you could find something in the old papers."

"When did they build Sage Lake?"

"Oh, about twenty years ago; before my time, anyway. I was still living in Menard."

Sage Lake was man-made, but I didn't know how they'd gained access to the land, or who'd owned it. Condemning private land could cause some grudges, but I didn't think they'd last twenty years.

Diane was frowning. "You know, that's the only specific thing I heard anyone say against the Judge. He really was universally liked."

"Well, somebody didn't like him," I said. "I'm still going to talk to June and IdaMae Dorfman. They've both been around long enough to remember some of the Judge's history."

"Just be careful, okay, Jolie? You know what always happens to the heroine in books."

"Protagonist," I corrected. "And, of course, I know. 'Drugged, mugged, bugged, kidnapped, threatened, beat-up, intimidated, spied on, followed, chased, etc.'" We'd learned it in a writing seminar. "Don't worry, that's art, not life."

"Yeah, well, keep something else in mind," Diane said. "In this particular instance, life has been imitating art." She shook her head. "I wish we had access to the police information. Too bad we couldn't enlist Rhonda's help."

"Not a good idea," I said. "Oh, but I do know a little more." I told her about the perfume that Andy had been looking for.

Diane looked surprised. "Trey's mother used to wear Youth Dew, but she lives in Palm Beach now."

"Do you know of anyone else?"

"No," she said slowly, still thinking about it. "But doesn't it seem kind of dumb for a smart murderer? You wouldn't want to leave your perfume behind, and that's a pretty distinctive one."

"I know. It's been bothering me." I stood up and reached for my notebook. "I don't feel like I'm very good company tonight; I think I'll go home and do some hard thinking. Maybe I'll shake something loose."

"Why don't you spend the night here?"

"Why?"

"I don't like the thought of you being at home alone."

I picked up my purse and began fumbling through it, looking for my keys. "Think about it rationally. The murderer has me exactly where he wants me. Why hurt me?"

Diane shook her head as we began walking through the house to the front door. "Rationally, I know you're right, but something inside me isn't agreeing."

I heard a car pull up outside and then doors slamming. Diane looked at her watch. "That must be Trey."

The front door opened and Randy came in, his face still blotchy with red patches from the fight. He saw me and dropped his eyes. "Hi, Jolie."

"Hi, Randy. Sorry you guys lost the game. And I'm sorry about the fight."

He shrugged, his eyes still on the carpet. "That's okay."

He started off for his room and Trey came in. "Jolie." He said it as if he were disappointed to see me and trying to hide it.

He didn't offer any explanation, instead he gave Diane a quick kiss. "Hi."

"Hi, yourself," she said. "How was the pizza?"

"Fine. Do we have any Tums?"

I laughed. "I'd better go. See you later."

"No, wait a minute, Jolie," Trey said. "If you have time, I think we need to talk."

I looked at Diane, then at Trey. "Okay."

I followed them into the formal living room. It had sandy gray rock walls with hunter green accents and two bowls of fresh flowers.

Trey waited until Diane and I were seated and then he pulled a crumpled piece of paper from his pocket. It was dirty, with little tears in the surface. He handed it to me.

Without a word I took it. The typing was clear and concise. So was the message. "Jolie Wyatt murdered the Judge. You'd better get rid of her or you don't stand a chance in the election. A friend."

Some friend.

I stared at the paper until Diane said, "Read it, Jolie. What does it say?"

I read it out loud, and when I finished I looked up to see her face turning white. "Where did it come from?" I asked Trey.

He debated his answer and finally told the truth. "Someone wrapped it around a rock and threw it through the window of my car."

"Oh my God . . ." Diane said.

Trey slipped an arm around her, but his eyes were watching me.

For a moment I was too stunned to speak. The small-town gossip had turned violent and that frightened me. I wasn't so concerned about myself as I was about my friends. And Jeremy. "I'm sorry this happened, Trey. I didn't stop to think how people might be judging you, too."

"Did you call the police?" Diane asked.

Trey shook his head no. "The rock must have been thrown while we were inside the restaurant eating. By the time I found it I thought it was better just to take the boys home; I'll call in a few minutes."

I felt sick. "Trey, I'm so sorry. I'll pay for the damages."

"Don't be ridiculous," Diane said.

"It's not your fault, Jolie," Trey added, "but I thought you needed to be warned." He looked meaningfully at me.

I jumped up and walked toward the fireplace, thinking hard. For the moment at least, Jeremy was safe with Matt, but how in the world was I going to protect my friends? Then again, maybe it was politically motivated. I turned and looked at Trey. "You'll never become mayor of Sage if this is how people are feeling," I said. "I think it would be better if I disassociated myself from your campaign."

"I don't know, Jolie . . ." Trey began.

"What if I sent a press release to Rhonda and the radio station?" I said. "I could do it early tomorrow and have a letter in the county clerk's office first thing Monday morning."

Diane shook her head. "Absolutely not!"

"Don't you see, Diane? I have to," I said. "It's the only way that Trey has even a slight chance." But it wasn't enough as long as people knew that Diane and I were still friends. "There's something else," I said. "I think it would be better if I didn't see you in public for a while, either."

Diane jerked back. "Jolie, how can you say that?"

"Because it's the only way."

"Is that all my friendship means to you?" Diane asked.

"Of course not. It's just a public gesture," I said. "It's just for the sake of Trey's campaign."

"Jolie," Diane said, "this is no time for you to be alone. Forget the whole idea."

The phone rang. Randy had his own line, so either Trey or Diane had to answer it. They exchanged a glance, and with a muffled sound of frustration Diane said, "I'll get the damn thing."

Trey stood in the middle of the room. He cleared his throat. "Look, Jolie, you really made my campaign take off—" I started to interrupt but he wouldn't let me. "And if I win it's a victory for you, too. I can't let you resign. It would be like denying everything you've done.''

"Right, except you can't win with me around."

Trey shrugged, then looked at me and smiled. "Frankly, my dear, I don't give a damn."

I couldn't help but smile back. "Nicely put."

"Anyway," he added, his voice serious again, "you need friends right now and it's the least I can do for you and for Matt."

It sounded like I had to be protected because of Matt, not for who I was.

Diane came back into the room, her eyes blazing.

"Who was on the phone?" Trey asked.

"No one important!" she snapped.

She wouldn't look at me, so I knew the call had been about me. Someone trying to warn her of the consequences of having me around.

It was what I needed to make my decision. Trey and Diane didn't have to approve of my resignation, or even know about it until Monday. I forced my voice to sound light. "Well, I'd better get going."

I started for the door and Diane went with me. "I'll call you tomorrow."

"Okay," I said, thinking that I'd unplug my phone. "'Bye." I almost ran outside, making sure that I closed the door behind me.

Instead of going straight for the Mazda, I had to look at Trey's car. It was a big silver Mercedes, but its usual perfection was marred. The driver's side window had a gaping hole with little shards of glass still trapped by the safety sealant. The hole looked like a wound. Carefully I reached out and touched the edge of it.

I whirled around and got in my car.

As soon as I was on the road I slammed my palm into the steering wheel. Something had to be done about all this, and I was just the person to do it.

NINE

IT WAS STILL midmorning when I headed for June's ranch, which was some twenty miles of rough road out of Purple Sage. It wasn't the storybook kind of place you'd expect for a famous writer. Instead it was typical, somewhat tacky, central Texas. The caliche road that lead to her gate was washboarded and pitted from too many rains without proper grading. The wildflowers that poked through the hard dirt to soak up the morning sunshine added a touch of unexpected civilization between the tall blooming yuccas and the rest of the foliage that was coated with a chalky film from the caliche.

Instead of a gate in the barbed-wire-and-cedar-post fence there was just an open space with a cattle guard. Everywhere I looked cactus and weeds were plentiful.

The Mazda kicked up a wake of dust as I slowed down and bumped over the cattle guard. June had a few cows and they could have been anywhere, including the road or her front porch. At June's place you could never be sure.

In another half mile the road took a turn, and I could see her house tucked into an oasis of lawn and trees. The house itself was an old wood-frame structure, with a wide raised concrete front porch and big square concrete posts to hold up the roof. Its only real charm came from the petunia-filled flower boxes under each of the windows. The flowers were a clear, fresh pink. Off to my left was the modern barn with a couple of acres of metal-fenced arena for working the horses.

As I parked at the edge of the grass and jumped out of the car, a cat looked up lazily from the porch, then went back to washing herself.

"Hello, Bratcat," I said, as I started up the steps. "Is June inside?"

The cat blinked once, and I knocked on the door.

"Is that you, Jolie? Come on in," June called from inside. I'd phoned earlier, so she was expecting me.

"Hi. Where are you?"

"In the kitchen. Come on back."

I went through the living room, which was sparsely furnished with a mixture of antiques and some fairly new pieces. On the scuffed wood floor was an oriental rug, and one wall was covered with bookshelves. That was the only thing all of us in the writers' group had in common: miles of books somewhere in our houses.

In the old-fashioned and barren kitchen, June was putting ice in two tall glasses. "Thought you might like something to drink. Iced tea, okay?"

The water of Texas.

"Wonderful."

She took out an old pink Fiestaware pitcher and filled both glasses. "Here you go. Let's sit in the living room. I don't know why this kitchen never cools off. Maybe it's me. I just got in."

I followed her out to the living room. "Have you been working Jupiter?"

"Not yet," she said, settling back with a soft sigh into an old recliner. "Oh, I've worked him a little, but I'm so mad at him for banging up his leg I'm afraid I'd be rough on the old fool."

I sat on the couch and felt myself relaxing. The nice thing about being way out in the country was that you couldn't take the outside world too seriously. It was simply too far away to be of that much concern. The tension began to ease out of my muscles and even my bones seemed less rigid.

"Oh, I've got something to show you," June said. "Take a look in that box beside you."

I twisted around to find a big brown shipping box on the floor beside the couch. "What is it?" I asked, opening the flaps and peeking inside. "Oh, your new book!" I pulled one out.

"Lucky number thirteen."

It was hardbound and the cover was in bright aquas with black lettering in an Art Deco style. It struck me again how different the real June Ingram was from her writing.

"It looks wonderful," I cooed, running my hand reverently over the cover. "I love this book. But then, all your books are wonderful."

"I'm rather pleased with it myself. I only wish Howard were here to see it." She heaved a small sigh that held no self-pity, just a touch of regret.

Howard had been June's husband. He had died in his early fifties, leaving June without the person she considered her best friend. As she told the story, after Howard's death she had begun writing letters to him, and even though she knew it was crazy, it made her feel as if they were still connected. After the letters she tried stories about the two of them. Finally someone had suggested that she utilize all that energy to create a book about their life together.

The initial manuscript had been a disaster, too filled with emotion to be any good. Then she came up with the idea of a mystery, using the two of them as the sleuths. June discovered that she was keeping Howard alive through her writing, so she continued, and those mysteries were the start of her very successful series. What I think is really fun is that Howard gets fan mail! Once, in a moment of weakness, June even admitted that she sometimes gets jealous of all the women who write to him.

June is a series of contradictions—some I like, some I don't. And at times I feel like I hardly know her at all. One thing I do like about her all the time is her writing. On paper she and Howard are as witty as characters in a Neil Simon play.

Carefully, I turned a few pages of the new book and noticed a phrase that I had suggested. I have to admit to a small swell of pride. Okay, so it's not the same as a ten-week run on the best-seller list, but at least it was a start.

"So how are you doing, Jolie?"

I put the book back in the box. "Right now my life is shit, June. Pure unadulterated cow manure, without the fancy packaging."

"We create our lives, Jolie."

"Not this mess."

For a moment she scowled, then the expression slipped away. "I'd forgotten about the Judge's murder. I'm a little out of touch out here, which I have to admit I like. How are things going with that?"

I sipped some tea, then put my glass on the table. "Not too good." I started from the beginning and rambled my way through the events of the past two days. The only thing I left out was my discussion with Trey and Diane the night before. I felt a sense of loss when I realized that I had to stay away from Diane until they caught the Judge's murderer. First Matt, now Diane and Trey. My life was turning into a series of empty spaces where there had once been people I loved.

I pushed that thought aside and went on with the story. When I finished I was filled with an unfocused anger. "I feel like someone is out to get me, June, and they're doing a damn good job of it."

She nodded sympathetically. "Maybe this is one of those times when life dumps on you for no good reason. I've certainly had an experience or two with that."

I stood up and found myself moving just to keep the anger tamped down. "You know what really pisses me off?" I said, finally stopping to look at her. "What if someone is doing it to me on purpose?"

"Jolie, you're taking this personally, and I don't think this is a personal vendetta against you. It sounds to me like someone killed the Judge using your murder plan because it was simple."

"I don't care about their motives," I said. "The result is still the same. For me and for Jeremy."

June was silent a moment, her lips pursed in thought. "The best lawman I've ever met is our own sheriff; you know Mac Donelly, don't you? Maybe you could persuade him to take an interest in the investigation. Especially since Andy could be called a suspect."

I found it interesting that both June and Diane had been the ones to bring up Andy as a candidate for our murderer. It wasn't that I disagreed, but my main complaint against Andy was more basic: instead of protecting me as a policeman is supposed to do, he was one of my harassers. And even if his

actions were part of his official duties, on some level I thought
he should know me better than to believe I could kill.

"I'd rather talk to you," I said. "You've been in Purple Sage
a long time, and you knew the Judge. Can you think of any
enemies he had? There must have been at least one or two."

"Jolie, I think you have real life confused with fantasy. How
is your writing going?"

Her out-of-the-blue question stopped me. "What?"

"How much writing are you doing?"

"A little, but who can write when all this is going on?"

"You." June sat forward, her voice taking on the no-non-
sence tone I'd heard so often before. "Jolie, get your ass home,
sit it in front of your computer, and don't get up until you've
finished your book. And then edit, and polish the manuscript
so it's ready to go to your agent. By that time the Judge's murder will be taken care of."

I was so surprised it took me a moment to respond. "Yeah,
but what if I get arrested?"

"You won't. Innocent people don't go to prison."

"Have you watched *60 Minutes* lately?"

"Certainly there are a few mistakes, but by and large I have
great faith in the judicial system. So should you." June became even more firm. "Jolie, you are a writer. Writers write.
They don't get in and muck up a real police investigation."

"Does that mean you won't tell me about the Judge?"

She nodded. "That's exactly what I mean. The only thing
you can do is talk to the sheriff. If you're not willing to do that,
then forget the whole business."

I couldn't believe it. I had expected an ally. If not that, at the
very least I'd expected June to sympathize and give me what
information she could.

I stood up. "I don't think you fully understand my situation."

"I think I do." June stood also. "Before you do anything
rash, give yourself some time to think. At least consider my
suggestion."

Right—sit around and let the police arrest me. Let Jeremy be the target of more insults and fists. Let every rotten kid in Purple Sage throw rocks through my friends' windows.

"I'll think about what you said." I started for the door, then paused. It seemed strange that June wasn't willing to help me. I wondered what her stake in all of this was.

I turned and said, "June, can I use your bathroom?"

"Sure. Off the hall there. You know where it is."

"Thanks." I walked down the hall. So, June didn't think I should get involved, huh? Well, everyone was entitled to their own opinion, but I didn't have to accept it. Nor did I have to take their advice.

I slipped into the bathroom and closed the door. I poked around quietly. In the shower was some shampoo and a bar of soap. Nothing feminine or scented. I flushed the toilet and used the sound as cover to open the medicine cabinet. No perfumes at all. I don't know why I was disappointed—I'd expected as much.

Next, I turned on the water in the sink, and gently closed the cabinet door. It made a slight popping sound, but unless June was in the hall listening she couldn't have heard it. Finally I turned off the water and went out to join my hostess.

"I guess I'd better get going," I said.

June walked me to the door. "Look, Jolie, I know I sounded harsh before, but I was just being realistic. Writing mysteries doesn't give you the expertise to go out and investigate one of your own. Here, put your hand on this wood."

I did as she said, sliding my hand along the ridge of the door frame. "Okay."

"This is real, solid and hard, right? Well, we can write about it, and turn it into something soft and foamy with our words. We can make it flip sideways, or we can paint it pink. But that's just on paper. In reality, this will still be a solid wooden door frame, and you don't have the skills to alter it. You're confusing what you can do on paper with what you can do in real life. I think that's a very dangerous mistake."

I took my hand off the door frame and moved it to the knob "Thanks, June."

"Go home and write."

"I will," I said, willing to agree to anything to get away from there.

ON THE WAY BACK to Purple Sage, I started thinking about the field of wildflowers that had been behind our house when I was a child. There had been something magical about that field, filled with tiny yellow mustard flowers on thin feathery stalks of fresh green. I had been small enough to disappear among them, and I'd made a hideout where I would stay, making up stories and creating my own world. My older brother couldn't find me, and my younger sister was too little to follow.

For some reason I was feeling homesick and I wanted to go back to that field. Oh, the rational adult side of me knew that it was gone, probably replaced with something mundane like a convenience store, but that didn't stop the yearning.

My subconscious apparently made its own plans while I dreamed of other things.

When I got back to Purple Sage I parked near the court-house. Mac Donelly, the sheriff, officed on the second floor.

TEN

"WHAT DO YOU mean, it's not your jurisdiction?" I asked. "It happened in this county, didn't it? As the sheriff you are the ranking law-enforcement officer, aren't you?" I knew he was; I'd researched it for my book.

Mac took off his hat, rubbed the white space above his forehead where there used to be hair, and put his hat back on. It was his way of wringing his hands. "Jolie, I can see you're upset by this, but I can't go steppin' on toes. When something happens inside the city it's off limits to me. That's the way we do our business and it's not just here in Purple Sage—it's in every county in the state." Mac saw my face and softened. "You know I'd help if I could."

I looked out the window to where a group of pigeons were strutting around the second-story sill, pecking at bits of leftover food. Mac had probably put the food out there himself, but his good heart wasn't helping me any.

A big black grackle came swooping toward the window, scattering the pigeons. Now that's what I call assertiveness. Maybe I needed some more of that.

"Mac, I realize that there are rules covering jurisdiction, but having Andy investigate the Judge's murder has got to be a conflict of interest." I said the phrase *conflict of interest* like I knew what I was talking about. "Andy helped me with my manuscript. He read part of it. He knew as much about the murder I created as I did. Surely someone should realize that he's a suspect, too?"

"Well, now, from your position, I can see where you might say that, but from Bill Tieman's point of view, it's overstating the case. He's got no reason to believe Andy would kill the Judge."

I put my hands on Mac's desk. "Maybe not, but consider this for a minute. Everyone in town is sure I murdered the

Judge, and I just happen to be Trey's campaign manager. It's going to get Bill Tieman elected mayor, and leave the chief of police job vacant. Guess who's going to move up to fill that slot? Andy Sawyer." I paused to let him follow my thinking. When he began to nod, I went on. "It sure gives him a good reason for dragging his feet on the investigation and focusing on me."

"I'm beginning to see your point." He rubbed his hand across his face. "But, you see, Jolie, that puts us back into the middle of a big problem. Bill's only got four other patrolmen, and that's all they are. They don't have the training or the skill to cover a murder like this one."

"Which is why you should be handling it."

His hat came off again. Not a good sign. He leaned closer to me, his face troubled but firm. "Jolie, I can't do a thing unless I'm invited. I sure wish I could help you, but my hands are tied."

And then I remembered that Mac was an elected official, too, and he was up for reelection.

With a sigh I stood up.

"I know it's real frustrating for you," Mac said. "But you've got to understand some things, Jolie. Andy's probably hard-pressed to find two more people in this whole county who'd had a run-in with the Judge. No doubt he's looking for other motives or suspects and just hasn't found any yet." He paused and glanced at the coatrack near the door, probably so he wouldn't have to meet my eyes. "One more thing. Lawmen don't much believe in coincidence. And you got two powerful coincidences against you, don't you see?"

"I see." And I still didn't like it.

He faced me again. "Now, don't go getting upset. Andy'll find the right person, you just got to have a little faith."

"It's disappearing fast," I said. "Isn't there someone else I could talk to? I mean, besides Bill Tieman?"

"The mayor might could help, except he's out of the country right now."

He was always out of the country. The man was on a permanent junket—he should have run for senator or something.

I thanked Mac for his time and left, thinking again of that field of mustard flowers where I used to hide.

THE SQUARE WAS as busy as it ever got, jammed with shoppers and tourists. This was Saturday, what Matt used to kiddingly call "double-stamp day." According to him, back in the sixties and seventies, the grocery stores gave double Gold Stamps on Saturday and Wednesday, enticing all the women who lived out in the country to come to town for their weekly shopping. The habit remained, although the stamps were long gone.

I turned left and went two blocks to the Purple Sage *Tribune*. It was a big three-story gray brick building that squatted over half a block. Someone had tried to update it in the fifties without much success. They'd added large picture windows that were always dirty and never used. Old newsprint covered the inside of them, I suppose so the few office supplies and greeting cards the *Trib* sold wouldn't yellow in the sun.

It was a little before noon, and the office-cum-office-supply-store was still open. I parked the car and went inside. Even on the best of days the *Tribune* headquarters were dreary. After leaving the sunshine, they looked worse than usual. I went to the counter and tapped the little silver bell to let them know they had a customer.

A teenage girl came out. "Hi, can I help you?"

"I was looking for Rhonda. Is she around?"

The girl moved closer. "No, she went..." She stopped in midsentence, her mouth dropping open half an inch. Obviously she recognized me and had heard the rumors just like everyone else. She took two shuffling steps backward before she spoke again. "She's not here."

"Is she going to be back?"

"I, uh, don't know. I mean, I'm not sure."

Fair enough. Rhonda had her own schedule, and Morris Pratt, the owner of the *Tribune*, didn't care what it was, since Rhonda was as close to a star reporter as you could have in Purple Sage. Practically his only reporter.

"Well, how about if I leave a message for her?" I asked. "Can I do that?"

"Uh, sure. I guess."

The poor girl was torn between fear and fascination. Billy the Kid must have elicited the same kind of response.

I picked up a piece of paper from the counter and took a pen from a display. "Here, I'll write it out. Just give it to her if she comes back."

The young girl nodded, her mouth still open. Maybe she was just a mouth breather.

I left the office and headed toward home.

As I whipped up Main I noticed the Captain, a solitary figure in white, trudging along the cracked sidewalk. He was carrying a couple of sacks and munching on something that looked like it had come from the bakery.

The bakery! IdaMae Dorfman was on my list of people to talk with. I slowed down and hung a cautious U-turn, only to discover that her parking lot was jammed with cars.

I pulled in next door at the library and then made my way back to the bakery. Besides the locals, there were some tourists who'd stopped off to pick up some of IdaMae's homemade goodies. Two high school girls were filling white sacks and making change as fast as they could. The glass cases were beginning to empty, which is why the bakery closed at one o'clock on Saturdays. I looked around for IdaMae, but I didn't see her.

"Hi, is IdaMae here?"

"Huh?" One of the high school girls, too harried to really look at me, stuck her head through the door behind her and yelled. "IdaMae, there's someone here to see you."

IdaMae came out, saw me, and gestured with a sly toss of her head for me to follow her into the back. As soon as I was through the door, she pulled me farther along and then into a hot cramped office that only had room for a desk and two plastic avocado green chairs that rubbed against the walls.

"Jolie, what are you up to?"

"I came at a bad time, didn't I?"

IdaMae slid around behind the desk and sat. "Nah. I try not to mess with the crowd out there on Saturdays. If I come out, them tourists start asking for recipes! Like I'm gonna give 'em to 'em. I don't even have 'em writ down. I just keep 'em up here in my head.'' She tapped a gnarly finger against the white hair at her temple. ''Sit down, take a load off. How're you doin', girl?''

''I'm fine,'' I said, sitting on one of the hard plastic chairs. ''I was looking for a little information.''

Her eyes narrowed and she looked shrewd. ''I suppose I could trade a little information with you. I been hearin' that you're under suspicion for killing the Judge. Is that true?''

''It's true that Andy has talked with me twice. I didn't kill the Judge, if that's what you're asking.''

IdaMae hooted with laughter. ''Didn't figure that you did. Pretty clever way of doin' someone in, though. I heard you made up a murder just like that for your book. That true, too?''

''I'm afraid so,'' I said. ''But where did you hear it?''

''Let's see, I think it was from LouAnn over to the cafe. Yeah, I'm sure she was tellin' me about it. And then Carl at the grocery store, too.''

''Never mind,'' I said, realizing I'd been right about the difficulty of tracking the rumors.

''You know,'' IdaMae said, ''if I was to pick someone to get hisself killed, the Judge would'a been last one on the list. Leastways, nowadays.''

''IdaMae, everyone thinks the Judge was so wonderful, but you just said 'nowadays.' Does that mean he didn't used to be so popular?''

''Oh, he was always pretty well liked.''

''Then why did you say that?''

''Oh, I got my reasons. Don't suppose they're all that secret,'' she said with a shrug. ''When he first become judge, he thought that made him better'n everyone else. He once said, in private, of course, that there weren't a person around who wouldn't come before him eventually, and they'd best be on his good side when they did.''

''And that's why you didn't like him?''

''Among other things.''

''What other things?''

IdaMae leaned forward on her bony elbows. "Just what are you up to, Jolie? Are you doin' Andy's job for him?"

I couldn't lean forward—my knees were already pressed against the desk—but I made eye contact. "I seem to have a personal interest in this; I just want to make sure that Andy gets the right person. Which isn't me."

IdaMae nodded. "Sounds fair, but I got a little problem." She opened the bottom desk drawer, leaned back, and put her feet on the edge of the drawer. "Anyone who'd murder the Judge probably had good reason and they've got my sympathy. I don't know as I'd want 'em gettin' caught."

"Why not?"

"Jolie," she said, with her own particular shit-eating grin, "there's some things I'll tell you and some things that just ain't nobody's business but mine."

And this was obviously one of those things that was nobody's business but hers. Fine. I didn't see IdaMae killing the Judge and I wasn't about to annoy her by pushing that particular point. "Okay, IdaMae, *but*, if Andy doesn't get the right person, he's liable to settle for me."

"Well, it don't seem right for them to pin somethin' like this on you." Her eyes fixed on mine with fierce intensity. "If I was you, I'd go lookin' into some of the deals the Judge had cooked up before he became the Patron Saint of Purple Sage."

"Before? When was that?"

"About twenty, thirty years ago. He wasn't never poor, but it was right about then that he got real rich." She put her feet on the floor and turned around to face me. "See, the Judge had a cousin or something who was in the legislature and he knew everything that was comin' down the pike. He, the cousin, that is, knew when they was gonna be buyin' land for the post office, so he bought it up first and sold it off at a handsome profit. The Judge didn't get in on that, but he was right in there afterward."

"Didn't people suspect him of having inside information?"

"Shoot, most people knew what was goin' on, but who was going to say anything?" She paused to think. "It was just after I was openin' the bakery, 'cuz I remember the streets was tore up with bulldozers. No, maybe the bulldozers was for the new gas lines."

I took a breath and tried to get her moving back on a more productive track. "So, did the Judge do anything that hurt a specific person?"

One of the high school girls poked her head in the door. "IdaMae, some lady is asking for you. Says she knows you."

"So, who is it?" IdaMae asked.

The girl looked sheepish. "I forgot her name. I'm sorry, we're just so swamped."

"I'll be out in five minutes," IdaMae said as the girl left. "Damn, but it's tough to get good help." She sat up. "Jolie, best I can recollect, the Judge got richest off the lake, but I don't remember much more about it than that."

"That was a government project, wasn't it?"

"Yeah, and that's where he had his best connections. After he got so rich he become all holy, so's now everyone loves him. Well, not everyone, I expect, since someone killed him." She stood up. "I'd best get out there. Can't leave 'em alone forever."

"Thanks for your help," I said as I slipped out of the office after IdaMae.

"I'll think some more on it," IdaMae promised.

I waved good-bye and hurried outside, picking my way through the cars to where I'd parked next door. Interesting, both IdaMae and Diane had mentioned the lake. Obviously that was my starting place, and I planned to check it out right after lunch.

ELEVEN

RHONDA WAS TAPPING away at a computer in an office no bigger than most utility rooms. It was dirtier, though, in desperate need of repainting. On the dingy institutional green wall was a bulletin board with yellowed meeting notices and clippings of stories from surrounding papers that had been sent by one of the *Trib* reporters. Not the kind of place to encourage creativity.

"Where's Morris?" I asked.

Rhonda shrugged. "He's never here on Saturdays, so I use his office. Actually, I use his office all the time; he's got the only computer." She saved the file she'd been working on and then turned to me. "So, how are you? From what I hear, things aren't going too well."

I don't know why I wanted to accuse her of starting the rumors. Rhonda rarely gossiped, but her calm acceptance of the situation annoyed me.

"Things are lousy, which you must already know," I said. "I was kind of hoping you'd be able to help."

"Me? How?"

"I wanted to go through the old *Tribunes*. Is that possible? From, say, about the sixties to the seventies? Do you have them on microfilm?"

She didn't bother to ask why. Instead she rolled her eyes. "Are you sure you're up to this?"

"Why?"

She stood up. "Come with me and I'll show you."

I followed her out through the supply area and over to a door that was the same pale green as the office. It was also coated with a layer of smudged fingerprints and accumulated grime. She opened the door and pulled on a string hanging overhead. A bare light flicked on so that I could see a wooden staircase.

"Where do these go?" I asked.

"You're going to love this," Rhonda said. "If I ever need inspiration for my books, I just come up here."

We went up the stairs, did a sharp right-angle turn, and then instead of exiting, went up another flight. When she pushed open the door on the third floor I was almost overwhelmed by the sickening smell of bat guano mixed with dust and mold.

"This is disgusting," I said, wishing I didn't have to breathe.

"It gets worse."

"Oh, good."

In the dim light I could make out a wide hallway with doors opening off either side of it. Some were open, others were shut. Probably painted shut, and for good reason. One of the doors had a sign that said *RALPH PRATT INSURANCE*. Inside I could see a desk sitting at an angle because it only had three legs. There was also a broken lamp on the floor and a scattering of papers, all covered with enough dust to send any Gothic heroine's heart into a frantic flutter. Or maybe she'd just run for her broom and mop.

We kept on going, and I was busy trying not to touch anything, hoping against hope that there was going to be a very modern office at the end of that sloping hallway to hell. I knew better, but the romantic in me refused to give up the faith.

A few more doors down and Rhonda stopped. "Abandon all hope, ye who enter here."

She shoved open the door and I was almost relieved. The layer of dust wasn't quite as thick as everywhere else. It was hot, though, and the smell was still nauseating, but there was a window that could possibly be opened. At least there was light, and fairly modern three-drawer files. Rows and rows of them.

"You keep the microfilm in here?"

Rhonda grinned. "We've only put the last ten years on microfilm. You want anything before that, you get the real thing." She pulled open a file drawer and I saw neatly folded *Tribunes,* the paper yellowed. "Welcome to the dark ages."

"Why me?" I groaned.

"Ask and you shall receive. You asked, and I just delivered." Now that she had enjoyed my reaction to the upstairs dungeons of the *Trib,* Rhonda leaned against a rickety table and got serious. "Are you really thinking about going through this mess?"

I nodded. "I was. I guess I still am."

"You want to tell me why?"

"Research."

She continued to look at me and finally must have decided to accept my answer. With a shrug she straightened up. "Whatever. At least the papers were small back then. Usually only four pages an issue, and they only came out once a week. Well, I'll be downstairs for an hour or so. In case we lock up and you're still here I'd better show you the back way out or you'll be stuck here 'til Monday."

That gave me a shudder. "Where is it?"

"This way." We went to the farthest end of the hall and there was another door, identical to all the others. "The back stairs. At the bottom there's a door that leads into the alley. There's no dead bolt. In fact, if you get stuck and need back in, just jiggle the knob, and push the door hard. Morris calls it our fire escape, which, God knows, this place needs. It's a fire trap if there ever was one." She seemed to relish that thought.

"Well, thanks," I said, not really wanting to stay up there alone.

"No need to thank me; believe me in an hour or so, you won't." She went through the door and started down the back stairs.

With real reluctance I went back to the grimy file room. The first thing I tried to do was open the window, but it was caked with layers of paint that wouldn't budge. There was no air-conditioning and the combination of the heat and the smell was enough to discourage a normal person. Obviously, I was no longer normal.

I pulled open a few drawers and began to get a feel for the filing system. I wasn't even sure what I was looking for, maybe a miracle. Something on the lake, certainly.

I was sticky with sweat by the time I located it.

TWELVE

THERE WAS A PICTURE of the Judge, smiling into the camera and gesturing at the lake as if he personally had created it. He looked much younger, but that was to be expected since the date on the paper was July 1968.

There were four other men standing with him and, according to the caption, one was Luther Atwood, mayor of Purple Sage. He was Trey's dad, although I didn't see much family resemblance.

Also in the picture was a state engineer who'd headed the actual work, the president of the Purple Sage Chamber of Commerce, and the last man was listed as a state representative. The story was mostly comprised of quotes by the various dignitaries, saying how beneficial the lake was going to be to the people of Purple Sage. There was a sidebar that talked about the fish used to stock the lake, and another box gave statistics on the dam and the amounts of water it could handle. Apparently the lake was part of a flood-control system, although I'd never heard of any major floods in the county.

There was a vague mention that the project had taken over two years to complete. It didn't give me much to go on, but I went back to the drawer marked *JANUARY 1966* and began pulling out *Tribunes*. I will admit to a twinge of guilt as the brittle papers cracked and crumbled in my hands, but frankly the preservation I was most concerned about was my own.

The next story I found said the land for the lake had been acquired by the county, but didn't mention how that had been accomplished. There was a map in an April edition showing the outlines of the lake, and giving a few landmarks so residents could place it. I took a pen from my purse and made a sketch on the back of a deposit slip.

From there I began working backward, starting in December of 1966. I will admit to some digression. It was hard not to get caught up in the society news that mentioned the parents of my friends. Mr. and Mrs. Luther Atwood had given a barbecue in honor of their daughter Geneva's twelfth birthday. That was Trey's sister. The list of attendees included Matt's parents. The *Tribune* story went on to say that the guests were served brisket of beef, potato salad, homemade rolls, and lemonade. I wished there had been pictures.

On the next page was a short story about the suicide of a local man. His name caught me: Julio Chavez. Now I understood why I'd never heard anyone talk about Maria's father. Suicide isn't something that you bring up.

The *Trib* story said the body of Chavez was found with a gunshot wound to the head. Some kids out hunting heard the shot and discovered the pickup in a pasture not far from the proposed site for the new lake. Inside they found the body and the gun. With typical *Trib* caution, there was no mention of why he'd killed himself. There was, however, a long list of survivors. His wife, Aurelia Chavez; two sons, Hector and Julio, Jr.; one infant daughter, Maria; his mother, Mrs. Mercedes Chavez; and half a dozen others. Poor Maria.

With more attention to the task at hand, I began checking the legal notices as well as the regular news stories. I didn't find anything that looked promising, and by the time I had gotten through April of 1965, I was filthy dirty and getting discouraged. I looked out the grime-covered window and discovered that the sun had lowered considerably. My watch said that it was almost five. I replaced all the papers and made a note of where I'd stopped.

I used Morris's fire escape to let myself out.

MATT'S BRONCO WAS parked in front of my house and it was apparent that it was freshly washed and waxed. My car looked disreputable in comparison and I'm sure I didn't look much better. If I'd had anyplace else to go, I'd have gone there.

I dragged in the door, hoping irrationally that Matt had let Jeremy drive into town alone.

Matt was standing in the hall, watching Jeremy through the open door. He turned and saw me. "Jolie."

"Matt." Even for openers the conversation wasn't going well. "What are you two doing here?" I asked.

"Jeremy is getting some of his things."

I glanced in and saw Jeremy filling a duffel bag. "Moving out?"

Matt shifted. "Jolie, can we talk somewhere?"

I felt my spirits falling even farther. The only people who wanted to talk with me lately had things to say that I didn't want to hear.

"Sure. Let me just wash my hands first." I held them up and saw the streaks of dirt. They were worse than I'd realized.

"You might want to get your face, too," Matt said with a smile.

I went into the bathroom and saw what he meant. I did a quick rinse and then rejoined him in the hall. "Shall we go in the living room?" I asked.

"How about the patio?"

Obviously he wanted privacy—another bad sign. However, my mother had instilled so many good manners in me that I agreed. "Sure."

We went out through the sunroom. The white wrought-iron table and chairs stood out starkly on the brown brick patio. It was a soft evening and the scent of jasmine was heady. I looked at Matt and suppressed a sigh, remembering evenings in Austin when we'd sat on the patio of my house. Too bad those times were long ago and slipping farther away by the minute.

"Well?" I said, pushing back the memories.

Matt sat down, taking his time. I began to pick the brown leaves off the geranium.

"Jolie, would it be all right with you if Jeremy spent all next week with me?"

"Next week? What about school?"

"It's spring break."

Oh, hell, of course it was. I was certainly keeping up with Jeremy's life. "Sure, that's fine with me. I assume he's not playing baseball anymore this weekend."

"He didn't want to."

I could hardly blame him, and having him at Matt's seemed the best thing. "I'm just glad that he's got someplace else to go."

"But what about you?" Matt asked. "From what I've heard things can't be too pleasant for you right now, either."

He'd noticed; that was nice. Then I remembered that I wasn't supposed to want him in my new life. "I'll be fine," I said. I sounded like some kind of Christian martyr. Or the priggish schoolmarm.

"Jolie, don't do that. Talk to me."

Caught again. "I don't know what you want me to say, Matt. I'm not a child. 'Sticks and stones can break my bones . . .'"

"'But words can never harm me'? I'm not worried about the words; there's been more than a little violence."

"Just one rock," I said.

"And a murder."

That had slipped my mind. "Okay, so there's been some violence."

Matt moved the geranium aside and looked at me squarely. "Look, Jolie, I'm worried about you. The Judge is dead and someone used your murder to kill him. It seems that same someone is trying to make you the scapegoat. We have no idea what's going to happen next. I don't think you should be here alone."

His concern caused a familiar twitter in my stomach. Sometimes my body is a traitor to my more sensible brain, and I needed to be strong right now. It wasn't just a case of self-preservation, I was protecting Jeremy, too. I had spent twelve years supporting us and protecting us—I couldn't put our futures in the hands of anyone else. It would be too much like it had been before, when Jeremy was just a baby.

I was just twenty-two years old and my first husband, Steve, and I had only been married about a year when I found out I was pregnant. At first he'd been excited, just like I was. But then, as I grew more and more ungainly, he started working later and later. The night I delivered he didn't show up at the hospital until just before Jeremy's birth. My mother was there instead, asking every ten minutes where Steve could possibly be.

Like it was my responsibility to know. And on some level I believed it was my responsibility and I felt guilty that I couldn't jump up and go find him. Labor was a nightmare, but in the end I had Jeremy and that was all that mattered. I had thought my worries were over.

Then just a month and a half later, when I was still carrying around all the pregnancy fat and suffering from the worst of the postpartum blues, Steve came home one night around ten to announce that he was leaving. Leaving me, leaving Jeremy. He wasn't ready for all the responsibility. Besides, he'd met someone else. They were in love and she made him happy; she was fun.

All I could think about was Jeremy—our son—so little, so vulnerable. "What about Jeremy?" I had asked.

Steve had only shaken his head, with what I hoped was sadness. "Hey, I'm sorry, Jolie, but having a kid, being tied down like this, it just isn't for me, you know?"

All I'd said was, "Sure, I know."

While Steve packed, I sat in the living room, trying to figure out how I was going to live. When we'd first gotten married we'd sold both our cars and upgraded to a shiny new Renault. We'd also moved to Houston, away from my home and my family. I didn't have a job or any savings left. I was overweight, and I didn't have anything but maternity clothes to wear to interviews. There was exactly $43.27 in our checking account with rent due in four days. The rent was $125.

My litany was interrupted by the soft cry of my infant son, and I had walked into his dark room illuminated only by the teddy-bear nightlight and I had picked him up and held him. His warm tiny body had squirmed against mine and my heart had swollen almost to the bursting point.

As I listened to Steve dragging his things out of the apartment, I had made a vow that I would never, ever, let Jeremy down again. I would never place our lives in someone else's hands.

When Steve was finally ready to go, he had stuck his head in the door and said, "I'm sorry, babe, but I've got to do what's best for me. You understand."

"What about the car?" I had asked. "Can I keep it for a while? We'll have to sell it."

He had made a small sound, like a half laugh that never quite materialized. "Candy's waiting in the car for me now. I can hardly kick her out of it, can I?"

"But what about us? Jeremy and me?" I asked. "I don't have a job. I don't have any money—" My voice had risen and I could see Steve's look of distaste in response. Jeremy stirred in my arms. I lowered my voice and went on, "The rent is due."

"You can keep whatever's in the checking account, but I can't give you anything from my next paycheck—you know."

And then he was gone. I had spent the night on the rocker in Jeremy's room, holding him, cuddling him, feeding him.

It took me two days to get up the courage to call my parents, and they had come to rescue me and take me back to Dallas. My dad had acted as if this were a normal occurrence. As if I were coming home from college at the end of the term. My mother was silent, but somehow she made it clear that it was my fault that Steve had left. If only I'd been a better wife, smarter, prettier, if I hadn't gained so much weight when I was pregnant or if I'd kept the house better. She never came right out and said those things but I heard them in my head, just the same. And I beat myself with them.

I never saw Steve again. During the divorce his lawyer handled everything, and even after the judge decreed that I was to get child support and half the value of the car, Steve never came through. He was gone by then, long gone, and I never got any money. Or closure.

But I did keep my promise to Jeremy: I never trusted his future, his well-being, to anyone, until Matt. And when the marriage had gotten rocky all the old memories and the fears that clung to them came back to me. I hadn't worked in three years. My savings had dwindled to under $2,000, hardly enough to pay for the move, the deposits, and first and last months' rent.

I had let us become vulnerable to the point of dependence, and that, more than anything else, had to end.

"Jolie," Matt said, interrupting my thoughts, "you can't stay here alone—it isn't safe."

I had the urge to shake like a water-logged dog to rid myself of the memories that were still surrounding me. "I'm sorry, Matt, but I can't leave town," I said. "Andy's made it very clear that I have to stay."

"You could come out to the ranch."

"No!"

"Why?"

"It wouldn't work, not for either of us. You wouldn't be comfortable having me." I focused on his hands as I spoke, and had this totally unreasonable urge to reach out and touch them.

"I think safety is the issue, not comfort," Matt said.

I'd been feeling flattered by his concern, and maybe even tempted, but his last remark made it apparent the offer was merely to satisfy his sense of duty. I was embarrassed that I'd misunderstood. "No, thank you," I said, firmly.

He let out an exasperated breath. "Can you go to your mother's?"

"She's traveling. I don't even know where she is. Besides, Andy wouldn't allow it."

"To hell with Andy."

"He's the officer in charge of the investigation. He could put a restraining order on me, or whatever it's called. I'd rather not push him into that."

Matt shifted. "Have you talked with a lawyer?"

"Not yet, but I plan to." I stood up. "I'd like to talk to Jeremy for a minute."

With the same rigid clamp to his jaw that I'd seen many times before, Matt watched me go.

Jeremy was standing in the hall, his duffel bag a heavy lump beside him.

"Hi, honey," I said with a tight smile. "I understand you want to spend the week out at the ranch. I think that's a good idea."

"You're coming, too, aren't you?"

"I can't," I said in the practiced tone that mothers use when they refuse to hear any discussion on a subject. "Is Matt going to be with you all week? I don't want you out there alone."

Jeremy was frowning. "Yeah, he's going to stay the whole time. Except for Tuesday night. He's got to go to Austin. He's seeing somebody named Ruth and sometimes—"

I cut him off. "I don't want to know about it," I said too quickly. I made myself smile again. "I'm going to miss having you around."

"I don't know if I should go, since you're staying here. You might need me."

"You sound just like Matt," I said. "Not to worry, I can take care of myself. If anything comes up that I can't handle, I'll call." He didn't look convinced so I added, "Look, why don't you come into town on Tuesday and we can have dinner together? I'll fix something special."

"You have your writers' group."

"Not until seven. We can spend the afternoon together; maybe work on that new computer mystery you got."

Jeremy nodded, not out of any need of his own, but more likely to satisfy mine. "Okay." He reached for the duffel. "I guess we'd better get going. Where's Matt?"

"He's out on the patio."

"I'll get him." Jeremy left the duffel and called out the back door to Matt, who was already on his way in. "Are you ready to go?" Jeremy asked.

Matt looked at me. "I'm ready." He reached down and picked up Jeremy's bag as if it were light.

"Show-off," I said.

Jeremy grinned. "Muscles, Mom." Matt didn't smile.

I walked with them to the Bronco and hugged Jeremy good-bye. As they drove off, I wondered why they were always going places, and I was always being left behind.

THIRTEEN

"YOU SEE," Maria was saying as we zipped along the highway, "I want a wound that causes a lot of blood, because blood is so symbolic."

"How about a nosebleed?" I asked.

"That's disgusting, Jolie. How much sympathy could she get for a nosebleed?" Maria demanded. "I considered a head wound, but the symbolism would be stronger if the blood were on her skirt. I need something romantic."

"Romantic?"

"Wounds can be romantic." She stifled a yawn. "Sorry, I wrote until almost two last night."

"I don't know how you manage to fit everything you do into just twenty-four hours a day."

"Careful planning and precise execution."

That may be one hell of a method for getting things done, but it sounded to me like a terrible way to live your life.

In a few miles the two lanes turned into four and a bit more traffic appeared, although I couldn't figure out where the cars had come from. Maria and I were on our way to Brownwood. It was my idea. I'd invited her because I wanted to see a movie and Purple Sage doesn't have a movie theater. I'd also invited her because I wanted information.

"I'm really glad you could come with me," I said. "Sundays in Purple Sage are like a prelude to death."

"Now you're doing it. Talking about death."

"I have an excuse; I write mysteries. Anyway, I was afraid when you said your brother was in town, you'd want to stay and visit with him."

"Hector? No way. You probably didn't notice, but he's about the most macho male on the planet," she said.

Actually, I had noticed. The two times I'd seen Hector, I'd felt as if the room were heading for a testosterone overload. "Some men are like that," I said politely.

"Yeah. I mean, I love my brother, but I don't talk to him if I can avoid it. Besides, it won't hurt him any to take care of Mom for a while."

"How is your mother?"

Maria shifted in her seat and I could sense the shrug. "She's sick."

I looked at her. "Now who's being macho?"

She let out a small sigh, and stared out the window. After a while she started talking, her voice quiet and without the usual animation. "My mother is going downhill. I can almost see the changes every day. She drifts in and out of reality. Sometimes she calls me Honoria, some old friend of hers, and talks about things that happened thirty years ago as if they were yesterday. You can't believe the kind of things..." Maria turned to me, her voice changing. "I've got someone to take care of her some of the time, but I can't afford full-time help. My biggest fear is that she'll wander off and then forget where she lives." She paused and finished even more quietly. "I'm going to have to put her in some kind of a home soon, and I can't even think about it."

I offered my thoughts slowly and gently. "It might not be so terrible for her. It might even be better. And for you."

"I know; it's not that. It would be better for both of us. It's the money. It always comes back to the damn money."

"What about your brothers? Can't they help?"

There was bitterness in Maria's voice. "Hector doesn't have a spare dime. I've asked Julio, and he's willing enough, but what good is a hundred dollars a month going to do? Those places are expensive."

"No insurance?"

Maria shook her head. "No insurance covers Alzheimer's."

"Have you tried getting the money from somewhere else?" I asked.

Some strong emotion flashed across her face, as if I'd meant welfare. That would be worse than death, considering Maria's pride.

I added, "I mean, are there any other relatives . . ." I let my words trail off. "Never mind, it's none of my business."

With a visible effort Maria relaxed. After a moment, she spoke lightly. "This was supposed to be fun and at the moment I'm not having fun."

"I could juggle. . . ." I removed both hands from the steering wheel.

"Let's just talk about something else," Maria said. I put my hands back as she asked, "How's the job hunting?"

"That's not fun, either."

"Okay. What about the police investigation?"

Just the topic I wanted to talk to her about, although I planned to take things slowly. "I don't know much of anything about it. Andy doesn't talk to me, except to ask questions."

"Andy's been to the house twice. What an asshole!" Maria was back to her fiery self. Watching the changes in her made me think of fire and ice. All flaming passion in her personal life; icy professionalism in her business. "You know, when you stop to think about it," she went on, "everything we've had to put up with is Diane's fault."

"Diane's?"

Maria leaned toward me. "Her and her damn realism. If she hadn't insisted you talk to Andy about how your murder would be investigated, none of this would be happening to us."

Except that I'd followed up on Diane's suggestion because it was a good one. "I thought it would be good for the book."

"'If it's good for the book, it's bad for the heroine,'" Maria quoted. That's what they'd taught us at a writing seminar.

"I think in my case there's a new twist to it," I said. "It was good for my book, but bad for the author."

"It'll turn out okay."

"I hope."

"It will. And it's given me an idea for my next project," Maria said. "I'm going to do a mystery. So," she went on, "tell me what you know. Did Andy say anything useful when he talked to you?"

"I didn't think it was very useful," I said, hearing the irony in my answer. "He told me in very nice words that I wasn't to leave town."

"No! That's terrible. What a rotten thing to say! Why would he do that?"

"Because I'm a suspect."

"Does he have even one shred of evidence against you?"

"Haven't you heard? I wrote the book on murder, at least according to everyone in Purple Sage. I have the only can of Pest Out sold in town for the past several months. I had a fight with the old—" I edited my description "—man. And I don't have an alibi. People have gone to the electric chair for less. Or the room where they give the lethal injections."

"No motive."

But all the circumstantial evidence was there, which made me regret that I hadn't stayed in town and spent the time reading old *Tribunes*. "Maria, you talked to the Judge the day he died," I said. "Did he do anything, say anything, that was out of the ordinary? Talk like there was someone who hated him?"

"The Judge?" she said with a quick laugh. "He wouldn't say something like that. He was the great man, remember? Besides, he didn't talk to me at all. To him I was just a servant."

"But he did tell you that a writer was coming by."

"Only because he wanted to make sure I had his house clean in time. He just wanted me to hurry and get out of there."

"What time was that? What time did you leave?"

She twisted awkwardly in her seat, straining against the seat belt so she could see me better. "Jolie, you sound like Perry Mason."

"It's just that you were there. In his house. Maybe you saw something or overheard something. I don't know, something!"

"Believe me, if I had, I would have remembered by now," she said, making a face. "Andy's made me tell him about that day at least a dozen times. I know everything I cleaned, and in what order. There just wasn't anything unusual."

I thought if I asked the right question, maybe it would trigger something that Andy had missed. "Did the Judge say what time the writer was coming?"

Another shake of her head. "Sorry, no."

I thought some more. "Okay, but he did try to hurry you out, right? Did he say what time he wanted you to leave?"

"Sorry, no. I left about four-thirty, and he was watching the clock as I went out the door."

"Maria, you grew up in Purple Sage, did you ever hear of any shady deals the Judge was involved in?"

"I was a kid when I was growing up! Kids don't listen to adults talk. And, I left for UT when I was seventeen." She looked out the window of the car, and pointed. "Go left up here at the Y."

I veered left. I was out of questions, anyway.

I HATED THE FILM. It was one of those semi-artsy, quasi-suspenseful spy-thrillers, dripping with pregnant pauses that inevitably lead to a sex scene. I was having a terrible time watching them. They reminded me of Matt and the good parts of our marriage. I especially missed the times after making love when we would be lying together, talking about things that were of no consequence, just feeling the warmth of each other's body. I missed the sound of his voice and drifting off to sleep with my head on his chest, feeling the rhythmic rise and fall of his breathing.

I must have made a sound, because Maria leaned over and whispered, "Are you okay?"

"Fine," I said softly. I had to get out of there. "I'll be back. Want anything?"

She shook her head no, and I got up and left.

I took refuge in the rest room, spending as much time as I could redoing my makeup, recombing my hair, and cleaning out my purse. Then I went out to the lobby. Another film must have been about to begin, because there were lines of people at the snack bar. I got into one of them and, when I reached the counter, realized I had to buy something. I ordered a tub of buttered popcorn and a diet Coke, thinking there was logic in that somewhere.

When I got my food I turned around, and almost knocked over Morris Pratt, Rhonda's boss at the *Trib.*

"Hi," I said.

"Uh, uh, Jolie."

At least he had my name right. Morris was in his early thirties, and while he wasn't considered much of a newspaperman, he didn't really need to be. His dad had started the newspaper, family money kept it going, and he had Rhonda to dig up the dirt. He did have a claim to fame: he was Purple Sage's only devotee of GQ. His pants were properly pleated, his shirt baggy, and his shoes shiny new Guccis.

"How are you?" I asked.

He stood as if planted, right in my way, too stupefied to move. "Uh, fine. Uh, what are you doing up here?"

"Watching a movie."

"Oh, of course." He laughed, but it came out too loud and too hearty. His eyes, soft chocolate brown behind Ralph Lauren glasses, were trained on a movie poster hanging above my head. "Guess everyone needs a little break now and then."

Was he including murderers? It sounded like it. He laughed again, this time with less vigor. His eyes focused on me for just a second, then flicked quickly away. "Well, it was a, uh, good seeing you," he said.

"Good seeing you, too," I said.

"Sure," but he was already sidling away his hands fumbling in his wallet. The man was scared to death of me.

I went back into the theater, and spent the rest of the movie planning what I was going to do as soon as I got back to Purple Sage.

FOURTEEN

WHEN I STOPPED the car in front of Maria's house, she jumped out and started swearing. "Damn that Hector! He's gone." Maria's VW and a big old Buick were in the driveway. "God, I hope Mom is okay."

I raced after her, across the tiny lawn hemmed in by huge flower beds. Maria flung open the door of the old stucco house and called out. "Mother?"

There was no answer. We hurried through a crowded living room, and a big old-fashioned kitchen, then out the back door. Her mother was stooped over a small garden, using a hoe carefully between the rows of sprouting plants.

As the screened wooden door slammed, Mrs. Chavez looked up in surprise. "Oh, it's you, Maria. You startled me."

Maria stopped and I almost ran into her. She moved more slowly toward her mother. "Where is Hector? Did he go home?"

"Yes, he wanted to visit some friends on the way back." She smiled at me. "He's such a busy little boy." Her words held the lilt of a Spanish accent.

Maria turned to look at me. "False alarm. Damn it, I wish Hector had waited for me." She went to the back door, apparently forgetting her mother entirely. "Come on in, Jolie."

I started to say something to Mrs. Chavez, but she'd moved away and was gazing distractedly at the chain-link fence. I followed Maria.

"I've got a good mind to call Hector!" Maria snapped as she threw her purse on the Formica kitchen table.

"He won't be in Dallas, yet."

"Yeah, but I could leave a pretty nasty message on his answering machine." Maria opened the refrigerator. "I need to go to the grocery store. Now I'll have to leave Mother alone again!" She closed the refrigerator firmly.

"If it would help, I could wait here while you go."

Maria looked surprised, then shook her head. "No, thanks. Mom can stay alone for a few minutes."

"It's no big deal."

She seemed to think about it. "I wouldn't be more than fifteen minutes; I'll hurry."

"Take your time."

Maria picked up her purse from the table where she'd thrown it. "I don't like this, Jolie, but I don't see any other way." She sounded as if she were doing me a favor instead of the other way around. Maybe it was just misdirected anger from her upset with Hector.

"I'll see you in a little bit," I said, as she walked out, her head held high.

I stayed in the kitchen, wondering how you baby-sat a grown woman. Mrs. Chavez had gone back to the garden, but she was just looking at it now. I had expected her body to be frail, but it wasn't. Her arms and hands were well muscled, probably from her gardening.

After a few minutes my mind gravitated to the Judge's murder. Perfume. Feeling like a horrible sneak, I tiptoed into the hallway and looked in the bathroom. The sink was small, old, and freestanding. There was no space for anything on its pitted porcelain surface. The medicine cabinet was practically empty. No doubt Maria had emptied it to make sure her mother didn't get into something dangerous.

There were no other cabinets at all. I went back into the kitchen and looked out the window. Mrs. Chavez was sitting on an old rusted metal chair, staring at the sky. I tiptoed into Maria's room.

On her dresser was a tray filled with perfumes: Giorgio, Silence, Fidgi, Jontue, Tea Rose, Pavi Elle, and Gucci. There were also jars of scented creams, but no Youth Dew.

I hurried out to check on Mrs. Chavez. As I looked out the back door, she turned around and caught me watching. I went outside to join her, trying to behave as if I hadn't been searching her house. It wasn't easy, considering I felt I'd been about as rude as a guest can be.

"Your flower beds out front are going to be spectacular in a few days," I said with a smile.

"Yes, they are. I'm quite a gardener. They say I can grow anything." She was facing the sun and squinting as she stared at me.

Maria was attractive, but Mrs. Chavez must have been stunning in her younger years. She had the same high cheekbones as Maria, and the same thick dark hair, with only a few silver streaks. It was in a tight bun, pulling the skin on her face almost smooth. "Where did Maria go?" she asked.

"To the store," I said.

She nodded wisely. "I heard her complaining about Hector. She has such a temper!" She looked at me. "I know you're one of Maria's friends, but I don't remember you."

"I'm sorry, I should have introduced myself. I'm Jolie Wyatt. I met you a couple of months ago," I said. "I'm in Maria's writing group."

"Wyatt? Are you related to Matthew?"

"His ex-wife," I said.

Suddenly she had a reference point. "You're the one they say murdered the Judge."

I could feel my shoulders slump. "That's what they're saying, but it's not true."

She reached over and patted my hand. "I know it's not, child. I'm just an old woman who says things she should not." She took me by the arm. "Come into the kitchen and we'll have some lemonade. You should protect your fair skin from the sun."

We went inside and she sat down at the Formica table. She didn't go for the drink she'd offered, instead she stared at me. "I don't remember you. Who are you?"

"Jolie Wyatt," I said again. "A friend of Maria's."

"Please, sit down. I'm sure Maria won't be long."

I sat, and wondered what to say next.

Mrs. Chavez filled the silence. "Wyatt? Did you kill the Judge?"

"No, of course not."

"Someone said you did. Jolie Wyatt. That's the name." She let out a long sigh. "People die. Even the Judge." A tear appeared in the corner of her eye and she wiped it away, raising her proud chin.

"You knew the Judge?"

She stared into space, and I wondered if her mind had drifted off. Then she spoke. "Yes, of course. But everyone knows the Judge. Purple Sage is small, and he's an important man."

Her tenses had changed, as if he were still alive. I leaned forward. "Mrs. Chavez, can you think of a reason why someone would kill the Judge?"

Her black eyes focused hard on me. "It was senseless! There can be no good reason to kill a man like that." I suddenly saw more than just the physical resemblance to Maria.

She got up and took a glass from the cupboard, filled it with water, then left it on the counter. She began to look out the window over the sink. After a few minutes she turned around and saw me.

"Oh, hello." Her face registered surprise.

"I'm Jolie," I said, as if it were the first time. "I'm waiting for Maria."

"Oh. Nice to meet you, Jolie." She stopped and looked startled. "Did you ask me a question?"

I was beginning to understand Maria's worries about her mother.

"It isn't important," I said.

"No. Tell me." She looked concerned, as if it mattered a great deal. "You did ask me a question. What was it?"

"I asked about the Judge."

Relief crossed her face, followed by a smile. "Yes, the Judge. Such an important man." She sat down.

"Someone didn't like him."

She made a huffing sound. "Foolish! His heart is always in the right place. Always."

"Oh, I'm sure you're right," I said, quickly.

She didn't seem to notice. Her voice grew soft, pensive. "Life always ends with death. Even in life, we are all the victims of death. It comes and takes those we love." She looked down at her hands; they were coated with a fine sprinkling of dirt from the garden. "Oh! Just look at my hands! I must go wash them." She stood up. "You must excuse me." And then she disappeared into another room.

There didn't seem anything for me to do but sit and watch her go. I felt sorry for both Maria and her mother, and then I got worried. What was Mrs. Chavez doing? I stood up and looked in the hallway. She was sitting on her bed, her hands still dirty, flipping with agitation through a magazine. I slipped back to the kitchen, wondering what to do next.

Luckily Maria was back in just a few minutes. She was almost breathless as she dashed in carrying just one bag of groceries.

"Where's my mother?"

"In the other room," I said, standing up. "She's fine."

Maria dropped the sack on the table. "Good. Did she talk to you?"

"A little."

"Was she . . . did she seem okay?"

"She seemed a little distracted at the end, but I probably just wasn't very good company," I said. Maria nodded as I picked up my purse. "Well, I'd better get going."

"Give me a minute and I'll walk with you." Maria checked on her mother, then followed me outside. "Thanks for staying, Jolie."

"You're welcome." I went past Maria's car and looked at the old Buick. "Whose car is that?"

"Oh, my mother's."

"Does she drive?"

"She's not supposed to, but sometimes she does. Usually I hide her keys, but she's good at finding them." She watched me climb into the Mazda. "Well, thanks again."

"Thanks for going with me." I waved good-bye, and drove off feeling like I was escaping.

FIFTEEN

I HEADED TOWARD the Purple Sage *Tribune*. A few minutes later as I braked for a stop sign, I realized that the Judge's house was on the next block. I moved ahead slowly, wanting a little better look.

The exterior was as impressive as always. It was huge, two stories, with fake marble columns and a wide circular drive sheltered by massive old oak trees.

Directly across the street from it was a simple wood-frame house, and the Captain, as always in his white, was sitting on his porch rocking.

I turned back to the Judge's and noticed a fairly new BMW parked in the driveway and a woman loading something into the trunk. When she heard my car she looked up and waved for me to stop.

It was Lisa Perry, the Judge's niece. She lived in Dallas, and I knew her because she and Matt were friends. On her infrequent visits, she and her husband had come out to the ranch. We'd hit it off right away, so it had always been fun to have them down.

I stopped the car, turned off the motor, and walked toward her. She straightened up and smiled. "Hi, Jolie. Boy, is it great to see you!"

"Me?"

"I needed a friendly face, desperately! This is a horrible job. Come on in, you look like you could use something to drink."

Without waiting for my answer she led me into the house. I'd never been inside the Judge's home before, and I'll admit to a little flutter of nerves, like the old man might suddenly appear and tell me to get out.

Lisa, slim in her jeans and baggy work shirt, gestured to the room in general. It was filled with antique furniture, and littered with books and boxes. "Have a seat if you can find one;

be careful, there's still fingerprint powder in places I missed. I'm going to wash my hands. Will iced tea be okay?''

"Fine."

She disappeared through a huge archway, and I wandered around, admiring things. The furniture was magnificent. A bookcase with a leaded-glass front stood against the far wall, and a huge picture window filled the wall on my right. The drapes were a pale yellow that exactly matched the Queen Anne sofa with its delicate curves and glowing wood. What I could see of the polished floor looked like walnut, although a massive oriental rug covered most of it.

I peeked into the next room, and discovered a formal dining room with a delicate crystal chandelier over the silken wood table. I moved a heavy velvet drape in one corner and discovered a butler's pantry, complete with sink and warming oven.

I turned at the soft sound of footsteps behind me. "This is magnificent," I said, as Lisa held out a glass to me.

"Uncle Judge definitely knew how to live. Here's your tea. It's not sweetened; I hope that's okay."

"Fine," I said, taking a sip and wondering if she knew that I was the prime suspect for her uncle's murder.

"Let's go in the back; I'm dying for a cigarette, and even with my uncle dead I'd feel guilty about smoking in here. I'm afraid he'd come back and haunt me."

I followed her through a modern kitchen and into a breakfast nook that was all glass and sunshine. "I'm sorry about your uncle's death," I said. "I would have come by sooner to offer my condolences, but I didn't realize you were in town."

She plopped down at a small white table, and put her feet up on one of the yellow vinyl chairs. "Oh, that's okay; I haven't seen anyone since I've been here except the people at the funeral and the police," she said, pulling cigarettes and a lighter from her pocket. "Have a seat." I sat down across from her as she lit a cigarette and pulled a half-full ashtray closer.

Interesting how something as small as a cigarette can shift our thinking. I suddenly saw the Judge as a real person. He had a niece who smoked and he complained about it. He probably complained about dandelions in his yard and IRS forms, too.

just like the rest of us, which allowed for a lot of human flaws and foibles that I hadn't thought about before.

"Can you believe what a mess this house is?" Lisa asked. "I know in a few weeks I'll realize that Uncle Judge is gone and start missing him, but at the moment, all I can think of is the stuff that has to be done. And the fact that he was murdered. Odd, isn't it?" I nodded, watching as she brushed a lock of dark curls off her forehead. Then she went on, "I mean, for someone to murder Uncle Judge...it just seems so..." She fumbled for a word as she took a puff of her cigarette. "So, unnecessary. He was old; he couldn't have lived much longer, anyway. And they did it so cleverly, using that poison. It seems almost fiendish. That's a weird word."

I had to tell her. "I don't know how to say this, but you're going to hear it anyway." I paused, feeling her dark eyes watching me. "Lisa, you must not be getting out much in Purple Sage, because apparently you've missed the gossip."

"The only place I've been is the funeral home, where people kept patting me like I was ten years old," she said. "So, what's the gossip? Anything juicy?"

I nodded. "People in town are blaming me for your uncle's murder."

She started to laugh, saw how serious I was, and said, "You? That's ridiculous, Jolie."

I explained as best I could about my manuscript, and the method for murder. I skimmed over the argument I'd had with her uncle in the courthouse, but I did tell, in detail, about Andy taking the can of Pest Out from my garage. When I was finished, I shook my head. "I almost feel responsible. If I hadn't written that damn book, maybe he wouldn't have died."

She stubbed out her cigarette. "That's really shitty."

"I know," I said. "I'm so sorry."

"Not that; it's not your fault if some loony steals an idea from your book. I meant about people blaming you. And the police coming after you. Jesus, Jolie, it sounds like they've damn near got enough to take it to the grand jury."

My heart contracted. I'd forgotten that Lisa was a public defender in Dallas. "Oh, hell."

"Hell is right. Especially because I can't think of a single real motive for his murder. I've talked with the police a couple of times, and I haven't been much help. Believe me, I've gone over that in my mind a lot, and I can't come up with anything. It certainly can't be money; he left every penny to his dear alma mater."

"You're kidding?" I asked, taking a gulp of my tea.

She shook her head. "It was arranged years ago. He's going to have a building named after him or some damn thing. Like the university needs the money. They own half the state as it is."

"What about the rest of his stuff? Didn't he collect books, or something?"

She reached for another cigarette. "Lord, yes! He's probably turning over in his grave right now, knowing I'm not handling them right. Most of those are going to the university, too."

"What about his other things?"

"Museums. Or they'll be sold and the university gets the money."

"And insurance?"

Lisa laughed. "He didn't believe in it. Uncle Judge said that was like betting against yourself."

"So, what do you get out of the deal?" I asked. "It looks like you're doing all the work."

Lisa took a long drag of her cigarette, and as she exhaled, waved the smoke away. "I get the joy of the leftovers. It's my own fault, though; he always felt that I was on the wrong side of the law. He wanted me to be a district attorney instead of wasting my brains and education 'defending that scum.' That's a direct quote, in case you hadn't heard it before. I heard it all the time, at least once every visit."

"That's hardly fair." And it was certainly a new side of the Judge's personality. This afternoon was becoming a real eye-opener. "We need people like you."

"Oh, I know. I probably shouldn't have said that; Uncle Judge was sweet to me and I guess to most people. God, the way everyone talked at the funeral I thought they were getting ready to canonize him!"

"Well, he was pretty generous."

"I guess so, but it seemed to me he always demanded a whole lot in return. I guess that's why in the last couple of years he stopped giving his money away."

"He did?"

"Well, that's not exactly true, either." She stopped to think about it. "He must have quit about a year ago. I think he was pissed because he hadn't been reelected. He said he didn't feel that he was being properly appreciated, but between you and me, I think he just wanted people to grovel." She sipped some tea.

"I never heard anything like that."

"Oh, he was coy about it, but that's the way he felt privately." She wriggled her toes, stretched, and then put her feet on the floor. "Remember when he gave ten thousand dollars for the new library? Well, then he got all pissed off because he said they were ordering what he considered trash books."

"Our library? You're kidding? What kind of trash?"

"Anything with a lot of swearing or sex. He said it was always gratuitous. He thought *Ordinary People* was filled with filth."

I had an idea. "What did he think of June Ingram's books?"

"Oh, he thought June Ingram hung the moon. He said her books were classic detection in the purest sense. No sex, no swearing, and no violence. Mostly puzzle, which is what he thought a mystery ought to be."

"Maria said a writer was supposed to come by that night. The night he was killed."

"Well, he certainly considered June a writer." Lisa put her empty glass on the table and looked at me. "You can't possibly be thinking that June Ingram killed my uncle?"

"Oh, no. I didn't mean that," I said. "But, someone had to have been there. Someone has to know something about his murder."

She nodded, for a moment deep in thought. Then she shrugged. "He lived a pretty isolated existence in the last year." She shook her head. "We may never know the whole truth."

We sat for a moment in silence and then Lisa stood up, stretching again. She put her cigarette out as a final gesture.

I stood, too. "Can I give you a hand with anything?"

"No, thanks, I wish you could. Right now I'm sorting, and I'm afraid that I'm the only one who can do it. I've got to get rid of things that no one else would want." She grinned. "Since the university gets the house, they also get the joy of hiring someone to clean it up and get it ready for sale."

She picked up both our glasses and headed for the kitchen.

I followed her. "Lisa, you haven't noticed anything funny in the house, have you? Or anything missing?"

"Who would know? The police were all over, but this place is huge, and every corner is crammed with stuff."

"Oh."

She put the glasses in the dishwasher and turned to look at me. "You're really worried about the police investigation, aren't you?"

"Shouldn't I be?"

"No." Her voice became firm and professional. "Look, I shouldn't have said what I did about the grand jury. All they've got against you is circumstantial evidence, and that's not going to be sufficient to convict." I didn't say anything, and after a moment she added, "If you're worried, though, I'll give you the name of one hell of a good lawyer in Dallas. He could get you off even if you did kill my uncle. Even if you killed him in the middle of the square with a crowd watching."

"I didn't," I said.

"Then don't worry about it." She leaned against the counter. "Finkman is incredible; of course, he charges the earth for his services, but with Matt's money you can afford it."

I swallowed before I said, "Matt and I are divorced."

"You're kidding!" she said. "When did that happen?"

"The official final part was two months ago."

"Jesus, Jolie, how did your life get to be such a mess? What did you do? Piss off your fairy godmother? Go on a mirror-breaking spree? Throw slugs in a wishing well?"

"Beats me. And now I don't even have a job. I'm trying to find one in Austin, but I kind of wanted to let Jeremy finish this school year."

"So what are you doing for money?"

"Luckily, it doesn't take much in Purple Sage. Matt's giving me child support, which I didn't even ask for. Anyway, that's been enough so far. I do have a little bit of savings. Oh, hell, it'll work out, it always does." I said it with less conviction than I had five days before to Jeremy. Of course, a lot had happened in those five days. "Look, I'd better get going."

She slid an arm around my shoulder as we went toward the front door. "Well, it was great seeing you. I'm in the middle of a big trial and I've got to get back to Dallas, otherwise I'd stay and help you muddle through this mess."

"Thanks. I wish you were going to be here. It's nice to know that someone believes in my innocence."

"That's why I became a public defender."

We hugged good-bye at the car. "It was great seeing you, Lisa."

"You, too. Just remember to call if you need anything. And when you get settled in Austin, call me with your number."

I promised I would, then headed for the *Trib*.

I PARKED MY CAR on the street at the mouth of the alley and kept looking over my shoulder as I walked to the back door of the building. Even in the late afternoon sunshine I felt uneasy. Going into someone's office without their knowing about it is not my style. Under other circumstances I would have called Morris and asked his permission. As it was, I couldn't: he was in Brownwood.

I gave the door one tug and twisted the knob; it opened as easily as if I'd used a key.

There was plenty of light coming through the filthy window, but instinctively I turned on the switch. When I finally closed the door it locked with the tiniest click. I almost went into cardiac arrest at the finality of that little sound, knowing that I was officially breaking and entering. I kept reminding myself that Rhonda had invited me to come back, well, perhaps not exactly invited, but she had told me how to get in.

The stairs were just as dim and narrow as I'd remembered, and the smell of bat guano just as nauseating. There were sounds, too. Joints cracked and windows rattled in the softest breeze. On my last visit I had attributed those noises to people working downstairs, only today, on a Sunday afternoon, the building was empty.

I gave myself a mental shove, and started up the steps.

"Rhonda? Are you here yet?" I called. As if I had planned to meet her. I can be so clever under pressure. "Rhonda? We'd better get to work on that research."

My words bounced off the walls and echoed back to me softly.

SIXTEEN

At first I only found stories about the Judge's generosity, stories that pointed up why he had been called the Patron Saint of Purple Sage.

For example, in 1965 Judge Osler had chaired the United Way drive, and when the campaign had failed to reach its goal he had donated almost $3,000 to make up the difference. Another time he had given $1,000 for trees to be planted around the square. He was pictured with the trees that were little more than sticks. Today, they were huge and full, almost reaching the top of the courthouse.

Then stories of the lake started cropping up. I discovered that the original plans had called for it to be several miles wider than the final size. According to the *Trib* story, it was narrowed to save money, although the citizens were assured it would still be large enough for recreation and to handle the overflow if the dam had to be opened.

And I found a list of families whose land was to be flooded. Theodore Ingram, Herbert Porter, Robert Quinton, Enrique Gomez, and Angus Schmidt.

The room was growing dimmer as the sun slid behind the courthouse. Above me I imagined I could hear the whisper of bats as the animals began waking.

I snatched up the copy of the *Trib* and scooted down the front stairs to the offices. When I got to the bottom, I opened the door and called out.

"Anybody here?"

Silence, except for the rattle of brown paper on the windows caused by the draft when I opened the door. The big room was in shadow, dim and empty.

"Hello?" I called again.

Nothing this time. I whipped over to the copy machine, turned it on, and counted seconds until the green light stopped blinking and it was warmed up. As soon as I had turned and folded the paper enough to copy the whole story along with the map of the lake, I clicked off the machine and ran back upstairs.

I didn't know why I was getting spooked, but I was. I began to hear more flutterings from the attic. I noticed cars passing by on the street below. Each time one stopped, presumably at the light, my heart did an irregular tattoo until the sound of the motor moved on.

I shoved the last two newspapers back into their drawers and slammed the files shut. The sun was all but gone by now, and the room was getting dark. I grabbed up my purse and the copies I'd made, and dashed for the back door, racing down the stairs.

I was at the landing, ready to start down the second flight, when I heard the knob on the door below me rattle.

I froze, trapped like the criminal I was.

The door rattled ominously again and then swung inward.

"Jolie Wyatt!"

My heart slammed to a halt. Framed in the doorway was Andy Sawyer.

"God, you scared me!" I said, slowly making my way down the stairs.

When I reached the bottom, he towered over me. One hand was resting on his holster and his legs were spread and braced as if he were about to pull out his gun.

"You want to tell me what you were doing in there?"

I tried to speak naturally, but I was having trouble breathing. "I was going to do some research. For a book."

He moved his hand away from his gun, but he didn't relax his stance. "So Morris knows you're here?"

"Well, not exactly." There was a hint of guilt in my voice. I made myself sound more confident. "Rhonda is the one who helped me yesterday, and she's the one who told me how to get back in today. I was only upstairs in the file room."

He shifted his broad shoulders, and shook his head. "I've been looking all over town for you. You mind coming down to the station with me?"

"The police station? Why?"

"I need to get your fingerprints. It's just a formality."

He held the door for me as if it were a social occasion, but I didn't feel sociable. I scuttled past Andy, afraid he might grab me. "Why don't I follow you over?" I asked. "My car is just around the corner."

"I know."

He locked the door, then we started walking together down the dim alleyway. I kept some distance between us. "Will it take long?" I asked.

"Shouldn't."

"Good." I pulled out my keys.

We reached the end of the alley and I saw his police car parked next to my Mazda. Without a word I went to it, climbed in, and started the motor. I didn't even look back as I drove the few blocks to the new police station. When I pulled into the lot Andy cruised in beside me. He held the front door for me and guided me back to his office.

I had only been in the police station once before. In typical Purple Sage fashion there had been an open house when the building was first put into use, but I'd only stayed long enough to see the dispatcher's area. Now I was in the back of the building, and I noticed another door off to the right with a large glass window. Through the window I could see jail cells.

"This will only take a few minutes," Andy said, reaching into a wire basket on his gray metal desk. He pulled out a sheet of paper with squares for each fingerprint, just one more indignity.

"Why do you need my fingerprints?" I asked as Andy rolled my left thumb across the paper. "Is it important?"

He moved on to my index finger. "We got prints off that can of Pest Out and we have to identify them."

"We both know that mine are on there."

"Can't rule yours out until I know what yours look like." He kept his grip on my hand until he'd finished with it, then switched to the other one.

"How much of that stuff was missing from the can?" I asked. What I really wanted to know was if the murderer had used my Pest Out.

"About a cup and a quarter."

"Oh."

"You could have mismeasured," Andy suggested. "Or some of it could have evaporated."

Or someone could have sneaked into my garage, poured out a quarter of a cup, distilled it, and used it to kill the Judge. I couldn't think about that. "Were you following me?" I asked.

"Nope. I'd been to your house, but you weren't there. I was just making the rounds when I spotted your car. Lucky for me."

Why didn't I feel so lucky? "I'm thinking of getting a lawyer," I said.

Andy finished with my little finger. "That's certainly your right, although I don't see why you'd bother unless you've got something to hide."

I snatched my hand away. "Of course I don't have anything to hide! Damn it, Andy, this whole thing is making me crazy. I can't go anywhere without people talking about me; it's horrible."

He sat down in his chair and focused his steady gaze on me. "Then if I were you, I'd cooperate like crazy to get this investigation over and done with."

"I thought I had been! What more do you want from me? I've told you everything I know." I took a breath. "Andy, I didn't kill the Judge and I don't know who did. It could be anyone. For all I know, it could be you." I hadn't meant to say that. I didn't really believe it, I was just fighting back blindly.

Andy looked me over. He finished with his eyes locked on mine. When the silence was enough to make me scream he nodded slowly. "Why would you say a thing like that?"

Because fear made me stupid. "Because you knew as much about using Pest Out for murder as I did."

"Have you mentioned this to Chief Tieman?"

"No."

He sat as still as stone. "I wouldn't if I were you. I'm your only chance right now. If he pulls me off this case, you'll get some rookie trying to make himself a hero. You'll be indicted first thing. I don't think they've got enough for a conviction, but it could be pretty unpleasant in the meantime."

My knees began to wobble. If he was trying to frighten me, he was doing a very good job. Or was he just trying to keep me quiet? "Can I go?"

He nodded. "We're finished here."

"Thank you." I picked up my purse and hurried out the door on my shaky legs. Fear also made me fast.

As SOON AS I got home, I called George Tyler, a lawyer friend of mine in Austin.

"Hey, Jolie, I haven't heard from you in ages! How's life treating you?"

I started to give him the highlights, and since he was an old friend George made soothing comments that spurred me on. Pretty soon he'd heard the whole story. "And the worst of it," I said, "is that I'm afraid they might bring charges against me, and that would be horrible for Jeremy."

"Not to mention for you. Look, Jo, I'm glad you called. You do need an attorney, but I'm not your man. You need someone who's a criminal lawyer, and I handle civil cases."

"Aren't they expensive? I don't have a job—"

"Whoa, it's okay. You won't need a fortune. I know a guy who takes a lot of cases just because he cares. I think running rings around those small-town lawyers would appeal to him. His name is Morgan Winchell and I think you should give him a call." Then he gave me the number.

It wasn't exactly Racehorse Haynes, but I knew the name and from what I'd heard he was good.

"Thanks so much, George," I said, beginning to feel better. "I'll call him first thing in the morning. Oh, and thanks for listening; I really owe you one."

"And I intend to collect. Dinner the first week you move back. My treat."

FIRST THING Monday morning I called Morgan Winchell's office, only to learn that he was in court and probably would be for several days. "Perhaps his associate could help you," the secretary added.

I assured her that he couldn't and left my number for Winchell.

"It could be next week," she went on. "This trial is going to take some time."

"I'll wait."

Then I hung up, gathered my things, and headed for the courthouse, arriving at 10 a.m. sharp, resignation in hand. In just seconds I would officially no longer be Trey's campaign manager. Jim Moody reached over the scarred wooden counter and took the document. He read over my careful wording twice before he said anything.

"I knew this was coming," he said, rubbing a hand across his thin gray hair. "I don't much like what's gone on with the mayor's race. This sure doesn't help it any."

I had no idea where his sympathies were on the matter. "I don't understand," I finally said.

He shrugged. "I know politics is dirty business, but they aren't supposed to be. Not in Purple Sage, at least. If I'd been here, the Judge never would have gotten away with taking Trey's spending report from you. He was probably just teasing you, anyway. 'Course, then he fell...." He shook his head, his pale eyes sad. "I keep thinking if I'd been in the office, none of this ever would have happened...." He stopped, and stared at me.

"Wait a minute, Jim," I said, firmly. "If you're hinting that I killed the Judge over some stupid report, you're way off base. I didn't. I didn't kill him for any reason. And I'm getting damn sick and tired of being accused of it!"

Jim looked me over for a minute. "I'm glad to hear you say so. You know, I always believed you had gumption; I couldn't figure why you were taking all the talk lying down unless you were guilty."

"Lying down? I'm not taking it lying down, but I can hardly go around the square punching out everyone who thinks I killed the Judge!"

He grinned, showing me a mouthful of dentures. "Come to think of it, I don't s'pose you can," he said.

"Jim, I'm doing some research on the Judge, and I need your help."

He looked surprised and took a step backward, giving me a view of his pouched belly hanging over his Sansabelt slacks. "Me? What do you want from me?"

"I have to go back through the old deeds of trust. I'm trying to locate some land that changed hands."

"That's public record," he said with relief. "You've got the right to go through any of those you want. Come on back, I'll show you where."

The file room of the courthouse looked far better than the one at the *Tribune* but that was only on the surface. The abundance of light made the mold around the edges of the books just that much more visible. And, yes, it did smell, but not as badly as bat guano.

"It's from that time when the roof leaked so bad," Jim explained, as he left me to search in solitude.

I won't go into the intricacies of Jim's filing system, but it was inconvenient, to say the least. It took almost forty-five minutes of fumbling before I made my first find. There were two sales together; Herbert Porter and Angus Schmidt had sold their property to the county. Those were two of the men whose land was going to be flooded for the lake. The price was a whopping $67.50 an acre, but the sales didn't appear to be forced.

"Hey, Jolie, how's it going?" Jim's secretary, Cynthia Golman, was standing in the doorway.

I grabbed at the desk to steady myself; her sudden appearance had jolted me. "Oh, Cynthia, hi."

She moved forward awkwardly in her old tight jeans. When she stopped the toes of her boots were pointed inward. IdaMae called her pigeon-toed, plain and as kind as they come.

"Listen, Jolie, I just wanted to say I'm real sorry about the way people are talking about you." Her pale eyebrows came together in concentration. "I feel real bad at how you're being treated."

"Thanks. It's nice to know that someone's on my side."

"Well, I sure am! The Judge was gettin' old and cranky, and you aren't the only one in this town has had a run-in with him. I know for a fact that Andy Sawyer had words with him too."

I dropped my hand from the desk. "Andy did? Really?"

She nodded. "Oh, yeah. It was about the last case the Judge presided over, so it was a while back, but still, Andy knows the Judge wasn't all that perfect."

"What did Andy and the Judge argue about?"

"There wasn't no argument," Cynthia said with a grin. "It was over some burglary case, and the Judge thought Andy did a piss-poor job with the evidence. The guy got off, and then the Judge called Andy into his chambers. Boy, he reamed Andy out but good! And Andy couldn't say boo back, because if he had, the Judge would have been on his case forever."

That little bit of news certainly changed the complexion of things. Andy had a motive to kill the Judge. It was weak; still, Andy knew how it felt to get in an argument with the Judge. It had to make him sympathetic toward me.

"Well, I got to get to work," Cynthia said. "Don't repeat what I told you, okay?"

"I won't."

"And hang tough."

I promised I would, and as soon as she left, started flipping through the pages again. I felt as if I'd had some minor victory and it was spurring me on.

I found names that didn't mean a thing to me. Kruger, Friedman, Smith. I began to scratch at my arms and neck absently. Simmons, French, Correll. I scratched some more. Pilsner, Tumbrel, Minton. Apparently some little bugs lived in the pages of those books, and they'd discovered me. Worse, they liked me. I scratched frantically as I moved on.

Then I found a sale involving two names I knew well: Ingram and Osler. Judge Volney Osler bought a parcel of land from

Theodore Ingram. June's father-in-law had sold his land to the Judge; I couldn't believe it. I copied down the information carefully between sneezes and scratches, then kept going.

More deeds that didn't concern me. The pages began to blur as my eyes watered from the mold. Bikel, Johnston, Tobler. I thought that was what they said, I couldn't be sure. Hadley, Windemere, Chavez, Bierkman.

Chavez? I dug a tissue from my purse and wiped my eyes. The Judge had bought 100 acres of land from Maria's father, and the price was high for back then. Eighty-one dollars an acre. Between sneezes I wrote down everything pertinent to the sale, then closed the book with a loud thump. I'd come back another day.

I blew my nose as I left, wondering what it all meant.

Outside I ran into June Ingram, hurrying along in her scuffed running shoes. "Jolie?" she said, stopping to look me over. "What's the matter? Do you have a cold?"

I sneezed. "Mold."

June nodded. "Allergies are terrible this time of year. Well, it's a good time to stay indoors and write. You are writing, aren't you?"

"A lot," I lied.

"Good. I'll expect to see those rewritten chapters tomorrow night." She turned toward her pickup. "See you."

Which meant I had to write. Maybe it was better. I could escape into a world that was orderly. A world that had a happy ending.

SEVENTEEN

"MOM, I STILL THINK you ought to talk to Matt," Jeremy said. He wasn't angry with me anymore, instead I heard the tinge of worry in his voice.

"I know you do," I said, poking at the roast beef that was on my plate. Jeremy was eating heartily and I was picking at my food; it was a reversal of our roles of only five years before. Amazing how fast he was growing up. "I just don't feel comfortable about going to Matt. Besides, I really don't think he can help."

"Why don't you at least give him a chance? He's a Wyatt, Mom, he's got strings he can pull."

"You're an adopted Wyatt. Can you pull strings, too?"

Jeremy grinned. "Give me five years."

I got up from my chair and brought the carton of milk to re-fill Jeremy's glass. "There's cobbler for dessert. By the way, when is Matt picking you up?"

"I don't know. He might spend the night in Austin."

I didn't want to hear about it. "Oh. Well, good, then we'll have some time when I get home tonight."

"You haven't answered my question," Jeremy said.

I sat down and placed my napkin back on my lap. "That's not true. I did answer your question, it just wasn't the answer you wanted."

He swallowed a chunk of beef whole so he could respond. "You won't tell me why you won't talk to Matt."

I began to wonder if having Jeremy spend the day had been a mistake. While it had started out well enough with the two of us working, Jeremy on one of his computer games and me on my book, he was now back to his old self. Maybe I was, too.

"Jeremy, do you remember Susie Waddel?"

"Ancient history," he said with an embarrassed shrug.

Susie had been his girlfriend for over a year in Austin. "Exactly. Would you go to her now and ask her for a favor?"

"I hate it when you use logic. Besides, it isn't the same thing. Susie doesn't have any clout and Matt does."

"Now, you didn't answer my question."

Jeremy pushed a carrot to the side of his plate. "Then why don't you just pretend that Matt isn't your ex-husband? Just pretend that he's my father. Do it for me."

I rolled my eyes. "What a manipulator," I said, glancing over at the clock. I was late, so I jumped up to clear the table. "Look, I'm going to have to go, do you want any more?"

"No, I'm full."

"The cobbler is right here," I said pointing. "You might want to warm a bowl of it in the microwave. Oh, and there's ice cream in the freezer."

"Mother, I'm not two years old," Jeremy said, rising. "Would you just do me a favor? Would you just think about talking to Matt?"

His hazel eyes were serious as they focused on me. I wished I could make him understand. "Honey, I know you think that Matt can fix everything, but he can't. Not this time." I waited for Jeremy to say something, but he didn't. "If the police really build a case against me they aren't going to drop it on Matt's say-so."

"He could get you a good lawyer. He said he would."

I started for the hall. "I already called a lawyer in Austin," I said.

"You did? What did he say?"

I turned around to face him. "I didn't get to talk to him. He's in court this week but he's supposed to call me."

"Then you are scared," Jeremy said.

"Not scared, concerned." It was a lie and it bothered me. Before the divorce Jeremy and I had had a very open relationship; I wanted to get back to that kind of communication. I sat down at the table and pulled Jeremy in to the chair next to me. "The truth is that I am a little scared, but I keep reminding myself that my fears are all based on nebulous what-ifs. They're probably not even rational. Especially since everyone I've talked to, including two lawyers, has said that I don't really have anything to worry about. Andy will find the right person."

"And what if he doesn't?" Jeremy said, his body statue still.

"Well, you remember Lisa Perry, the Judge's niece?" He nodded that he did and I went on. "She's a public defender in Dallas, and she says they don't have near enough for a conviction." I looked at his face, suddenly young and pale. I wished there were some magic that I could perform to make all our problems go away. "You're scared, too, aren't you?"

Jeremy nodded. "Yeah. The whole town is talking about how you killed the Judge."

"Not the whole town," I said, reaching over and touching his arm. "A lot of people believe in me. Important people like Jim Moody and Trey and Diane."

"They do? Did you call Diane back?"

"Not yet," I hedged. I didn't want to talk with her just yet, and I didn't want to explain why to Jeremy. I went back to my original thought. "The sheriff thinks I'm innocent, too, so take the gossip with a grain of salt, okay? Take it with a whole shaker of salt."

He looked a little better. "Okay."

"Besides," I said, rising, "I'm doing a little checking on the Judge myself. I'm getting pretty good at it, too."

"Great, my mom the private investigator." But he had a crooked half smile on his face.

"I've got to run," I said. "I'll see you when I get back."

"And if you need money for a lawyer, you know Matt will help," Jeremy added, standing in the kitchen doorway watching me as I grabbed my manuscript and purse.

"Oh, I know, but I won't need Matt's money."

"Okay, Lone Ranger," Jeremy said with a shake of his head.

"WELL, I THINK exclusivity is ridiculous," Maria was saying as she came through the door with Diane. "That agent I talked with said that on a first book you need to get as many people to read it as possible. I think I should send query letters to a dozen people."

Diane shut the museum door. "But Maria, you volunteered not to send your manuscript to anyone else while that editor had it."

"Hi, there," I said.

Diane nodded, and Maria looked in my direction.

"What do you think, Jolie?" Maria asked. "The editor has had my book for over four months."

I sat down. "Beats me. You could ask June."

Maria put down her notebook and purse. "She doesn't keep up with that kind of stuff; she's published, well known. It's totally different for her."

"I'm going to make popcorn," Diane said, dropping her manuscript on the table, ducking into the kitchen, and leaving me with Maria.

"This whole business sucks," Maria snarled.

The hum of the microwave came from the other room.

"Maybe you could write her a letter?"

"That would probably just piss her off and then she'd have an excuse not to buy my book."

It sounded to me like the editor was in a no-win situation, but I could also understand Maria's frustration.

"Why don't you just quit worrying about it and work on your new book?" I suggested.

That was a mistake. "I am working, but that doesn't mean I can quit trying to sell my first manuscript!"

The sound of corn popping came from the kitchen. I wished it would hurry so Diane would come back and save me. I tried a less volatile subject. "How's your business going? Picked up any new customers?"

"Jolie, I don't come here to talk about cleaning houses," Maria said, snapping out the words. "I need help with a marketing problem. What would you do in my place?"

I let out a breath. "I don't know, Maria."

The microwave dinged to signal that it was finished—saved by the bell, literally. More reinforcements arrived in the form of Rhonda and Liz Street. Liz, looking like she was dressed from a Goodwill clearance sale, stopped and sniffed. "Eau de Livre."

"Popcorn," Diane said, coming out of the kitchen with a heaping bowl.

"To you perhaps," Liz said. "But every time I come into this room, I smell popcorn and the scent of newly printed manuscript pages. The aroma of books in the making."

Newly printed manuscript pages have no scent that I've noticed, but no one corrected her.

Rhonda bounded to the table, her blond ponytail flying. "We've had popcorn ever since we started meeting, so it reminds me of books, too."

June came in. "Am I the last? I hope I'm not late. It's been a very busy day." She was in her jeans and tennis shoes, as usual, and her gray hair was sticking out like brittle hay.

"You're right on time," Diane said, putting the bowl on the center of the table.

The rest of the group gathered around as if it were a Peanuts Thanksgiving dinner. June sat down in a chair and everyone followed her lead, placing manuscript pages in front of them.

"Everyone has something to read tonight?" June asked.

We all nodded and I said, "I redid chapters twenty-four and twenty-five. God, I hope they work."

"No prejudicing the jury," June said.

Rhonda started grinning. "I don't think you should use the word *jury* around Jolie. She almost ended up in jail Sunday night."

"What?"

I looked at Rhonda. "How did you find out about that?"

"Andy talked to Morris and I was there." Even her ponytail seemed to be quivering with mirth. The woman was definitely not herself.

Liz looked at me. "This could be another book in the making. Are we going to hear the whole story, or are we just going to have to wonder?"

"Let Rhonda tell it," I said. "I don't quite see the humor, yet."

Everyone turned to Rhonda, who was still grinning. "Oh, lighten up, Jolie. Nothing really happened, and you have to admit, it was funny. See, Jolie was doing some research, going through the old *Tribs* on Saturday. I told her that if she some-how locked herself out all she had to do was turn the knob and jiggle the back door to get in. So she did, but she did it Sunday afternoon when the place was supposed to be empty."

"And Andy saw me coming out of the building," I said with finality.

"The way Andy tells it," Rhonda went on, ignoring my comment, "is that he was in the alley, just checking the door, and then, from inside the building, he heard this clomping noise. He said it was real fast, and he finally realized it was someone coming down the stairs. He said even the footsteps sounded guilty! So, he jerks open the door and he's reaching for his gun when he finds Jolie frozen on the stairs. It must have been hysterical!"

"A riot," I said.

June slid on her reading glasses. "Obviously Jolie doesn't think it was so amusing."

"It was just a misunderstanding," I said.

Maria frowned. "Was this after we got back from Brownwood? What was so urgent?"

"Nothing," I said. "I just had some free time and I thought I'd spend it productively."

Diane tilted her head and turned her eyes to me. It was the first time that evening that she'd really looked at me. "You could have called Morris. He'd have been happy to let you in the building."

No doubt she'd heard I'd resigned from Trey's campaign. I also hadn't returned her calls.

"I don't really think it matters now," I said.

Rhonda leaned forward. "Now, come on, Jolie, tell the truth. In retrospect, it is funny, isn't it?"

"In six months remind me to laugh," I said.

"And think of it this way," Liz said, adjusting some flowing piece of material around her neck. "You did it for your art."

Rhonda snickered. "Art, hell. She's poking around trying to find out who killed the Judge."

June frowned and looked at me over her reading glasses. "I thought you weren't going to keep on with that?"

"Who said I was?" I asked.

"I do," Rhonda said. "Your car was out in front of the Judge's house the other day. Sunday afternoon. Having a chat with his niece?"

"Lisa Perry is a friend of mine."

"Sure, sure."

They were all watching me, their expressions ranging from accusation to glee. "Look, I'm doing what I have to do, okay? Since none of you are under suspicion, it's not the same for you."

For the first time Rhonda looked serious. "Hey, it's okay, Jolie. I'm sorry I brought it up. You do whatever you think you have to do."

"Thank you; I intend to."

"Have you found anything out?" Maria asked.

At least she seemed sympathetic. "I'm working on some stuff."

June snorted. "Jolie, what could you possibly accomplish? All you're going to do is screw up the police investigation."

When it came to matters of plotting, editing, or grammar— in fact, anything to do with writing—we always bowed to June's superior wisdom; she was the font of all knowledge. But I was getting tired of her self-righteous pronouncements about how the rest of the world worked, too.

"Oh, really?" I said with a bite in my words. "I've already discovered a number of interesting facts. This whole thing could be over and done with in a few days."

That silenced her.

"DAMN IT, JOLIE," Diane snapped. "Why in the hell would you say anything so stupid?"

The others were all gone and we were standing in a pool of light in the dark parking lot.

"What was so terrible?"

"Everything! If one of those women murdered the Judge you just announced to them that you're dangerous. Jesus! How could you do that?"

"Because I got pissed off!" I said. "I'm only human, Diane, and I'm feeling frustrated and useless. I'm also tired of June Ingram's advice."

"June's just pragmatic."

"Pessimistic," I said. "And what about Rhonda? Normally she's a robot, and tonight she's all cutesy giggles. At my expense."

Diane started to say something, closed her mouth, and thought a moment. "She has been acting strangely lately, hasn't she?"

"No shit." I exchanged a look with Diane. "She's been this way ever since the night the Judge was killed."

A long, slow pensive nod. "That's exactly when it started. That night she was excited. Almost quivering."

"Even IdaMae noticed it at the political reception."

Diane looked around the dark lot. "Let's go sit in the car and talk."

We got in and she started the engine.

"Where are we going?" I asked.

She pulled her car over next to mine. "I want to keep an eye on the Mazda." She looked over at it. "I don't have a good feeling about tonight. Not at all."

"You're overdoing it," I said, but I could feel the hairs on my arm bristling. "Look, Diane, I'm sorry I haven't called you back. I guess that was pretty rude."

"It certainly was! You want to tell me why you did it? And why you decided to resign without even a courtesy call to me or Trey?"

I lifted my shoulders in a shrug. "I thought it would be easier that way. I'm giving Trey a better chance at being elected. I didn't want to cause any problems," I said.

Diane turned in her seat; her nostrils were flaring. "Well, I think we should have some say in that! What do you think, you can protect Trey and me, *and* bail yourself out of this jam without help from anyone? Who do you think you are, the Terminator?''

It sounded so much like something Jeremy might say that I almost smiled. "No, I don't have the muscles. But I don't see that it's really anyone else's problem."

"You don't listen! Jolie, you have friends; friends are there to help. That's why God made friends, idiot!" She was angrier than I'd seen her in quite a while and there was a gut-level hurt, too. "That's exactly the kind of stupid thing that got you divorced from Matt. The old make-your-stand-and-then-cut-and-run routine."

I paused as the realization sank in. "Oh, God, I've done it again." I barely heard my own words.

"You damn sure have, and I don't appreciate it!"

I sat in the darkness and let the extent of my stupidity wash over me. And my stubbornness. I could see how it had altered events all through my life. Finally I raised my head enough to look at her. "I'm sorry, Diane, I just didn't think." Then I added, "Like you said, my usual."

She let out a long breath. "I'm sorry, too. I shouldn't have said that."

"It's okay. I deserved it."

"No," she said. "I was just angry and I popped off. Forgive me?"

"If you'll forgive me."

"You got it."

I took a few deep breaths. "God, no wonder my life is such a mess."

"Forget that kind of thinking, Jolie. Everything will turn out fine, isn't that what you always say?" She smiled as if to coax me into smiling back. I didn't.

"Used to say."

"Come on," she said. "Your resignation can be remedied pretty easily. I have a wonderful idea; you and I can have lunch tomorrow at the most public place in this town, the Sage Cafe. Then tomorrow night, Trey and I will both take you to dinner at the country club. We'll show people that we're backing you, and vice versa."

"I'll think it over."

"Don't waste the brainpower, it's already been decided," she said with a finality that I wasn't willing to challenge. "Now, I talked with Trey about the Judge."

"And?"

She made a face. "Nothing. He thought he remembered his dad talking about some shady deal with the lake, but he was too young to pay any attention. He just doesn't remember."

"Well, hell. Tell him to forget dinner if he can't do better than that." We smiled at each other and then I went on. "Actually, I'm already looking into the construction of the lake because IdaMae mentioned the same thing. Our Patron Saint wasn't all that good until he got rich, and IdaMae says he got rich over the lake."

"Interesting."

"Isn't it? I've been making notes as I go along, but so far I haven't made much sense of them."

"Maybe I can help. How about if I come over tomorrow? Together we'll go through what you've got."

"Are you sure you want to do that?"

"I insist."

"You're on," I said, with a smile. "Oh, and what about Trey's car? Did he call the police?"

"Uh-huh, but he got one of the eager-beaver patrolmen since Andy's so busy." She shrugged. "I doubt we'll ever find out who did it."

"Damn."

"It's not that important. No one got hurt and that's what counts."

"I guess you're right," I said. "Well, I'd better run. Jeremy's at the house, and I don't like leaving him alone."

"Okay." She leaned over and gave me an awkward hug. "I'll wait until you get in your car."

"I'll be fine," I said, opening the door. "And thanks, Diane. You're terrific."

"And don't you forget it, either!"

I unlocked my car, checking to make sure it was empty before I climbed in. Diane waved good-bye as I pulled out of the lot. She followed me for a few blocks, then turned off toward her house.

I *did* feel better. I had allies; maybe I could even get Diane to help me look up records at the courthouse. The job wouldn't be so awful if someone were there to commiserate.

When I pulled into the driveway I saw that the lights were on at the house. It meant that Matt wasn't back and Jeremy was still there. Another ally.

The garage door was open, just like I'd left it, and I pulled straight in and turned off the engine. The garage was now pitch black.

I walked around the car, carrying my manuscript in one hand and my purse in the other. I juggled the manuscript, finally putting the bulky thing under my arm until I could reach up for the rope to pull down the big garage door. Only a smattering of light from the kitchen window illuminated my fumbling. Finally my hand brushed the rope. I was being careful because the door was heavy and one of the springs was broken—sometimes it would come crashing down and I needed to be ready to jump out of the way.

A sound came from behind me.

I whirled around, letting go of the cord. "Jeremy?"

No answer.

Just a cat, I told myself, reaching up again. I got a solid grip on the cord and gave it a yank. There was a thunderous clattering as the door closed. Then there was another sound behind me. I spun around one more time, but I was too late. Something hit me and I went down hard.

EIGHTEEN

I WOKE UP on the cool concrete. My body felt delicate, like when I'd had a migraine headache and had taken too many pills to get rid of it. I couldn't feel the pain, but I knew it was there, lurking somewhere inside my head waiting for me to make one wrong move.

Jeremy was leaning over me, his hands on my shoulders, as if he were about to shake me.

"Don't," I said.

"Are you okay? I thought you were dead!"

"No, I'm not hurt," I said, trying to raise up. The pain leaped through my neck into my forehead like a jagged fork of lightning. I groaned and lay back down.

"I called nine-one-one. Don't move."

"I won't." I closed my eyes.

"I called Matt on his car phone, too."

"You what—" But I stopped when I saw his pinched and frightened face. "It's okay," I said. In the distance I heard the shrill whine of an ambulance siren. It was getting closer. I hoped they'd kill the siren before they got too close.

"They got away, Mom. I couldn't go after them, because I didn't want to leave you."

"Where am I?"

"In the garage. Don't you remember? Are you going to be okay?"

"I'll be fine, Jeremy." I was speaking softly, trying not to jar anything. "They must have hit me on the back of the neck." I reached back and winced at the pain. The skin wasn't broken, so there was no blood.

The wail of the siren seemed to be splitting my head. There was a squeal of tires, a flash of bright light, and then blessed silence. It was followed too closely by the slamming of doors and the sound of running feet. I heard the voices, but I didn't open my eyes.

"What happened?" a male voice asked. Skip Jefferson. He ran the local funeral home and ambulance service.

"Someone hit her," I heard Jeremy say. "On the back of the neck. Is she going to be okay?"

"Move out of the way, and let me have a look at her."

He checked my pulse and opened one eye to look at my pupil.

"She's got a concussion. Probably mild," Skip said. "No breaks in the skin. Of course, her skull could be fractured. We'd better transport her to the hospital."

"No siren," I said as firmly as I could. "And, Jeremy, lock up everything. Come with me."

The next half hour or so was mercifully hazy. Getting me on the stretcher was not a pleasant experience, nor was the ride to the hospital. Once there, they ran me through the long hall to the emergency room. I do remember Jeremy coming in and out of the room where I was treated, and I think I heard Matt's voice.

"How did this happen?" Dr. Baxter asked.

It was Jeremy who responded. "Someone hit her in the garage."

"Dear gracious God in heaven! Are you sure about this?"

"I'm sure," I said.

"I'll have to call the police at some point."

I think I dozed off until the gentle but intrusive poking and prodding by Dr. Baxter woke me up. He started talking again, this time saying that what I needed most was rest. I tried to keep my eyes open to watch his face as I listened. I was only partially successful.

"Jolie, nothing's broken, luckily. The blow was to the back of the head, but the weapon must have skimmed down to your neck, too. Or, maybe you got hit on the neck and you hurt your head when you fell. In any case, you're going to be very sore tomorrow. What I can't tell about is internal hemorrhaging, so I'm giving you a coagulant. I'm also giving you a shot, which should relax you, but your body will take over in a few minutes as soon as things quiet down." His voice faded for a moment. "She'll be much better in the morning. I'll arrange for a room."

I wasn't sure he was still talking to me, but it didn't matter.

"Home," I said. "I want to go home."

It wasn't heroic posturing on my account; I didn't want Jeremy alone at the house. I didn't want the house empty, either. Whoever had been there might come back, and I didn't want them doing any further damage to anyone or anything.

I even had the irrational thought that someone might steal my computer disk with my book on it. Eight months' worth of work would be gone.

"Jolie," Dr. Baxter said, "you need to rest for a few days, and I think the hospital will be the best place for that."

I opened my eyes and winced at the light. "No, I don't want Jeremy alone." I noticed Matt near the corner of the room. He was walking toward the table where I was lying. I felt the shot beginning to take effect as my muscles relaxed.

"Doc," Matt said, "I could stay at their house for a couple of days, if that would work for you."

I tried to raise up, changed my mind, and said, "Why are you asking him? Ask me; it's my house!" I closed my eyes again. I felt very far away when my eyes were closed.

Someone patted my arm. "Irritability is a sign of shock." It was the doctor.

"It's *still* my house," I mumbled.

Matt said, "Doc, why don't you give me a moment alone with her?"

Feet shuffled and moved away. I felt someone's presence near me. I opened one eye to discover that Matt and I were alone in the blinding whiteness of the tiny cubicle.

"Jolie, I'm sorry; that was thoughtless of me."

"Yes, it was," I responded, although I could barely hear my own words, so I doubted that he could. I raised my voice. "I don't want Jeremy alone. I want to be able to protect him. And my book. What if they get my book?"

"To hell with the book. If someone is after you, you'll be safest here in the hospital."

That had to be a joke. "The average age of the staff at the Wilmot County Hospital is somewhere around a hundred. Unless they've been teaching karate to the Sunshine Ladies, I don't see who's going to protect me. Maybe I should pack a pistol."

His face was serious, but I could hear the suppressed smile in his voice. "You must be feeling better. Look, we could take you to the ranch. Then Jeremy and I can both watch over you."

"I don't want to go to the ranch."

He pursed his lips. "Jolie, you're making this difficult."

"No, I'm not. That's your house, and I don't feel comfortable there. I'd hate it." I couldn't face that house; it would be like reliving my failure.

"Fine, then we'll take you to your house, but I'm staying, too. I don't know karate, but I've got several guns."

"Fine." It wasn't really what I wanted either, but I was out of energy. I closed my eyes, letting the drug-induced haziness take over my mind and body.

"MOM? ARE YOU AWAKE?" Jeremy was standing a foot or so from the edge of my bed, holding a tray in his hands. Bright sunshine was coming through the windows.

"I'm awake," I said, not really sure yet.

"Here, Matt said you need to eat something. Are you hungry?"

My stomach did a slow flip. I was hungry, but there were other things on my mind. "Is Matt here?"

"Yeah, he spent the night," Jeremy said, juggling the tray. "Do you want this?"

"Yes, wait a minute; let me sit up." I tried to follow action to words, but the inside of my head began screaming. I suddenly wanted to cry. "This isn't going to be as easy as I thought."

Jeremy slid the tray onto the night table. "It's okay, Mom. I can help."

Jeremy got the pillows into position, and I slid gently upward until I could sit without too much pain. My neck felt much the same as it had when I'd accidentally put my dad's car in a ditch after a high school football game.

"Here you go," Jeremy said, setting the tray on my lap.

There were fluffy and steaming scrambled eggs, toast, two kinds of jam on a saucer, and orange juice. The kind of breakfast that Matt had served me himself when we were first married.

There was even a stem of bluebonnets in one of my vases. I didn't remind Jeremy that it was illegal to pick wildflowers.

"Is everything okay?" Jeremy asked.

I shoved down the memories. "It all looks wonderful. Thank you." I picked up a fork and took a few bites.

"Oh, and Diane has called three times. I think she thinks that Matt is holding you hostage or something. You'd better call her."

The food was bringing me back to life. "Anything else?"

"Uh-huh. You have to take those pills." He pointed to a green pill and a pink capsule lying beside the orange juice.

I took them both in one swallow and then rubbed my neck. "When I get my hands on whoever did this, they're going to be very sorry."

Jeremy grinned. "That's what Matt says, too."

"Matt will have to stand in line behind me if he wants to get the guy who did this. I suffered the most; I get them first." I went back to eating, and Jeremy lurked nearby, straightening the covers and neatly rearranging things on my dresser. After a while I knew that something was up: Jeremy is not compulsively neat. "Okay, what else do you have to tell me?"

Jeremy looked up. "Well, it's really nothing."

"Then tell me."

He came closer. "I'm not supposed to worry you with it."

"That really worries me."

There was a chair not far from the bed, a kitchen chair I hadn't noticed before. Apparently someone had been watching me sleep. I tried not to wonder who, and concentrated instead on Jeremy. He pulled the chair over next to the bed and sat down.

"Well, it's like this, Mom," he began, then stopped.

It was a bad starting place; I'd heard that phrase in the past and it never preceded good news.

"Go on."

"The police want to talk to you," he said.

"That's it?"

"Well . . ."

"Jeremy, I am not well. I may not live long enough to hear the rest of this. Spit it out."

He grinned. "Andy was here twice this morning and Matt wouldn't let him see you. I thought Matt was going to punch him out."

I'd always thought the infamous Wyatt clout was more subtle. "Well, I can talk to Andy now. Call the police station and tell him I'm available." I thought about it. "No, tell him half an hour. I've got to get dressed first." Just the thought of getting out of bed and wrestling into clothes made my head hurt worse.

"Is that a good idea?" Jeremy asked.

I didn't think so. "Bring me the phone. Maybe I'll just call him and get it handled that way. What time is it, anyway?"

"Ten-thirty."

"What day is it?"

Jeremy frowned. "It's Wednesday. Don't you remember?"

"Of course, I just didn't know how long I'd slept." I sipped my coffee and Jeremy moved the vase to the table beside my bed, then slid the tray off my lap. "I'll be right back with the phone."

"Thank you for breakfast, honey. It was wonderful." I hesitated. "And thank Matt, too."

Jeremy smiled as he went out the door.

I put down the coffee cup and lay back on the pillow. It felt so good to close my eyes.

THE NEXT TIME I woke up there were voices outside my bedroom door. Male voices, speaking in angry whispers.

"She is asleep, damn it, and you're not going to wake her up."

"That's what you keep telling me, but I can't wait any longer."

"You're going to have to."

The voices were getting louder.

I got up slowly, determined to put a stop to what sounded like the prelude to a fistfight. I got my robe from the closet and sort of slid toward the door, pulling on the robe as I went.

"You have no right to keep me out. This is an official investigation."

"She's not well."

"Dr. Baxter said she would be able to talk to me."

I opened the door. Matt was just on the other side of it, his back to me, his legs apart and his fists clenched. On the other side of him was Andy in an identical stance. Neither one noticed me for a moment.

"I'm here," I said. Matt swung around. Andy stared at me. I tried to smile. "You guys woke me up. If you'll just give me a minute, Andy, I'll talk to you."

Andy shot Matt a triumphant look, but Matt was too busy to notice. He put his hands on my shoulders. "Are you sure you should be up?"

"No," I said honestly, feeling warmth where his hands touched me. I stepped back away from him. "And if we've got anything for a headache, I could use a double dose. First I need to brush my teeth, then I'll be out." I closed the door softly.

I noticed the clock as I passed it on the way to the bathroom. Two-thirty.

Even my teeth hurt, and I brushed them as gently as I could. Then I ran my fingers through my hair, decided that was overdoing it, and went out to face the police.

NINETEEN

"THEN YOU DIDN'T SEE or hear anything?" Andy asked.

"Nothing," I repeated. I was beginning to think the man was slow. "It was dark and there was some movement that caught my attention, but that was all."

Although Matt had volunteered to stay with me during my interview with Andy, I had sent him away. I didn't want to get used to having him around again.

"Did you smell anything?" Andy asked. "A perfume? Aftershave?"

I focused hard on him and started to shake my head. I realized that was a bad idea and said, "Sorry, no." I started to ask if he was referring to Estée Lauder's Youth Dew, but didn't.

"Why do you think someone would hide in your garage, and then attack you? Any names or reasons come to mind?"

At the moment I had a great deal on my mind, but the thoughts were jumbled by the presence of a monstrous headache. I wanted to stop talking and close my eyes. I wanted to lie down; I wanted heavy-duty drugs. Then I remembered Diane. "Maybe you'd better talk to Diane Atwood."

Andy looked up, surprised. "You think Diane hit you?"

"Oh, no, nothing like that. In fact, she's the only one who couldn't have done it. We sat outside after group and talked. She followed me partway home, so there's no way she could have beat me to the garage." I shifted a little, hoping to get more comfortable, and finally decided it wasn't possible. "She might have some ideas, though. She's been worried about me. About something I said at the writers' group."

"And what was that?"

I told him as few words as possible. Then I shifted again and let out a soft groan, hoping he'd get the hint.

Andy looked concerned. "Have you taken anything for the pain?"

I shrugged, then winced. "I did just before I came in here. They'll kick in soon." I hoped.

He leaned forward. "You know, Jolie, this may be the best thing that has ever happened to you."

"It doesn't feel that way."

"No pain, no gain," he said with a grin.

I grimaced, not from the headache. "Bad," I said.

"Yeah, well maybe this will let you off the hook with some of the people in town. They might stop talking about you."

"What about you? Will you leave me alone?"

"I'm just doing my job."

I got serious. "You know, Andy, what I don't understand is why someone would do this. Does it seem dumb on the part of the murderer? For all he knew, or she, I could have been arrested tomorrow. Why screw it all up by going after me?"

Andy leaned forward. "Maybe you weren't supposed to live through this."

"What?"

"Jeremy heard your car; when you didn't come in right away he went to look for you. Close as I can figure, when he slammed the back door your assailant ran off."

"Oh my God. He could have been hurt."

"Yeah, but he probably saved your life." Andy shifted in the small wicker rocker.

I was suddenly cold, and I wrapped the robe around me tighter. "But still, why kill me? I was suspect number one. The murderer was safe, at least as far as he knew."

"Maybe you were on to something, something you said to your writers' group. Maybe you sounded more dangerous than you really are."

I remembered Diane's diatribe after the meeting. I felt sick. I had brought the attack on myself.

"Talk to Diane," I said. "She can explain it all."

"I intend to." He closed his notebook and seemed to think for a moment. "Maybe the murderer has a weak spot, and he was afraid you'd found it. Or were going to." Andy grew still. "There is another explanation."

"Oh?"

"You could have done this to yourself."

"What?" I couldn't believe it. The man was insane. "You're hallucinating, Andy! How could I hit myself on the back of the neck?"

"You could have let the garage door fall on you."

"How can you say that? And what about Jeremy? He says he saw someone."

Andy tilted his head a little. "It was dark. He heard a noise, and thought there was someone else. Or maybe he's lying."

I put my hand to my forehead, hoping to ease the pain that was dancing inside of it. "You need a vacation, Andy. Either I'm guilty or I'm innocent; make up your mind."

"That's not my job. I just get enough to indict. Jury makes the final decision."

I closed my eyes.

When Andy spoke again his tone was almost conversational, as if he hadn't accused me of anything at all. "So everyone was at your group last night, including Liz Street?"

"Yes."

"And any one of them had time to beat you home, except Diane Atwood. They knew that you'd been researching the old *Tribunes,* and that you'd talked to Lisa Perry, the Judge's niece. Does that about cover the specifics?"

"That's it."

I heard the doorbell ring. Andy stood up. "Sounds like you've got company. Oh, by the way, we've fingerprinted your garage and car already, so you can use them if you want."

"But you didn't find any prints except mine."

"They've all been sent in to the national computer, and after I fingerprint the members of your writers' group, we'll have something to compare. At least now I know who to check." He looked at me gravely. "Get some rest."

He left, no doubt passing Matt in the other room. They must have been civil, because I didn't hear any loud voices.

Matt came in.

"Jolie?" Matt said, giving me a searching look. "Rhonda's here to see you. You look pale."

"I'm fine, Matt."

"Are you sure? You really don't look good, Jolie."

"Thanks, I needed that," I said lightly.

Matt continued to watch me.

"Matt, it's okay, I want to talk with Rhonda."

He left the room shooting me what appeared to be an annoyed look.

My spirits sank even further. I'd had the distinct feeling that something had broken the night before, something more than my head. I'd been sure that I was in the clear and now the police could take over and find the murderer. Instead, I was still a suspect. Accused of even attacking myself. And Matt was around, seeing me at my weakest.

I curled into the couch, letting the cushions cradle me.

"Hi, Jolie. How are you?" Rhonda asked as she slipped quietly in the door. "You look pale."

I shifted my body. "Of course I'm pale. No makeup."

"Oh, right. So, how are you feeling?"

"Better," I said, trying to sound it. "How did you find out?"

Rhonda grinned as she lowered herself into the chair. "The cop shop. I go there first thing every morning, and this morning I found a very interesting report on you. Got attacked, huh?"

"One of these days, your wicked ways are going to catch up with you."

For a moment she looked startled, then she relaxed. "Well, let's hope not."

"Did you tell anyone else?"

"Me? No, of course not," she said. "Well, I did mention it to Morris. I mean, he owns the *Trib,* and we discussed running a story. The police asked me not to...yet, so I guess we'll wait. Oh, and I called Diane since you two are so close. I thought you'd want her to know."

"That's fine," I said.

She took a breath and bit her lip. "Listen, I uh, wanted to mention something to you. It's kind of a message from Morris. He was really sorry to hear what happened to you. He sent his sympathies."

It sounded like he thought I was dead. "That's nice."

Matt came in, his annoyance with me apparently forgotten. He handed me a tall glass of iced tea with a straw. The kind that bends, no less.

"Thanks," I said.

"You're welcome." He touched my hand briefly, so quickly that it might have been an accident. Then he turned to Rhonda. "Do you want anything, Rhonda?"

"Oh, no, thanks."

"Well, I'll leave you two alone, then." He gave me a quick wave and disappeared.

Rhonda watched him go, her eyes on the back of his jeans. "He's taking care of you? God, all that and gorgeous, too."

"Buddy Wayne's good-looking, too," I said.

Rhonda looked for a minute as if she didn't remember her own husband. "Oh, right. He's okay." She furrowed her eyebrows. "Now, what were we talking about?"

"You were just delivering Morris's sympathies."

"Yeah, I was. He, uh . . ." The sentence fizzled out and she stared at me.

"He what?" I asked.

She began to rock, taking her time. "Well, it's just that he was really upset to hear about what happened. Your getting hurt and all. And he, uh, well, then he remembered that you'd been in our building on Sunday." She leaned forward, picking up speed. "If someone had attacked you Sunday, when no one was there, you might be dead right now. So, from now on Morris thought maybe it would be better if you didn't go up there. I mean, because he would feel terrible if something happened to you."

"Well, that's very thoughtful of Morris," I said. I'd intended to sound sweet and compliant; sarcasm slipped out between the words. "Then I certainly won't be going back up there."

"Oh, no," Rhonda said. "You can still do your research. I didn't mean you shouldn't look through the old papers."

"Then what did you mean?"

She leaned forward, very earnest. "Just let us know first. Come by during office hours, and Morris will take you up there, and stay with you. Or me, I guess. Just make sure that one of us is with you...." She tilted her head, her tone coated with concern. "That way you'll be safe."

Unless, of course, Rhonda murdered the Judge. But what about Morris? What did he have to do with this? An accomplice? The whole thing was too bizarre. Maybe Morris was merely protecting himself from a possible lawsuit, in case something did happen to me on his property. Jeremy could sue for millions, which Morris didn't have. It might mean that Morris would have to give up his designer clothes.

The doorbell rang softly in the background.

"If I need any more information," I said, "I'll get either you or Morris to go with me."

Rhonda let out a relieved breath. "That's great. Then we won't have to worry about you." She jumped up. "Well, I guess I'd better go. You probably need to get some rest."

"Thanks for coming by," I said, not even trying to raise up.

"Oh, you're welcome. I was worried about you, but I can see that you're doing fine. Much better. Well, see you."

Things were getting curiouser and curiouser, as Alice said in Wonderland.

"I told you!" Diane said as she swept in and sat down on the rocker. "I just knew something horrible was going to happen."

"Congratulations, you were right. I hope you're happy."

"Well, I didn't cause it," she said. "Jolie, I'm just so relieved that it wasn't any worse. You could be dead right now."

"If that's what you came to tell me, you've wasted a trip. Andy already said it."

"He did?" She sat forward. "And Matt is here taking care of you?"

"You noticed."

She studied my face for a moment. "How is that working out?"

"I'm kind of..." I began, but we were interrupted.

Matt came in. "I thought I might run out to the ranch and get a change of clothes. Jeremy will be here and I won't be gone more than an hour. Are you comfortable with that, Jolie?"

I wanted him to go. Forever. And I wanted him to stay. "Sure."

"Diane," Matt said, seriously, "guard her. I'll be back as fast as I can."

"Take your time," Diane offered, as he left with a last wave. Then she touched my hand. "How is your head, by the way?"

I moved it experimentally. The aspirin seemed to be working. "Better. No rockets shooting through it."

"Matt said it was just a concussion, is that right?"

"I guess so. There was no blood, anyway."

She smiled. "Well that's not very colorful." Then she became serious again. "Now, tell me about Andy."

I repeated the things I'd said to him, and told her Andy's alternative theory.

When I was finished, Diane's eyes were blazing. "Jolie, that's ridiculous! Who would let a garage door crash down on them? You'd have to be crazy."

"Or desperate. Which I suppose someone would be if they'd killed another person and were about to get caught."

She jumped up and began to pace. "This is worse than I thought. It's time to get busy."

Her intensity made my head ache. "Diane, there's nothing that I can do. Not right now, anyway."

"You said you took notes on the things you've found out, where are they?"

"On the computer table. The pink spiral notebook."

She walked across the room and picked it up. "This one?"

"Yes," I said. "But they aren't very complete."

The door opened and Jeremy popped in. "Mom, Matt said I was to make sure that you took your pill. It's time for the green one." He placed it in my hand. "Sorry to interrupt." And then he whisked himself back out the door.

"This place is like an airport with everyone dashing in and out," Diane said as I downed the pill. She began to look at my notes. "Are you tired?"

My eyelids drooped at the question. "I don't know, maybe a little."

"Well, close your eyes," she said. "You can take a nap, while I do some reading."

TWENTY

By THE NEXT afternoon I felt much better physically; mentally I was confused and frustrated. It seemed I had done nothing but sleep, eat, and read, the whole time hiding in my bedroom. Jeremy had popped in and out with messages and food.

"Do you want anything else?" he asked from the doorway.

"No, I think I can manage just fine."

"Then can I go out for a while? I won't be gone long."

"I don't know if you should be alone."

He paused. "Oh, I won't be alone. You know, Randy is going to come by."

"Baseball?" I asked. When he nodded, I agreed. "Sure, go ahead and have fun."

"I already locked all the doors, but if someone tries to get in, call nine-one-one."

I raised one eyebrow slowly. It drives Jeremy crazy; he thinks he should be the only one in the world who can manage that little trick. I mimicked the annoyed tone Jeremy often used on me. "I'm not two years old, you know."

He grinned as he dashed out the door, and then stuck his head back in. "Don't forget, Matt's coming at five to cook dinner."

"I can hardly wait."

Jeremy shook his head and left.

As soon as he was gone, I wobbled to the bathroom. The hot water helped, and by the time I was out and getting dressed I felt much more stable. I even did my makeup and fixed my hair. My head didn't hurt at all, although it might have been because of all the pills I was taking. I put on my aerobic shoes, bending over carefully to tie them. There was no dizziness, no pain.

I stood up, grinning to myself. What I needed was a little action. I resented being watched constantly, as if I might suddenly up and die.

I wandered out to the kitchen, and then into the sunroom. It was a beautiful day. The world had changed in the past two days; everything was beginning to green up. The grass that had been a yellow brown was now turning a soft emerald. Flowers were poking out of the ground, displaying the brilliant colors of spring. In my two-day absence, the trees had put out some fresh leaves.

I started for the garage, but not before I locked the door and tucked the key in my pocket. It was the first time I'd seen the garage since I'd been attacked, and it too was undergoing a metamorphosis. The vines that covered the far side were changing from winter brown to a soft lime green. Amazing how quickly spring takes over. And how it wiped away any frightening feelings I might have had toward the place.

The heavy double-wide door was still closed, and it took more effort than I'd exerted lately to raise it up. I winced as a small shot of pain grabbed my neck. To hell with it; no pain, no gain, as Andy had said. For a moment I looked at the door above me. Then I gave a tug on the rope and jumped back. The heavy door came down with a resounding crash.

Andy had been right; I could have inflicted the damage on myself.

"Jolie? Are you okay?"

I whirled around quickly. It was Diane, just walking down the driveway.

"I'm fine," I said. "You startled me."

She looked me over anxiously. "Did the door hit you? Did it slip?"

"I was testing a theory." We started toward the backyard and I explained what Andy had said.

Diane scowled. She was wearing jeans and clutching my spiral notebook to her chest. "I still think he's crazy."

I used my key to let us in. "Well, that's always an option."

"Are you supposed to be up? Where are Matt and Jeremy?" she asked as she followed me to the kitchen.

I shrugged carefully. "I don't know where Matt is, but Jeremy is playing baseball with Randy."

She stopped. "Randy is at his grandmother's in Menard."

Forty miles away. My heart contracted and for just a moment I panicked. Why would Jeremy lie to me? Where could he be? Was he safe? I stepped into the hall to look out the window beside the door. The sky was clear blue and the world was bright with sunshine. Surely nothing bad could happen on such a beautiful day.

And then Jeremy came into my line of sight; he was on his bike, wheeling down the street as fast as he could. He applied the brakes hard, leaving long black skid marks on the asphalt. Then he spun around and rode to the far end of the block to do it all over again.

"Look," I said, sadness tugging at me. Jeremy was no doubt avoiding his friends because of me. "He's by himself."

Diane moved closer to watch. "It's not your fault, you know."

"I know," I said, the hurt wrenching at me. "But it feels like my fault."

She touched my arm lightly and we stood there, side by side for a few minutes. I was grateful for her understanding, but it still didn't stop the way I was feeling over Jeremy. I wanted so much to protect him, and I seemed to be doing nothing but bringing him unhappiness.

"Come on," Diane said, gently pulling me away from the window. "We can't help Jeremy standing here. Let's get something to drink and run over your notes."

"Sure," I said, following her into the kitchen, willing my attention onto other things. "You're right. Jeremy was probably just going stir-crazy." I stopped. "But he lied to me."

"All kids lie to their parents. I'll bet you did, too," Diane said. She cocked her head and gave me a half smile. "Even I did."

"Not you! You always told me you were too busy what with chores and all your school projects. And 4-H."

"If I'd spent half the time with that calf that my mom thought I did, I could have trained it to sit up and speak."

I smiled. "Thanks." I opened the refrigerator, poured out tea for both of us and sat at the table. Diane took the chair beside me, placing my notebook in front of her. "So, what did you think of my notes?" I asked.

"They make for some pretty interesting reading. Oh, part of it I knew already, like the Judge's generosity. That's common knowledge, of course, but the question it brings up is why someone would kill him when he was so good."

"He was still human. You should know there was more to him than his reputation."

"But I've been here longer than you. Almost seventeen years, and it's harder for me to get beyond it. Strange, huh? Especially since he was backing Trey's opponent in the mayoral race."

We had a saying at the advertising agency: Perception is reality. If you told a person something often enough, they believed it. Diane was only proving the maxim true once again.

"According to Lisa, you know, the Judge's niece, he could be just as rotten as the next person when he wanted to. Well, she didn't say exactly that, but close. And she said that he liked people to grovel when he gave money."

"Maybe, but he never said so publicly," Diane argued.

"And he quit giving money about a year or so ago," I said, then stopped. "That's right after he didn't get reelected."

"I didn't realize he'd stopped giving money."

"So, did anything in my notes strike you as a motive?"

"Actually, yes. The lake. The Judge bought two pieces of property in that vicinity around the time of the planning. And people from those families are in our writers' group and knew about your murder."

"I thought that was a pretty interesting coincidence, too."

"Too much coincidence. And you wrote that IdaMae said he got rich about that time. His whole reputation changed. But there's a down side," she said. "Why kill someone for something that happened that long ago?"

I picked up my glass, took a drink, and then set it down. "Wait a minute. If what I was doing wasn't getting me close to the Judge's murderer, why did someone come after me? I must have found something important."

There was a *thunk* as she put her glass on the table. "Right! What if you were looking in the right place for the wrong thing?"

"Of course! That's it!" I stopped. "I don't have any idea what we're talking about."

Diane's smooth brow wrinkled with a frown. "Come to think of it, neither do I."

"Too bad we can't find out where everyone was when I got hit." I rubbed my neck carefully. The pain was coming back, so I got up and took two aspirin from the cupboard.

"Head hurt?" Diane asked.

"Preventative medicine."

She nodded, then went back to our original discussion. "How many people knew you were checking out the Judge's past? I mean, besides our writers' group?"

"I don't know. I don't think anyone," I said, picking up my tea and swallowing the pills.

"I still can't believe you popped off and said what you did."

"I don't even remember what I said." I sat back down. "And, please, don't tell me."

"Fine, I won't. But, if I were writing that scene, I couldn't have made it any more dangerous or stupid." She went on quite calmly. "The problem is that you weren't specific enough to give us any clues. Rhonda mentioned the *Tribune,* and the Judge's niece, but that was all. It covers a lot of territory. So, here's what I think. First, we can rule out an inheritance as the motive. I just can't see the trustees of the University of Texas coming down here and knocking off the Judge."

"Okay."

"But I do think we need to keep looking into this lake thing."

"June Ingram," I said softly, trying to imagine her as a murderer.

"There could be others."

I went on slowly. "Maybe, but she's the only one who's old enough to have been involved in what happened when the lake was built. Maria was just a baby. So were most of the others, come to think of it. Rhonda was maybe five, Liz was only ten years old or so. So was Andy."

Diane closed her eyes for a moment. I could almost hear her very organized brain clicking away as it categorized my suspects, and then searched for additional information on the Judge. A very slender Nero Wolfe.

Finally she opened her eyes and picked up the notebook. "Actually, this thing has brought up more questions than answers. Like Liz's comment that she hated the Judge. When did she say that?"

"At the political reception."

"And why? She's only been back a couple of years; she left when she was in her early twenties. She should be number two on the list." She frowned at the notes. "Is there anything else you can think of?"

"You know almost everything that I do."

"But I'm going to know more. I'm going to pick up where you left off."

"Look, Diane, I thought that was a good idea the other night, but I've changed my mind. There's no sense giving the murderer a second target."

She stopped to pin me with a long stare. "Do you know what makes for a real friendship?"

It had to be a trick question, but I couldn't think of the trick answer. "What?"

"Give and take in equal parts. And you never take. Which means I can't give, and that's really crappy! If you want to remain my friend, I suggest you let me do something for you for once."

I was doing it again. I swallowed and said, "I'm sorry."

She watched me for a moment then said, "Good." She flipped open the notebook, stopping at a page that was filled with my handwriting. "You haven't checked out Andy's background at all and I just happen to have a cousin who's some kind of muckety-muck with the Houston Police Department; that's where Andy started out. I'm going to call him tonight and see what he can find out about Andy's record." She ran her finger down the page, flipped to the next one, and said, "And this whole thing with June is so nebulous. Especially since she was on a couple of boards with the Judge. The museum board of directors. The United Way. Maybe a couple more. Were they friends? Friendly enemies?''

"June won't talk," I reminded her.

"Not to you, but she told me to come out anytime I needed some help with my book." Diane grinned. "Did I tell you what a horrible time I'm having with my writing lately? And who knows? I might get a little information."

"Yeah, well don't bother to check her bathroom for perfume; I already did that."

"You did?" Shock, surprise.

"Yes, I did," I said. "And you needn't tell me what a rotten thing it was. I already know." I glanced at the clock; it was a little before one. "Since you're going to talk with June, then I'm going to have a short visit with Liz Street."

"You're supposed to be in bed, resting. You have a concussion."

"I heal quickly." I reached for the phone. "Besides, you have to take a little, too. Oh, shit. And give. Do you have Liz's phone number?"

"She doesn't have a phone, remember?"

Which was why we never knew if she was going to show up at our writers' group, and why we never worried if she didn't. "Well, then I'll just go and see if she's home."

I reached for my keys as Diane dug in her pocket for hers. "We'll meet back here at about five," she said. "Will that give you enough time?"

"I can't," I said. "Matt is coming back. I'd prefer he didn't know anything about this."

"Why?" She looked at me. "He's really making himself at home here. Have you wondered why?"

"No, and I don't want to think about it."

"I don't know, Jolie. Matt isn't the kind of man to do things without a good reason."

"Then maybe it's pity. It can't be anything else; he's seeing someone in Austin."

She looked concerned. "Are you sure? He hasn't mentioned anything to us about it."

"Jeremy told me."

"Oh." She cocked her head. "You could always fight fire with fire. If you wanted to."

"Yes. *If* I wanted to," I said.

"Message received." She picked up her purse. "I'll call you. If not tonight, first thing in the morning. What are you going to do with Jeremy?"

"He can come with me."

"He'll hate it," she said, "but what's a mother for if not to make a teenager's life miserable?"

TWENTY-ONE

LIZ'S HOUSE is an older country-style home with a wide porch that she's painted deep blue to match the rest of the trim. The wooden clapboard sides are a paler shade, giving it a story-book appearance.

I pulled up on the street under one of her massive pecan trees and got out of the car. Some kind of East Indian music was emanating from the house.

Jeremy got out of the car, too. "I'll be out here." He had his skateboard with him. "Are you doing this just so you can keep an eye on me?"

"No," I said. "It's so you can keep an eye on me. Matt would be furious if he found out that I took off alone for a couple of hours."

That seemed to salve his male ego. "Well, okay. But don't be too long."

I bit back the temptation to tell him not to go too far away. "Okay."

He scooted off, and with some reluctance I went up the concrete walk and onto the wood of the porch. Brass bells hung on the handle of the screen door. The wooden door behind it was open. I knocked and waited for some response. When none came I searched for a doorbell. There was one, and when I touched it I heard a delicate cacophony of chimes peal in the distance. Eventually Liz appeared.

"Jolie, what a nice surprise," she said, sweeping open the door. "I heard that you'd been attacked, or something. The rumors made it sound like you were at death's door in the hospital. Apparently the story was exaggerated."

"Greatly," I said as I stepped inside. The front room was wall-to-wall books, and on every shelf in front of the books were woven baskets and strange artifacts from around the world. The pale wood floor was littered with woven American

Indian rugs, huge pillows, and more baskets. The furniture consisted of an orange couch, a white armchair, and a big wicker lounger. Ferns draped gracefully from hanging baskets. "I hope I didn't catch you at a bad time?"

Liz gestured me to the chair and then sat on the lounger. She was dressed all in black, except for a scarlet belt and matching headband. Her feet were bare. "Not at all. I have been editing, and I need to clear my brain before I look at another word." She reclined gracefully. "So, you weren't irreparably damaged, how nice. Were you attacked at all, or was that simply more grapevine foolishness to enliven the lives of our poor bored Purple Sage-ites?"

"Well, someone did hit me, but it wasn't a big deal. I have a minor concussion, but I didn't have to stay in the hospital at all."

"I'm delighted."

"How's the editing going?" I asked.

She told me in detail. When she finally ran down, and I'd commiserated as much as I was capable of, she raised up a little on the recliner. "But I'm sure you didn't come to hear about my little annoyances. I'll bet you've come to talk about the Judge. Am I right?"

"Well, sort of," I said, realizing it was coy. "You grew up in Purple Sage and I just thought you might know something about the Judge that would help me."

"I know very little. Thank God, my memory has grown hazy."

"Oh," I said. "Well, do you remember anything about the creation of the lake? Was there something shady about that?"

"The lake? Lord, Jolie, I was practically a child. Well, a teen perhaps, but really not interested in politics."

"But you didn't like the Judge," I reminded her. "At the political reception, you said you hoped he was, ah..." I found myself hesitant to quote her. Maybe because she was staring at me, almost as if she were daring me to go on. "Well, I forget exactly what you said, but you made it sound like you weren't a fan of his."

"Certainly not a fan. What I said was that I wished I believed in hell so I could be sure he was burning in it." She tossed off the words casually, then waved them away. "A slip. I'm only human, and sometimes prejudiced, but aren't we all when it comes to other people?"

She was driving me crazy with her vagueness; especially when her words, if not her tone, held a lot of venom. "Can you be more specific? Why did you hate him?"

"Hate?" She pondered the word, allowing it time to roll through her mind. "I don't believe that I'm capable of hate. Oh, I'll admit to a bit of sporadic anger, but I meditate regularly these days and strong emotions simply don't coincide well with my serenity."

I was ready to strangle her. "Did he ever do anything to hurt you?"

"Jolie, you must realize that all people are merely divine instruments. They bring us lessons that we, on some other plane, have asked for and need to learn. I see now that he merely moved me." She smiled like some sort of madonna, but I noticed that her toes were clenched. "Quite literally, he moved me to New York, where I gained some modicum of success and was able to learn that true happiness doesn't come with money or prestige. One of the greatest lessons."

"That may be true, but there are outside factors affecting happiness. At the moment, Liz, I'm facing one hell of an unpleasant one. Frankly, if I can avoid the lesson of prison, I intend to."

She shrugged. "I wouldn't be concerned. You're basically a good person, Jolie, this will all work out as it's supposed to."

"But I'm still being persecuted. You've got to admit that even you would be getting a little worried if you were in my place."

"Would I?" She shook her head. "No, I don't think I would. The key is surrender, Jolie. Merely surrender."

I wasn't up for a religious discussion. I needed facts and I needed them in a hurry. I blurted out my question. "Well, will you at least tell me what the Judge did to you?"

She stood up. "A minor youthful peccadillo that the Judge felt demanded an unreasonable punishment. I left under what I believed was a cloud. Later, I realized that it was of my own creation and of no consequence to anyone else. Or to me, for that matter."

She made it sound like she'd been caught toilet-papering a house and the Judge had wanted to send her to the penitentiary. I stood up, too, since she obviously wasn't going to tell me anything useful if I asked straight-on. I tried one last question. "Something really smells good in here. Is that your perfume?"

"Perfume? Hardly. I'm allergic to all perfumes and I break out in a horrible rash. No, what you're smelling is incense. I burn it constantly; to raise the vibrations, although I'm sure that some residue of the scent clings to my clothes. Lovely, isn't it?"

It reminded me of love beads and peace signs. "Yes, nice," I said. "Well, I'm glad we talked." I just wished she'd said something useful.

From somewhere in the back of the house came the sound of what I would have sworn was a phone ringing.

"I wish I had more time," Liz said, leading me toward the front door. "But I must get back to my editing. Albert has a number of scholarly publications clamoring for his work, and it can't be sent out until I've finished."

Just then Albert appeared. "Liz, it's for you."

I turned around to look at her. "I thought you didn't have a phone."

She laughed, but it was brittle. "I detest the ringing of the phone, so I simply tell people I don't have one." She winked at me. "Don't give away my little secret."

"No, I won't. And you won't tell anyone we talked?"

"Of course not."

I thanked her for her time and left, wondering how much of Liz was real and how much pretense.

And wondering how I was going to find out the whole story on her "minor peccadillo."

As SOON AS WE got home I wrote down notes on my conversation with Liz. I was genuinely tired when Matt arrived, so I decided to take a nap while he and Jeremy fixed dinner.

When I woke up Jeremy was beside my bed, holding a tray with my meal.

I ate alone, and by the time I took the tray back to the kitchen, I discovered that the house was quiet. Computer-generated sounds were coming from behind Jeremy's closed door, along with some country music. I assumed he and Matt were together. It left me free to move around and get some air without fear of running into Matt.

I headed outside for the dark patio, where I could be alone to think.

Matt was already there, sitting at the wrought-iron table.

"Hi, how are you feeling?" he asked when he saw me.

"Oh, fine," I said. "I didn't realize you were here."

"It's a beautiful night." He pulled out a chair for me. "Here, sit down."

I started forward and tripped over a loose brick. If Matt hadn't reached out an arm to catch me, I would have fallen. As it was, I was still off balance and ended up sitting abruptly in his lap.

Matt laughed. "Well, that's one way to get a woman."

"Sorry," I said, jumping up and moving to my own chair.

"It wasn't that bad, was it?"

"Not appropriate. Jeremy told me you were seeing someone in Austin."

"He did? I see."

"It's none of my business," I said, not quite looking at him. "I'm sorry I mentioned it. I know you never would have said anything if I hadn't brought it up."

There was a pause, and then he said, "Meaning that I'm not very communicative?"

It hadn't been my intention to hurt him. "I didn't say that."

"That's okay," Matt said with a slight shake of his head. "I've been hearing that quite a bit recently."

"Oh. She's perceptive." I wondered if she was pretty, too.

"She seems to pick up on a lot of things about me. I suppose that's good, though. I'm learning a lot, and that is why I'm seeing her."

It didn't exactly sound like the passionate affair I'd imagined. "That's pretty cold-blooded."

"He looked surprised. "Why? That's what I pay her for."

"Pay her?" I stopped. "Are we talking about a woman you're dating?"

"Dating?" Matt laughed. "I'm not dating her, I'm seeing her professionally. She's a counselor."

"She is?" I was almost giddy with relief. "You're actually seeing a psychiatrist?"

"A counselor," he said. "You'd like her. Her name is Ruth and she's a very special person."

I didn't know how to respond, so I said, "That's nice."

My noncommittal comment effectively stopped the flow of communication between us. The silence seemed to stretch and expand, enveloping us in a bubble.

I sat back; the cool of the metal chair felt good against my body. It was a beautiful night. The air was spring soft and the sweet smells of verbena and jasmine drifted toward me. I looked at the dark sky and saw millions of glittering stars. That was the nice part of living in Purple Sage: you could see the stars.

It brought back vividly those times when Matt and I had sat on the porch at the ranch. There was an old wooden swing, and we'd sit side by side in the quiet spaciousness of the night. Back then I had talked to fill the silence; now it was Matt who seemed to feel the need to say something.

"How's your head?" he asked.

I shrugged. "Fine." It seemed so unimportant. If we were going to talk I wanted to say things that mattered. "Matt," I began tentatively, "why are you seeing a counselor?"

He took his time, letting the question float there between us. Finally he looked at me. "At first I went..." But he didn't finish it.

"Never mind. It's not important."

"No, if you asked you must want to know." The words came out simply. "I went because I wanted to get over the pain of our divorce."

The answer twisted my heart. I'd never thought about Matt hurting, too. I reached out toward him, but stopped, letting my hand drop to the geranium. "I'm sorry."

His smile was sad. "I know. At first, I didn't realize what it was all about. Ruth says that any loss brings pain. I'd lost my family, my whole way of life."

It brought up questions. If Matt had grieved for the loss of me, why hadn't he said something? I wanted to ask, but I couldn't. The carefully constructed wall that separated me from my feelings about Matt was beginning to slip.

I wanted to keep him talking, but not about loss. "Is the counseling helping?" I asked.

He thought about it. "My focus has changed."

I think I was disappointed. "I don't understand."

Matt looked at me, his dark eyes careful. "Jolie, it's hard to explain. Right now, what I'm doing is like starting life all over again. I'm relearning how to communicate. As you've pointed out, that's never been my strong suit."

"Is it so hard?"

"Not for you. I think that's what I found so appealing about you. Both you and Jeremy. You told me how you felt about things. You really let me see inside of you, and I felt so, so—" he searched for a word "—privileged. Somehow I'd found my way into the inner circle and it amazed me. I couldn't believe that the two of you would just let me in like that." He paused; his voice softened. "It humbled me."

I was so moved I forgot to be cautious. "Matt, what happened? What happened to us?"

A sadness slid over his face. "So many things. I couldn't give the openness back to you. Jolie, I didn't mean to be like that; I just didn't know any other way. I was the listener. In my family, when I was growing up, that was enough. I'm learning that it doesn't work in a marriage. It didn't work in ours, at any rate."

"It couldn't have been just you, though. I must have done things that made you unhappy." When he didn't say anything I leaned forward. "Please, Matt, talk to me. Tell me."

He reached across the table and touched my hand, gently stroking it with his fingers. "It wasn't your fault, Jolie."

"Dammit, Matt, that isn't fair. You're shutting me out again. Closing me off." I jerked my hand away and jumped up.

Matt was up too, and he grabbed my arm. "Jolie. Please."

I shook my arm free. "I don't need you, Matt. Not anymore."

"You never needed me," he said softly. "You always made that very clear."

I almost fell with the impact of his words. Words that carried the same meaning as the ones Diane had used. Even Jeremy had called me Lone Ranger. I caught the back of a chair and let my fingers press into the metal. "I didn't want to be just Mrs. Matt Wyatt," I said stiffly.

He shook his head slowly. "You never were."

I backed up, feeling defensive. "What does that mean?"

He moved in closer. "Only that you've always been your own person. You made Purple Sage your home, and challenged the status quo in a way that I never would have done." He watched me, waiting, but I didn't say anything, so he went on. "Who fought with the city to repair the Little League field?"

"You and Trey."

"No, Jolie, it was you," he said. "Trey and I finally came around, but we were willing to let things go on as they always had until you took your stand. You've never been just Matt Wyatt's wife."

I looked into his eyes. "And that was bad?"

He watched my face and said carefully, "I couldn't find my place in your life." He touched my cheek gently. "In the end, we both closed each other out."

I let my gaze fall to the dark brick. He was right, and it hurt to hear the truth. "I'm sorry."

He lifted my chin so that I couldn't avoid his eyes. "I'm sorry too, Jolie. I always wanted . . ." He watched my face for a long time, neither of us speaking. Finally he dropped his hands. "I wanted us to be friends, at least."

Friends. At least. "We can be friends," I said.

He smiled then, a sad smile, maybe because he saw what I was feeling.

"Good night, Matt," I said, half turning away. Then slowly, I turned back to face him. "And thank you."

"Thank you."

TWENTY-TWO

I HAD THOUGHT that since I wrote mysteries I'd have an advantage in discovering who had murdered the Judge. It was a misconception. In a book your protagonist follows a logical sequence, one that you create to get him to the final clues in the final chapter. You know exactly where to send him next to get the information needed to solve the crime.

In real life I had no such guideline. Not only did I not know who was important, I also didn't know who was telling the truth and who was lying. And I certainly didn't know where to go next.

I had a whole full life going on, too, which gave me some additional, and very interesting, things to think about.

I turned my attention back to the question of the Judge's murder, poring over my notes, as if finding one answer might answer all the questions in my life.

I made a list of all the things I needed to find out. Then I tried to prioritize it, but it was futile. By the time Diane called that morning I was feeling scattered, like I needed to charge off in a million directions at once.

"I feel like I'm caught in the middle of a big huge tangle of yarn," I said.

"What's your gut instinct?" Diane asked.

I tucked the phone between my shoulder and my ear, trying to concentrate on murder. My notebook was on my lap, the list of questions looking formidable. "That we can't do this."

"Defeatist."

"Well, you should see my list," I said, staring at it.

"You should see mine. Besides, there has to be a logical answer."

Did there? "What if some jerk came in from out of state and killed the Judge just for the joy of it."

"And by some bizarre coincidence was carrying a straight pin with the tip covered by your poison?"

"It's not my poison," I said. "But, I see your point. Okay, maybe that is a bit far-fetched." I stopped. "Wait a minute, what did you say?"

"That it couldn't be a bizarre coincidence because people don't just walk around carrying a straight pin covered with poison. Why? What are you thinking?"

My breathing seemed to quicken as an idea popped into my head. "Carrying a straight pin," I said. "How do you carry a straight pin? You can't, not for long; not if it's got nicotine on it. There's too much chance for it to slip, and if your finger even touched the poison you'd get deathly ill."

"So?"

"So the murderer had to carry this straight pin to the Judge's house."

"We don't know that for sure," Diane said.

"Of course we do." Now that I was on track, I expected her to keep up. "If the Judge had gone anywhere else, Andy would know by now and he'd be asking us if we'd been there."

"So?"

"So the murderer put the pin in one of those glass tubes that have perfume samples! Youth Dew!"

"Of course! That's brilliant, Jolie."

"Thank you." I didn't bask in the glory of my brilliance for long. "But that means anyone could have done it. I mean, they never actually wore the perfume or had a bottle of it. Just a sample that they dumped in a sink somewhere."

"Maybe. But at least it's something."

We seemed to be going backwards instead of forward. "Diane, do you have any theories? Or any favorites?"

She hesitated. "Could be any one of them. Rhonda, Maria, or Andy."

"You forgot June."

"I didn't forget her, I just don't see why she'd bother."

"Unrequited love?"

Diane laughed. "What a sick mind you have." Her voice, tinny over the phone line, became serious. "Last night I called my cousin in Houston and he's checking on Andy. We should know something in a couple of days.''

"Well, I talked with Liz. And guess what? She's got a phone. She's had one all along.''

I told her the rest of the story about Liz and her "minor peccadillo.''

It was almost impossible for me to really deep-down-believe that someone I knew would kill, but Liz was just odd enough to commit murder and find some way to justify it.

We both felt that Liz was one kind of person who would kill. The other type of murderer committed a crime of passion, and while ours looked cool and well planned, there might have been passion in the motive.

"I'm going to the courthouse later,'' Diane said. "I want to check on those land sales. Your notes are hard to read.''

"I was sneezing. It's tough to write and sneeze at the same time.''

"I'm not blaming, merely stating fact. How about if I meet you there? You can see if Liz's disagreement with the Judge was a legal one. You know, a case that he adjudicated.''

"Fine,'' I said. Except that we couldn't get our schedules to match. Diane had to join Trey for lunch with some of the movers and shakers in the Purple Sage political arena, and I didn't want Matt to know what I was up to. At that particular moment he was out at the ranch, but he could come back or call at any time.

"I almost forgot,'' I said. "Did you talk with June?''

"Mostly about writing. Boy, she can be hard.''

"I warned you, didn't I? So, did she tell you anything about the Judge? Or her father-in-law's land?''

"Not much,'' Diane admitted. "She said that when he sold the land he was in poor health, so it was a blessing. It gave him enough money to support himself until he died.''

"How very convenient.''

"Life's like that. Miracles happen.''

"Yeah, well, I hope a miracle comes my way, soon,'' I said, just before we wished each other luck and hung up.

I WENT STRAIGHT to the courthouse and Jim Moody's office.

"Court records?" he said, from behind the old counter. "Long as it's not too far back, it shouldn't be hard."

"What if it's twenty years ago?"

He shook his head sadly. "Then you've got a real tough job on your hands, Jolie. When the roof leaked, part of the county records got flooded. Oh, it didn't destroy the microfilm, but you'd be surprised how much damage sitting in water for a few years can do."

It explained the mold. "Didn't anyone clean them up?"

"Eventually, but you're talking about a lot of work. Doesn't happen overnight. Some of it didn't happen at all."

I was sorry to hear that, and I told him so as I followed him down the hall to the microfilm room. It didn't take long before I found out exactly what he was talking about. Some of the film was pitted and water-spotted. In other places I found more mold. What I didn't find was anything on Liz Street.

After two hours of searching, I gave up. I picked up my notebook and waved at Jim on my way out.

MATT AND JEREMY cooked a big dinner, and Jeremy set the table in the dining room, using the good china. There were fresh flowers, and I noticed that my son had even combed his hair. It was as if everyone were on their best behavior, trying to accomplish something that good manners would make possible.

Our conversation covered only neutral topics: Jeremy's computer game, the weather, my current book. I began to relax, and even took a second helping of brisket. Matt smiled approvingly and handed me the salt without my asking. He didn't offer the pepper; I never use it. When our hands brushed, we ignored it as if nothing had happened.

Then the phone rang. Naturally it was Jeremy who nearly jumped over the table in his haste to get to it.

I forgot about being on my best behavior and glowered. "Jeremy, don't do that again!" I said. At least it broke the unnatural politeness.

Matt grinned. "He'll slow down just as he gets to the telephone, and then answer in a bored voice."

We listened in silence, and Jeremy did exactly as Matt had predicted.

"Are you speaking from experience?" I asked.

Matt grinned. "Can't tell tales out of school, and that was definitely from high school."

"What? Girls called boys? In Purple Sage, Texas? I don't believe it."

"Well, we didn't talk about it, but every once in a while, if you got very lucky. Of course, we had to be very careful of what we said. Back then we had a six-party line, and two of the worst gossips in town were on mine."

The talk of girls must have jolted something in my subconscious, because suddenly my mind was on a new track.

Liz's last name hadn't been Street when she was growing up in Purple Sage. Street was her married name. I couldn't believe I hadn't realized it before!

"Matt, you know Liz Street, don't you?" I asked. "She's in my writers' group?"

He nodded slowly. "Purple Sage's only remaining flower child?"

"That's the one. Although she was fashion editor of the *New York Times* for a while."

"I just know her to say hello to."

"Did you know her in high school?"

If he was surprised at my sudden curiosity about Liz he didn't show it. "Actually, Elizabeth, that's what she was called back then, is about five years older than I am." He thought some more about her. "I don't remember her very well. Just that she had something to do with 4-H—sewing. I think. And she might have been valedictorian."

I took one final bite, chewed slowly, then swallowed. "Do you remember her maiden name?" I asked.

"Sure. Elizabeth Tandy," he said.

Elizabeth Tandy! No wonder I hadn't discovered anything under cases involving Liz Street.

I decided to go a little farther. "One more question. Do you remember anything about her getting in trouble? Something that might have resulted in legal action?"

He had finished eating by now and put his knife and fork down. "Legal action?" he asked. "Do you mean some involvement with the Judge?"

I shrugged, trying to be casual. "Well, I suppose it might have been. She just mentioned it yesterday, and I was curious."

"Yesterday?"

I swallowed. Yesterday I was supposed to have been in bed all day. "She called," I lied.

Matt leaned forward. "Jolie, I know that what you do is your business," he said. He sounded like a man forced against his better judgment to speak up on a controversial issue.

It was controversial. "It is my business."

"I know that. But if you're out poking around in the Judge's past, I think it's a very bad idea."

"Thanks for telling me," I said, jumping up and picking up plates at the same time. "I'll clear, since you cooked."

He picked up his plate and followed me to the kitchen. "Jolie, it could be dangerous. The murderer has already come after you once. What if he comes after you again? He could kill you."

"Let's not talk about this, okay?" I said, scraping dishes and shoving them in the dishwasher.

"Fine," Matt said, putting down his plate in front of me. "We won't discuss it. Except that I think you're being foolish."

I turned around to face him. "Matt, he could come after me regardless. If I was dangerous three days ago, I'm still a danger."

"Just think about what I said, all right?"

"Fine."

Matt was getting annoyed, too. "Or let me help."

"The infamous Wyatt clout?"

"I'm not thinking of buying anyone off, if that's what you meant. And frankly, Jolie, I wish you'd stop harping on my being a Wyatt. I didn't choose it, you know. And I am rather proud of it."

I had inadvertently struck an exposed nerve. "I'm sorry, I didn't mean that."

"I know you didn't, and now we're way off the subject." He shook his head. "Look, at least let me go with you when you go out. That way we know you'll be safe."

I kept my voice even and measured. "Matt, I really don't have any specific plans, but I'll think about what you said."

He began to study my face, probably to see if I was lying, so I went back to the dishes.

"Okay, Jolie," he said. "I guess that's all I can ask."

"Good," I said, turning around and heading for the dining room. "Oh, I was planning on going over to Diane's tonight. Don't worry, she's picking me up."

I heard the phone ring again as I put the last of the dishes in the sink. "Oh, and thanks for dinner. It was wonderful."

"You're welcome." He accepted the compliment as if it were a peace offering. "As you may have noticed, my cooking is improving."

"I've noticed. I think I've gained five pounds in the last few days."

He looked me up and down, then grinned. "Maybe two."

I decided I'd get home early.

Jeremy stuck his head in the door. "Mom, Diane's on the phone for you."

"Thanks, honey. I'll take it in the sunroom. You can wipe the counters."

Jeremy didn't even complain as I went out.

"Hello?" I said, putting the receiver to my ear.

"I think I've found something," Diane said. Her excitement was obvious.

"What?"

"Remember the deed of sale to Julio Chavez? At the same time as all the other sales to the county?"

"Of course. That was Maria's father. He committed suicide."

"Right. At first I thought it was strange that you mentioned his death in your notes, but I'm glad you did. Listen to this. He sold the land to the Judge exactly two weeks before he killed himself. Doesn't that seem odd?''

"Wow. I didn't realize the timing was so close. But wait a minute," I said, getting caught up in her discovery, "he sold the land for eighty-one dollars an acre."

"So?"

"I'm not clear on where his land was, the records are so screwed up, but it was near the lake." My brain was whirring. "Why would the Judge buy land that was going to be covered with water? Diane, the county only paid sixty-seven dollars an acre. The Judge wouldn't buy it just to take a loss. Would he?"

"I don't know, but I've got every county map that was ever made and I'm going to figure it out."

I thought about it for a minute. "Maria's mother said that the Judge's heart was always in the right place. I wondered at the time why she said it."

"When did you talk with her? Was she rational?"

"I think so," I said. "I stayed at Maria's house for a while Sunday, so Maria could go to the grocery store. I thought at the time that Mrs. Chavez knew the Judge."

"Her husband did, for sure. Look, we need to get to work on this. I'll come pick you up."

"Great, but there's something I want us to do first."

"I'm almost afraid to ask," Diane said. "What are we going to do?"

I dropped my voice just in case Matt was lurking nearby. "We're going to break into the *Tribune*."

TWENTY-THREE

"THIS IS HORRIBLE," Diane whispered as we tiptoed up the back stairs.

I was in the lead, wondering why I'd ever considered doing something so idiotic as breaking into the *Trib* office at night.

I had only a shaded flashlight beam to show the way, and the eerie darkness, hiding unseen horrors, seemed to press in from all sides. Diane had a flashlight, too, but we'd decided not to turn it on just yet. We wanted to be as quiet and inconspicuous as possible.

I got my first whiff of the noxious air; at least that was real. Unpleasant, perhaps, but not frightening. "Smell the bat guano?" I asked softly.

"I may not breathe the whole time."

I was trying to remember all the reasons that had made me brave enough to tackle the *Trib* in the dark. It had seemed the only way. If Rhonda was the murderer it would be even less safe to have her there watching.

Besides, Diane and I had decided that no one would be foolish enough to come after two of us, the old safety-in-numbers cliché. Not only that, we'd been cautious about getting to the *Trib*. We'd executed a number of diversionary tactics, like going to Diane's house first. Then we'd switched to Trey's big Mercedes. I'd been relieved to see that the smashed window had been fixed.

Despite all our precautions and rationalizations, when we reached the top of the stairs and opened the door, my skin felt clammy. Just peering into the blackness of the long hall was making me sweat.

I waited and listened. There was an uneasy silence, broken by the creaks and groans of an old building.

"Go on," Diane said, giving me a little nudge.

"I am." I led the way to the file room, my light barely piercing the gloom.

"What else is up here?" she asked.

"Abandoned offices," I said as I closed the door.

Diane clicked on her flashlight and carefully shaded it with her hand. "This is a nightmare," she said, looking around at the bulky shapes of the filing cabinets creating dark and distorted shadows in the dim light.

We were still speaking softly, as if someone on the street might hear us. From that distance they couldn't have, nor were there many people out. At nine-fifteen on a Friday night the streets of Purple Sage were empty except for the teenagers cruising Main in their parents' trucks.

"Here, put this over your flashlight," I said, pulling a roll of masking tape from my purse.

"I wish the windows had blinds." She took the tape, and between the two of us we cut the light sufficiently. "Now what?"

"Now we go through the files," I said. "I'm going to look for something on Liz. You can try the lake stories."

"And Maria's dad. I still think it's odd that he committed suicide so soon after he sold that land."

I slid open a drawer as quietly as I could. "This is where you need to look. I'll start down here."

I read the faded labels until I found the years I wanted, then pulled open another drawer. A spider crawled out. It had more right to be here than I did, so I flicked it away with my fingernail, then got a stack of papers. There was only one creaky table, and I shared it with Diane.

She was handling the yellowed *Tribunes* with great care to avoid crumbling them. She only swore occasionally.

"Damn. These things are falling apart. Why don't they put them on microfilm or something?"

I was reading newspapers in between worried glances toward the door. We couldn't have been followed, and no one in their right mind would come to the *Tribune* offices at night; still I kept watch. "Because nobody digs through them except idiots like us."

"Idiots is right."

I went through six months' worth of papers as quickly as I could, not letting myself get sidetracked by other stories as I had before. When I finished with one pile I put the papers back in the drawer and started on the next. By that time my hands were stained with ink and my senses were heightened by my prolonged case of nerves.

"Did you hear a car?" I asked.

Diane looked up and listened. The walls creaked and a stray puff of wind caused a whistle as it slid through a crack in a nearby window.

"Must have been over on Main," Diane said. "This place gives me the willies. I can't believe you ever came up here alone."

I couldn't believe I was there now. "Desperation," I muttered.

I started in on the next paper in my stack. The front page dealt with a big brush fire. I turned the page and skimmed each article.

"It's here!" I said.

"Be quiet. What have you got?"

It was a small story, only three paragraphs, almost buried among the grocery ads. Diane and I read it silently.

A Purple Sage youth, Elizabeth Tandy, was given probation today in the court of Judge Volney Osler, after having been indicted for growing an illegal substance.

A month ago, a patch of what was formerly thought to be a weed growing in a pasture near the Tandy home was discovered to be marijuana. The Tandy teenager, Elizabeth, admitted to police that she had grown the drug on a dare, but told this reporter that she had never smoked the dangerous substance.

Miss Tandy, a native Purple Sage-ite, graduated a year ago and has been working as a bookkeeper at the feedmill. Formerly she was active in 4-H and the Journalism Club at Purple Sage High School.

Diane made a face. "Sounds more like a social notice than a trial case."

"And I love the credits at the bottom. '. . . active in 4-H and the Journalism Club.' Brother!" I said. "And this part. 'She had never smoked the dangerous substance.' Give me a break!"

"I'll bet she made marijuana brownies and served them at 4-H meetings," Diane said with a quiet laugh. "But, it's not much of a motive for murder. The Judge was pretty soft with her."

"I know," I said, folding the paper, then putting them all back in the drawer. "How are you coming?"

"Well, I have a better idea—" She stopped talking suddenly, her whole body stiffening.

Somewhere in the building a door had slammed.

"Oh, my God!" I started grabbing for papers.

"The lights. Turn off your light!"

We turned off our flashlights, leaving us in total blackness. I could hear Diane breathing just beside me. I could also hear footsteps on the back stairs.

"They're coming!" I said in a whispered croak.

She grabbed me, and together we scurried to the door. I put my flashlight in my right hand, ready to use as a weapon if necessary.

The door at the end of the hall creaked open, and a pale reflection of light came from the crack at our feet. The footsteps were stealthy patters moving in our direction.

Diane and I clutched at each other.

The footfalls drew closer until they were just outside our door. Diane's nails dug into my skin. Neither of us breathed. Slowly, the steps went on down the hall. Another door opened, then closed softly.

I sucked in much-needed air and shook my arm loose from Diane's grip. She leaned forward and whispered, "We've got to get out of here."

I reached back and took her arm. My words were so quiet that I could barely hear them. "Follow me."

With great caution I slid forward, fumbling for the doorknob.

The hallway was dark and empty. Only the tiniest bit of light escaped from a crack under a doorway down the hall. I eased forward; Diane was as close as a shadow.

When we'd gone just a few feet, I heard the door at the bottom of the stairs open and close again. Then began another tread of footsteps climbing the stairs.

I whirled around. "Back!" I hissed. My heart was going so fast I was afraid I was going to have a coronary.

We scuttled back to the file room. I ducked inside, hitting my eye squarely against the corner of a file cabinet. I made a little sound, and Diane pushed me out of the way so she could get into the room. She was barely inside before the hall door opened. Our own door was still ajar but I didn't dare close it.

Diane and I huddled together in the darkness, waiting. I rubbed my eye. Then I forgot it. The footfalls coming toward us were louder, heavier than the others. We heard another door open. We waited.

Running now. Someone was running down the hall.

"Rhonda?" It was Morris Pratt's voice.

"Hi, I thought you'd never get here!" Her words were breathless. "Oh, I've missed you so much."

"Oh, and I've missed you."

I stuck my good eye to the crack in the door and saw Morris Pratt and Rhonda Hargis kissing passionately less than five feet from where we were hiding. Their mouths broke apart but their bodies were still clinging together.

"I almost couldn't get away tonight," Rhonda said. "It was awful, thinking that I couldn't see you. Oh, I love you."

He was kissing her eyes, her nose, her mouth, whispering things I couldn't hear.

Diane leaned closer to me. "Passion in the pits."

I nudged her with an elbow, and looked out the crack again. Rhonda and Morris had moved farther down the hall. I could just make out a door as he opened it for her. Then it closed behind them.

I grabbed Diane. "Let's go."

She pulled me back and whispered, "Let's put this stuff away."

"Are you crazy?"

"They'll never hear us. They're busy."

We threw the last of the papers into the open drawer, then slid it shut. I checked to see that the coast was clear, then like wraiths we slid toward the back door. Whatever Rhonda and Morris were doing didn't involve a lot of noise.

At the bottom of the stairs we threw ourselves outside into the cool alleyway.

"I can't believe it!" I said.

"Not yet," Diane said. She grabbed my arm and pulled me toward the Mercedes. It was on a shadowy street a block away from the *Trib* office. I yanked open my door and tumbled in.

Diane jumped in the other side. "By God, she is human!" She locked all the doors while I took in massive amounts of air.

"And now we know why she's been acting so strangely!" I finally said, looking in the backseat, just to make sure no one was hiding there. I saw headlights go on about two blocks behind us.

"What did you do to your eye?" Diane asked.

I turned around and fastened my seat belt. "Clipped it on the corner of the file cabinet. It hurts like hell." I pulled down the visor mirror to find out how much damage I'd done to myself, but it was hard to see in the darkness. "We can at least rule Rhonda out as a suspect."

Diane was pawing through her purse, searching for the keys. I looked in the mirror one more time and caught sight of the headlights still behind us. My scalp began to prickle.

"You're nuts," Diane said. "Just because she's having an affair doesn't mean she couldn't have committed a murder."

I didn't answer, and Diane asked, "What's wrong?"

"Look back."

She glanced up to the rearview mirror. "The lights?"

"They aren't moving."

"Have they been there the whole time?"

"No," I said, my eyes still fixed on my mirror. "They came on right after we got in the car."

"Well, shit." She yanked out the keys and started the car. "It's probably just kids."

"Maybe." But I kept watching. "It's a truck, I think. I don't know." The beating of my heart, which had just calmed to near normal, became erratic again.

"I forgot how quiet this area is at night," Diane said. She put the car into gear and we moved forward.

"Go slow," I said. The lights behind us slid forward.

She checked the rearview mirror. "They're following us," she said.

"I know."

"Should I go faster?" she asked.

"Yes." I held my breath and watched. "The lights are like the ones on a pickup. Who's got a pickup?"

"June. Andy. Liz has a Suburban."

"Oh, shit, Diane. We've got to do something."

She swung the car around a corner and speeded up, almost overshooting the stop sign on Main.

The headlights came around the corner, too. Closer now.

Diane saw them. "Hang on." She gunned the engine and we shot across Main, then she did a quick right, and another left. Two blocks later the lights reappeared.

"Oh, God," I said, my heart hammering. "They're still there."

"Not for long."

I was slammed back against the seat as we shot forward. She raced down Willow for two more blocks, then did another quick right, followed by a fast left. We were in an alley.

"Don't stop!" I said.

"I'm not going to."

We flew out of the alley and into a parking lot at an incredible speed.

"Where are we?" I demanded as we whipped behind a building.

"Backside of the country club."

"Get us around people."

"I am. Hold on."

She jumped a curb and we were racing across a grassy patch. There were trees in front of us, and she headed straight for them.

"What is this?" I asked.

"Ninth hole."

I saw a break in the trees and then we were through it. We were on a service road, narrow and twisty. Our headlights careened off the trees. Then the trees seemed to open up and we bounced onto pavement. We were only half a mile from her house.

"They're gone." Diane's voice was shaky.

So was mine. "And we're alive," I breathed.

"Is Matt still at your house?"

"He should be."

"Let's go there," Diane said. "It will be safer since Trey's not home."

I tried breathing normally; it was a new experience. I kept looking in the mirror, but there was only darkness behind us. "You think that was the murderer?"

"What do you think?" She sounded grim.

We passed houses, some dark, others with warming lights shining through the windows. There were streetlights. A kid's bicycle was half in a driveway, half in the street. It all looked so normal. She turned onto my street and into the driveway then shut off the engine. For a minute we both just sat there, letting our nerves settle. My hands were shaking.

"I don't ever want to do that again," Diane said.

"I still can't believe we got away."

Just then I heard the sound of an engine. I looked into the mirror in time to see a set of truck headlights pull into the driveway behind us.

We were trapped between the garage and our pursuer.

TWENTY-FOUR

WE SAT FACING forward, frozen like statues. Our eyes were fixed on the mirrors. The headlights glared at us. I watched with disbelief as the lights seemed to move away. They swung around and the vehicle backed up.

"What the..."

In the yellow reflection of the streetlight I saw the vehicle park on the street in front of my house. It was the Bronco. Matt climbed out.

"I don't believe it," Diane said, jumping out of the car. I went after her, grabbing her arm to stop her from saying anything, but I was too slow.

"Was that you following us?" Diane demanded.

"Yes," Matt said, his voice gruff. "I'm sorry if I frightened you.

Diane and I stood with our mouths open. There were so many things I wanted to yell at him, but none of them seemed sufficient to communicate the fury I felt.

"If that wasn't the dumbest damn thing!" I finally blurted.

"I think a number of dumb things have been done tonight," Matt said through clenched jaws.

Jeremy opened the front door and stuck his head out. "You're all back."

"Amazingly, we're all back. Safely," Matt said, letting Diane and me go in first.

"Wait just a damn minute, Matt..." I started, but Matt talked right over me.

"Jeremy, your mother and Diane and I need to have a private discussion. We'll be in the sunroom."

As soon as we got there and Matt had closed the door, I said, "Just what did you think you were doing tonight, anyway?"

"I might ask you the same thing. And what happened to your eye?"

Automatically I reached up to feel the faint puffiness. "Nothing much."

"Wait a minute," Diane said. "Matt, did you follow us when we left the house? Were you there the whole time?"

"Yes." That one word held back some strong emotion.

"Why?" I asked. "Why would you do something like that?"

"Why don't we sit down and discuss this calmly?" Matt said in a voice that he was trying hard to keep calm.

"Good idea," Diane said as she plopped down on the floor. "I don't think my knees would hold me up much longer."

Matt took the couch and I perched on the edge of the rocker. He looked at me, then at Diane. "I did follow you when you left the house, only because I was afraid that you were going to do something dangerous."

"We were perfectly safe!" I snapped.

A look of incredulity flashed across Matt's face. "Just how do you figure? Did you have any protection? Any weapon?" He stopped, took a breath, and spoke more calmly. "When I saw Rhonda come sneaking around the corner with her hands in her pockets, I was sure you were both going to be dead. What if she'd had a gun? What if she were the murderer?"

Diane ignored his dire words. "If you were so concerned that Rhonda was dangerous, why didn't you stop her?"

"I did start to follow her," Matt said. "Luckily I'd dropped back in a shadow, or Morris would have seen me. That's when I decided that they weren't bent on homicide."

"Marital suicide," Diane mumbled.

I'd been watching Matt and realized he was genuinely upset. "I guess you did have a few bad moments," I said.

"I was at the other end of the alley when you two came out." He looked straight at me. "You'll never know how relieved I was when I saw you."

I stared at him; he was still watching me. "Just how were you going to protect us?"

Matt had on a dark windbreaker and he unzipped it, pulling it open. He had a very serviceable pistol in a shoulder holster.

"Oh," I said. "So you were prepared."

He nodded and said evenly, "And I am sorry that I frightened you."

"And I'm sorry I snarled at you, Matt," Diane said, reaching over to pat his knee. "I do appreciate your concern."

My own words seemed forced. "I appreciate your concern, too."

"Now," Matt said, "why don't you just let this thing go? After all, it's a police matter."

I exchanged a look with Diane. She shook her head firmly. "It could also be a police crime, Matt." She explained about Andy.

Matt's eyebrows drew together in a frown. "Jolie told me that, but have you talked to anyone about it?"

"I have," I said. "I talked to the sheriff and he told me he couldn't get involved. Obviously Bill Tieman isn't going to be too concerned, which leaves me in a pretty precarious position. Andy might haul me up before the grand jury just to protect himself. And besides, why bother looking further when I look like the best culprit?"

Matt thought about that, then asked, "Have you found any connection between Andy and the Judge?"

"A small disagreement a year ago," Diane said. "But, that doesn't mean there wasn't more."

Matt took his time before he spoke. "Maybe I can help."

There was a long pause. Eventually, Diane pursed her lips, made some kind of decision, and looked at me. "He did grow up in Purple Sage," she said. "Maybe he'd remember something that would take us days to discover."

"Trey grew up here, too."

"And he has the worst memory of any human being in the Northern Hemisphere."

I still didn't want Matt involved. I didn't want Matt to get all tangled up in my life because of a murder. If he were going to be in my life I wanted him in some separate part that was all roses and romance. Besides, this wasn't how I had planned things.

"Fine," I said. "Tell Matt what's been going on." So it wasn't the way I wanted it. Maybe it would still be okay.

Diane told him why we'd gone to the *Trib*. She added some details that I'd so painstakingly tracked down earlier, and finally she pulled out her notebook.

"We've been keeping notes," she said. "We've still got a lot of questions that we can't seem to find answers to. Since you're here, you might be able to help."

I pulled out my own notebook. "But, Matt, I want you to realize one thing. I'm an adult; I do what I please, when I please. I won't listen to a lecture just because you don't agree."

Matt stared at me, and when he spoke his words were not at all what I expected. "I understand, Jolie. I respect your right to make decisions about your well-being." He looked at Diane, then back at me. "The way you respected my judgment when I bought Boris."

Boris was a stud horse that Matt had tried to turn into a workhorse. A nasty ill-tempered beast who attempted to kill every rider who came near him.

"What do you mean?" I asked, warily,.

Matt's voice was gentle, innocent. "You don't remember?"

"I remember," Diane said, not even trying to hide her amusement. "Jolie, after Boris threw Matt a couple of times you threatened to shoot that horse. Or Matt, I forget which."

Matt grinned at Diane. "But I'm sure she didn't lecture."

"She ranted and raved for an hour one day when I was there," Diane said. She reached up and nudged my leg. "Come on, Jolie, relax. Matt was only doing what you would have done if the situation were reversed."

"Enough." I jumped up. "If we're going to work, then let's get started."

"No problem," Matt said. "Why don't we go to the kitchen table where we can all sit down comfortably?"

"And I want coffee," Diane said, rising also. "This has been one of the longer nights of my life."

We moved into the kitchen, and Diane went over our notes while I brewed coffee. Watching the two of them reminded me of the first year that Matt and I had been married. Just like the times when the three of us would puzzle over how to approach the city council. Or when all four of us would be figuring out how to play a new board game. It was all so familiar, and yet so strange.

"I think the *Tribune* skimmed the surface on this story about Liz," Matt was saying. "It's coming back to me slowly, and I somehow remember that the chief of police didn't want to prosecute at all. It was the Judge who heard about it and used his power to get her indicted."

I poured coffee and put colorful mugs in front of both of them.

"Why would he do that?" Diane asked. "Why indict her and then let her off so easily?"

Matt looked puzzled. "I don't know. It does seem strange, doesn't it?"

Listening to Matt and Diane, I found that my own thoughts were beginning to clarify.

"Wait a minute," I said, sitting down between them. "Lisa said the Judge didn't like that she was a public defender. 'Defending that scum,' is the way she put it. What if the Judge just had a very moralistic streak? You know, a very pronounced sense of right and wrong?"

"Possible," Matt said.

"He became a judge for some reason. Maybe he just really couldn't stand the thought of crime, or wrongdoing, going unpunished."

"Yes," Diane said, "but he was known for being so light on local offenders."

"But the offense was still on their records," I argued. "That could be why he insisted that Liz be indicted, so it would be on her record."

"Well, that's pretty rotten," Diane said. "A drug arrest was a serous offense back in the sixties in this part of Texas. It could have ruined her life."

I leaned toward her. "It certainly could have."

"It was a long time ago," Matt said.

"Revenge can take a long time," I said.

"And it's a classic motive," Diane agreed.

Matt smiled. "I almost forgot that I was dealing with a couple of experts on the subject."

It had been so long since Matt had teased me, I'd almost forgotten he was capable of it. I stared at him, realized that no offense was meant, and went on. "Anyway, that leaves Liz as a suspect," I said. "But we still haven't uncovered anything about Rhonda."

"Except that she's having an affair," Matt said. "In the state of Texas, that's against the law."

Diane looked at Matt. "Wait. Are you thinking that somehow the Judge found out?"

"I'm just speculating. It is a possibility."

"Matt," I said. "Do you think we're right about the Judge's character? I mean, about him seeing things in black and white? You've known him, or at least of him, all your life."

Matt thought for a moment. "It seems to fit, but I know one way we can find out for sure." He stood up. "Let me go call Lisa. She can tell us."

He left the room and I looked at my watch. I couldn't believe it. It wasn't even ten-thirty.

Diane was pulling maps and copies of papers from a pocket at the back of her notebook. "This is what's driving me crazy," she said. "I can't ever seem to get all these pieced together enough to figure out where that land was that the Judge bought from Maria's dad or from Ted Ingram. I've got the coordinates; it should be easy. Have you got any Scotch-Tape?" she asked.

I opened a drawer and handed it to her. "What are you going to do?"

"Put this map together."

Matt came back, his teeth showing because of the big grin.

"Let me guess," I said. "Lisa agrees with us about the Judge."

"Exactly," Matt said, sitting down and picking up his coffee cup. "She said he believed wrongdoing should always be brought to light."

"Which means," I said, "that if the Judge found out about Rhonda and Morris, he might have thought it was his duty to tell Buddy Wayne."

Diane looked up from her maps. "That would be nasty. Buddy Wayne is not the most even-tempered guy in the world. Have you ever heard him at a Little League game?"

"You think Buddy Wayne should go on our list?" I asked.

Matt frowned. "As a murder suspect?"

"Well, if the Judge did find out about Rhonda's affair, and if he did tell Buddy Wayne, and Buddy Wayne got really pissed off..." I stopped. "Never mind. Too much conjecture. Besides, Buddy Wayne is not the subtle type. He'd never use my murder."

"He'd use his bare hands," Diane said.

"Diane, tell me more about Andy," Matt said.

"Ah, yes, Andy," she began, and then went on in detail.

I felt like I was drifting in and out of the discussion. At times I was involved, at other times I found myself a third party. I rubbed my forehead, wondering why life seemed so complicated.

"Is your headache back?" Matt asked.

I smiled. "No, I'm fine. Just impatient."

Matt nodded as if what I'd said made perfect sense, and then pointed to my notebook. "I keep seeing references to June Ingram. What's that all about?"

"Inconclusive evidence," Diane said.

I agreed. "I can't seem to find a decent motive, no matter how hard I try."

"And believe me, she's tried," Diane said.

"But it's not just personal prejudice on my part," I said. "Maria told us that the Judge was expecting a writer the evening he was killed. June is *the* writer in Purple Sage."

Matt was nodding. "Have you had an opportunity to check up on alibis?"

"The murderer would just lie," I said. "Besides, Andy can do that."

"I think maybe I'll talk to him," Matt said.

I turned to Diane. "Did you ever get back to your cousin about Andy?"

"Oh, hell, I forgot. I'll call him first thing in the morning."

"Okay," Matt said, "then what about Maria?"

"Now there's a puzzle," Diane said. She explained about the land sale and the suicide. The phone rang.

"Who would be calling this late?" I asked.

"Trey," Diane said. "I told him to call when he got back from Brownwood."

Matt reached up and grabbed the kitchen extension. Just like he lived there. "Hello? She's right here, Trey." He handed the phone to Diane.

"Hi, there," she said into the receiver. "How'd it go? Uh-huh. That's good. Sure, I'll be there in a few minutes." She hung up the phone. "I'm going to have to run. Can we finish this tomorrow? I'm exhausted. It's not the company, it's the activity."

I stood up to give her a hug. "And you performed admirably. If I ever buy a race car, you can drive it for me."

"Thanks, but I think I'm hanging up my driving gloves after tonight. At least all that hot-rodding in high school finally paid off."

Matt watched as she started picking up her things. "Why don't you leave your notes?" he suggested. "I'd like to look them over. Maybe I'll remember something that will be helpful."

"Okay. What's tomorrow? Saturday? Maybe we can get together in the morning."

"Fine with me," I said.

Matt walked her to her car, and then came back in as I was cleaning up the kitchen.

"How are you doing?" he asked.

"Oh, a little tired," I said with a shrug.

He watched me for a minute, then asked, "Are you still upset with me?"

I put the last mug in the dishwasher and unplugged the coffeepot. Finally I turned to look at him. "No, I guess not. At least your heart was in the right place."

Carefully he put his hands on my shoulders. "Yes, it is."

I didn't respond; I couldn't.

He leaned over and kissed me lightly on the forehead. "I'll take all this stuff with me. I'll be on the couch; call if you need me."

And then he picked up our notes and walked into the other room.

TWENTY-FIVE

I COULDN'T SLEEP.

While my body was fatigued, my mind was whirring with thoughts that wouldn't be laid to rest. Most of them were about Matt, and I didn't want to think about Matt, so I moved over onto my stomach and tried to concentrate on the Judge's murder.

There was nothing new to think about the Judge's murder. Besides, it wasn't holding my attention. I rolled onto my back.

I tried to capture the feeling of when I was a kid in that field of mustard flowers. It wouldn't come. I did various breathing and relaxation exercises, and after an hour I gave up.

The final solace is, of course, food, so I got up and crept silently to the kitchen, turning on only the dim light above the sink. In the cupboards I found a new loaf of French bread, and all the ingredients for Matt's famous spaghetti. At some point since his arrival, Matt had done some shopping.

Just to be sure, I looked in the crisper drawer of the refrigerator. A fresh head of lettuce, two kinds of cheese, ham roll, and Italian sausage. As one final check I peeked in the cookie jar. A dozen shortbread cookies. Matt had been planning to stay for the long haul, and he'd bought some of my favorite foods.

I had just stuffed a cookie in my mouth when I heard a sound behind me. I turned and found Matt. He was leaning against the doorjamb, his hair tousled as if he'd tried to sleep but had given up. He was wearing just his jeans, his chest glowing a golden color in the soft light.

"Hi," he said.

I swallowed the cookie almost whole and wiped the crumbs from my mouth. "Hi."

"I hope I didn't wake you."

"Nope." I got the last of the cookie down.

"I was going over the maps that Diane left." His eyes moved from my face to my body.

I was wearing what I call my French shift. It's silky white and the top has thin straps with just the tiniest amount of lace at the low neckline. From there it glides straight down to about four inches above my knees, except it clings in a few spots. Matt's eyes followed it down and then back up.

I could feel myself beginning to flush. Ridiculous, considering that I had been married to the man for three years. Instinctively, though, my hand went to the neckline.

"I'm sorry," Matt said, with a shake of his head as he straightened up. "I'd forgotten how beautiful you are."

"I'll get my robe," I said.

"Good idea," he said very seriously.

I went into the bedroom and grabbed the white Hopi coat that my mother had sent me from one of her travels. I slid it around my shoulders and belted it tightly at the waist. I don't know why it made me feel more secure, especially since Matt was still in just his jeans, but it did.

When I went back to the kitchen he was at the table, a glass of milk in front of him.

"Want some?" he asked.

I nodded. "I'll get it." I could feel him watching me as I got a glass and went to the refrigerator to pour the milk. "You've done some shopping," I said.

"Do you mind?"

I wasn't sure. "No, I guess someone had to. You're planning to make spaghetti."

"It was always one of your favorites." Then he smiled. "And it's one of the three things that I can cook."

I closed the refrigerator door and sat at the table, but I didn't say anything. I couldn't even look at him.

Matt reached across and touched my hand where it rested on the glass. "Jolie, I know I'm here at your sufferance, but I'd be lying if I said I haven't enjoyed it. I've missed you and Jeremy."

I took a long breath and stared at him in the soft light. Slowly I nodded. "You've been a great help."

"Like an orderly? Or a distant cousin?"

I shook my head. "No. More than that."

He waited for a while and when he spoke his voice was soft. "Are you sure you want to leave Purple Sage? A lot of people here love you, Jolie."

I almost laughed, but the mood was wrong. "Those people are talking about me, Matt. They're sure I'm a murderer."

He shook his head. "No, just a few. A few who don't count anyway, because they've always been jealous of you. You've got a lot of admirers."

"Name one."

"IdaMae." Matt smiled. "I can't even go to the bakery anymore without getting a lecture on what a fool I am. And Diane and Trey."

"Diane's a friend."

"That's right," he agreed. "And Diane doesn't warm to people easily. She did with you, and not because of me, either. Maybe it was because you started the writers' group, and if you hadn't done it, no one would have. Diane would never have become so serious about her writing, either. That's probably true of Maria and Rhonda, too."

"I also did it for myself," I said truthfully.

"The result is the same." His eyes, dark and warm, looked into mine. "I've missed you. I've missed seeing you, and being part of your life. Being here is almost like having my family back." He watched my face for a long time. "Jolie, there's something I've been wanting to say. This may not be the time or the place, but I have to say it." He paused, then went on, his voice like velvet. "I still love you."

I gulped. "Thank you."

Matt accepted my words, asking for nothing more. He touched my hand again. "Have you missed me? Maybe just a little?"

I nodded. "Yes. Of course."

He waited; my answer seemed to echo inside my head. Then he began to stroke my hand. "Jolie, do you think there's still a chance for us?"

"I don't know," I said softly.

"Time has passed, maybe we've gotten some perspective. I know I have."

My stomach was tight with fear and hope. "Matt, nothing changes unless we do."

"I know, and I've thought about that a lot. I think I have changed. Am changing. At least now I know some of the things not to do."

I bit my lip. "But what about me? I'm still the same."

He leaned forward, anxious to convince me. "You could come with me to Austin. Talk with Ruth, my counselor. She's a wonderful person, caring, supportive. She could guide us over the rocky parts."

I shook my head. "I don't know."

"Then don't go with me," he said. "Talk to someone else. See anyone you want, Jolie, what's important is that we still have all the things that made us happy to begin with. Those are the things that brought us together, and they can hold us together."

Out of sheer panic, I jumped up and started for the sink. Matt reached up and caught my arm and then stood beside me, just inches away. He took my fingers, holding them gently, then raised them to his mouth and kissed my hand. When he was finished, I was trembling.

Matt's voice sounded husky. "Jolie, I know I'm rushing you; you haven't had the time to think about this that I've had. I'm sorry about that. But you have to know that it's what I want."

I looked up into his dark eyes. "I'm afraid, Matt. You don't know how much it hurt before. I was just getting over you, or at least I was pretending to. The pain was going away." I could feel tears stinging my eyes again. I tried to sniff them back, but it didn't help. They slid onto my cheeks. "What if we couldn't make it work? I couldn't go through that again."

His arms went around me and he held me tightly against his chest. "You won't have to, not ever. I promise you, Jolie, I'd never let you go again."

"Oh, God." The tears began to flow in earnest. I dropped my head and began to talk. I told him again about Steve leaving Jeremy and me without even rent money and how much that had hurt and frightened me. And for the first time, I told Matt about my pledge never to be that dependent on someone else again.

"I'll set up a trust for Jeremy. And a savings account for you," Matt said. He mentioned figures that seemed astronomical. "You'll have complete control of both accounts so that you'll never have to be afraid again."

"Oh, Matt..."

He tried to wipe the tears from my cheeks, but more kept falling. "Hey, there's no reason to cry," he said. "You can have whatever you want, Jolie. However you want it."

I put my face against his chest and let the tears come. I wasn't crying for the present; the tears were those I'd refused to shed before. The ones I'd kept tightly balled inside of me, some that went all the way back to Steve, others from the divorce.

The hair on his chest tickled as I leaned against him, letting my shoulders relax. Matt began to knead my back gently, easing the tension. I tried to smile, but I knew my lips were wobbling. "I still love you, Matt."

He kissed me then. I could taste the salt of my tears. Both of his arms were wrapped around me tightly and my own hands were sliding along the silken skin of his back.

When the kiss was over I could feel his heart pounding and my knees felt weak. Matt touched my chin gently and tilted my head up. "I love you, Jolie."

Our eyes were locked. My heart was racing as fast as Matt's. He kissed me again.

"Matt, I don't know if I'm ready for this."

He held me close, his hand stroking my hair. "I know."

Finally I stepped back, but I kept my hands on his chest; I didn't want to lose contact. I needed time to adjust. Time to be sure. I couldn't make a mistake again, not for myself, and not for Jeremy.

"Matt, it's all happening so fast."

He ran his hand gently up and down my arm. "It doesn't seem that way to me, but I've been thinking about this, wanting it, ever since you left."

I half turned away, knowing I couldn't tell the truth if I were looking at him. "Matt, I love you. But I have to be sure this time. I can't do this to any of us, especially Jeremy, if it isn't going to work. He was as devastated as I was."

"There are no guarantees," Matt said quietly. "There's no proof that I can give you, except to tell you that I've never stopped loving you. And I'll do everything in my power to make our marriage work."

I faced him. "This is crazy; our divorce was just final."

Matt laughed softly. "Then we'll get the divorce annulled. Or we'll get remarried. We'll have the ceremony on the courthouse lawn and we'll invite the whole town!"

I tried to laugh too, but I couldn't. "Could we just take a day or two?"

He took a step closer, sliding both arms around me. "Jolie, you can take all the time you want. I'll be here when you're ready."

"And what if I'm never ready?"

"Then I'll just go on loving you. We can take our time, because that's the one thing we have, all the time in the world."

"Thank you," I said softly.

He kissed my forehead, then my eyes. "No, thank you." Then he straightened up. "And now, I suggest that if you want to wait, we have to stop kissing, or I'll get carried away. And carry you away. Literally."

He'd intended to break the mood, and I let him. It was difficult; I wasn't sure what I wanted. Guarantees perhaps, and as Matt had pointed out, life doesn't come with those.

I gestured to the table. "More milk? Cookies and milk?"

Matt's laugh was shaky. "That should cool me down."

I sat at the table and Matt joined me. We began to talk. Awkwardly at first, but the dim light and the late hour somehow made it easier. We started talking about Purple Sage, neutral things. Then about Jeremy, and about Matt's business. Matt told me things I'd never heard before, and for once, I was the one who listened.

"And in the future," he paused, holding my hand as if I might slip away. "If things work out, I want you to come with me on business trips. I realize now that at the end," he stopped and then went beyond the meaning of those words, "I wasn't home enough. I won't be gone so much. And when I am, I'd like you to be with me."

"My writing," I reminded him. "I'll need to write."

"We'll get you a notebook computer." He brought my hand up to his lips to kiss it. "You can write during the day, and at night we'll go out."

"What about Jeremy?" I asked.

"This summer we can take him along. Of course, he'll have to have his own room." Matt grinned. "He'll love it. He'll be ordering room service and bringing along computer games to play on the notebook when we go out. And, sometimes he'll go out with us."

I felt myself smiling. "You do have this all planned."

"I've had a lot of time for planning."

"You've forgotten something, Matt," I said very seriously. "I can't stay in Purple Sage if they don't solve the Judge's murder. Too many people would be watching me. And Jeremy. I couldn't live with that and it wouldn't be fair to expect Jeremy to."

Matt nodded. "I understand. I'll talk to Andy first thing in the morning and see how his investigation is coming along. If that doesn't work, I'll talk to his boss, Bill Tieman. Don't worry, Jolie, one way or the other we'll get this thing handled."

"More Wyatt clout?"

"Wyatt ingenuity," he said with a grin. "If Andy can't figure out who murdered the Judge, you and I can. Two Wyatts. Lots of ingenuity."

I laughed.

MUCH LATER I began to yawn. Matt stood up and put our glasses in the sink, then pulled me up. "Come along, Cinderella, it's time for you to get some rest."

"Is it midnight?" I asked.

"Well past," he said, kissing me softly before leading me to my bedroom door. "And you're still a princess."

I sighed. "You really think fairy tales can come true?"

He was serious, his eyes on mine. "That's our choice. We have to make them come true, but we can do that."

He kissed me good night, and with reluctance we parted.

"I love you," he said softly.

"I love you, too," I said, going alone into my bedroom.

I was only sure of one thing: that I still loved him. I wanted to see how that felt in daylight. Making love would break down the last barrier between us. I was glad that Matt understood my reluctance.

I wasn't sure that I did.

TWENTY-SIX

THE SUNSHINE FLOODING through my windows seemed brighter Saturday morning, despite the slight headache I had. I decided that the sunshine, and probably the headache, were well deserved. I went out to the kitchen and found Jeremy listening to the radio and drinking orange juice. Crumbs from toast were on the table and the counter.

"Good morning," I said. "You want to turn that down?" I pointed to the radio that was blaring out the latest country hit on KSGE.

He jumped up. "Sure. Hey, listen, Mom, I kind of wanted to go play baseball for a while. You mind?"

"Like you did last time?"

He wriggled uncomfortably. "I wasn't really doing anything. You know, just messing around. I mean it wasn't..."

I gave him a quick hug, and he accepted it graciously. "It's okay," I said. "Have fun. But, whatever you do, I don't want to end up reading about it in the *Tribune.*"

He grinned. "You won't."

The thought crossed my mind that he was up to something, although for the life of me I couldn't figure out what it could be. If he wasn't talking about it, I wasn't pushing. After all, I wasn't telling him everything that I was up to. "Where's Matt?" I asked.

"He left early. Had to go feed at the ranch. Bart's got the flu or something. Oh, and he said he was going to run a couple of other errands, too."

"So, when are you leaving?" I asked.

"I'm supposed to wait until Matt gets back." He looked me over carefully. "You look nice. Except for your eye. What happened? It's really gross."

I had done my best with makeup, and had thought the soft shadow gave me a haunting look, like something out of *Wuth-*

ering Heights. Apparently Jeremy didn't find it quite so romantic.

"Nothing. I bumped into a cabinet."

"Yeah, well maybe if you put a little makeup on it . . ."

"I did put makeup on it."

"Sorry," he said, but he didn't look contrite. "So, uh, what are you going to do today?"

An excellent question. "I don't know."

"Oh. I just thought maybe you had plans, or something," he said, as he swiped at the crumbs on the table with a paper towel. He even got a few.

"Jeremy, you're not yourself this morning. Are you up to something?"

His eyes got as big as saucers and just as dumb. "Me? What would I be up to? Want me to pour you some orange juice?"

I gave up. "Yes, please."

The phone rang, and for once I beat Jeremy to it. "Hello?"

"Hi, there," Diane said. "How's it going this morning?"

"I have a headache and Jeremy says I need to put more makeup on my eye. How are you?"

"About the same, except for the eye. Your voice sounds funny. Is something up?"

Amazing how perceptive Diane could be. With Jeremy there I could hardly explain what had gone on the night before between Matt and me, and I wanted to. She'd have been all for it, too. In fact, she'd probably have demanded to give away the bride or something equally odd.

"Nothing's up," I said. "How about with you?"

"I talked to my cousin. Guess what?"

"What?"

"Andy had a perfect record in Houston."

"Well, shit."

"I know. Wouldn't it be awful if he were just a good cop doing his job?"

"Yes. Especially since he's doing it so friggin' slow," I said. Then I remembered that Matt might be talking to Andy at that very minute. I glanced over at Jeremy, who was pretending not to listen. "So, are you coming over, Diane?"

"That's the other bad news. I have to drive over to Menard to get Randy. Apparently he and his grandmother have had all the familial togetherness that either one can stand. Want to drive over with me?"

It was tempting. "I'd better not. Matt's gone out to the ranch and I'd rather Jeremy weren't here alone. Not if we're going to be that far away."

Jeremy rolled his eyes and mouthed, "Go!"

I ignored him. "What time do you think you'll be back?"

"Well, that's the problem," she said. "Without an excuse I'll have to stay for a couple of hours at least. Maybe not until this afternoon."

"Don't worry about it. You've performed above and beyond the call of duty as it is. Take a break. Have some fun."

"At my mother's? You must be kidding. She'll have me in a stock pen working sheep if I'm not careful."

I laughed. "Well, then have a terrible time. Call me when you get back. Matt may have worked out something ingenious with the maps last night." Of course, if he had, it would have to have been before we talked. Or maybe afterward.

"He'd better not have."

She sounded possessive about the Judge's murder. Funny, I didn't feel quite that way anymore.

We said our good-byes and hung up. Then I drank my orange juice and fixed some toast. It seemed everyone had something important to do except me. Well, I could certainly find something.

I decided on laundry and vacuuming, on the theory that it would give me a chance to put my brain to work. I also put Jeremy to work.

"Why don't you sweep the patio? Okay?"

He grumbled but went, and I put a load of clothes in the washer and started cleaning the sunroom, carefully not thinking about Matt. Instead I concentrated on murder. The problem was that until we could pinpoint all the land that the Judge had bought, and the county had condemned, I wouldn't know who had motive. I remembered something vague about the lake being made smaller after the initial plans were drawn up. We still hadn't made a list of events in chronological order. We'd do that this afternoon and maybe then I could determine if the alteration of the size of the lake made a difference. As I vacuumed, I missed most of the corners, but an idea was taking form in my mind. Could some of that land have turned out to be lakefront property? Little flashes of lightning seemed to zing through my brain. That was it! What if the Judge had bought land that was designated for flooding and then, when they narrowed the lake, his newly acquired property became extremely valuable?

IdaMae had said that the Judge was wired into all the political happenings back then. He could have had inside information. Information that allowed him to buy land cheap, then develop it and sell off lots for a small fortune.

Jeremy's voice interrupted my thoughts. "Mom? Are you all right?"

"What?" I turned off the vacuum cleaner.

"You've been standing there for five minutes. I talked to you, but you were in some kind of a trance."

"Here, put this away," I shoved the vacuum cleaner into his hands. "I've got to check something."

I dashed into the living room and found our notes. Matt had left them in a neat pile on an end table. The maps were on top, with delicate ballpoint-pen markings circling two sections. Another darker circle showed the location of the lake today. Apparently he'd done more work than I'd thought. I sat down and tried to figure out what it all meant.

After a few minutes I had it. The land the Judge purchased from Julio Chavez had ended up being completely covered with water, but the Ingram land was only partially flooded. The biggest portion of it was now Sage Lake Estates. All expensive waterfront property.

Again Jeremy was standing there watching me. "What?" I asked.

"Can I go now?"

"Where?"

"Oh, you know, Just out."

I finally focused on him. "I thought you were supposed to wait until Matt got back."

He huffed impatiently. "Mo-om! Isn't this baby-sitting getting a little ridiculous?"

"No. Besides, you're baby-sitting me, remember?" I stood up. "I need to go downtown; you can come with me."

"Mother!"

"I mean it, Jeremy. Get your coat. We're going."

"My coat? It's seventy-five degrees out there."

"Never mind. I'll get my keys. Come on."

HE SAT IN watchful silence as I drove downtown. If I could help IdaMae separate fact from recipes, then maybe we could get someplace. We'd find a reason why June would kill the Judge thirty years after he'd screwed her father-in-law out of a lot of money.

"Stop the car," Jeremy practically yelled.

"What?" We were nearing the top of the sloping hill on Main just above the bakery. A familiar figure in all white, the Captain, was trudging along the sidewalk.

"Pull over, Mom! Let me out here." Jeremy was already fumbling for the door handle.

"Get a grip, Jeremy. Let me stop first," I said. There was no one behind me, so I eased over to the curb. "And what's the big deal about here?"

"Huh?" He grabbed the skateboard that was resting between his feet on the floor. "Oh, I'll ride down the hill."

There was smooth sidewalk all the way to the bakery.

I hesitated a moment, but he was already jumping out of the car. "Okay," I finally said. "But be careful. I'll meet you inside the bakery in five minutes."

"Ten," he said, slamming the door.

Inside the bakery I found wall-to-wall people all pushing toward the counter. With some judicious squirming I made it to the front.

"Is IdaMae in back?" I shouted to be heard above the noise.

One of the high school girls stopped unloading a tray of cookies just long enough to say, "Yeah, in her office."

Without waiting for anything more I dashed to the back office and found IdaMae smoking a cigarette in that little room, blowing the smoke out the open window like a kid afraid to get caught. She jumped when she saw me.

"Lord, Jolie, you scared me. I thought you was one of them nosy tourists." She waved away the cloud of smoke and pointed to the chair across the desk from her. "Sit down. What are you doin' here?"

"I came to see if you could help me. You seem to have the best memory in Purple Sage." It was bold-faced flattery but I was desperate.

IdaMae cackled with delight. "You want somethin', that's for sure. Okay, what is it?"

I scooted into the chair. "I just had a couple of questions."

"Is there somethin' wrong with your eye? Looks like you got a shiner."

"A small one," I said. "I bumped into a filing cabinet. It's a long story. Maybe I'll put it in a book someday."

"And I'll read it, too. Now, what was it you wanted?"

"Actually, I was hoping you could help me figure out why June Ingram might kill the Judge thirty years after he screwed her father-in-law out of money."

IdaMae blinked twice. "How did he do that?"

I told her about the land deal and profit I thought the Judge had made on it.

IdaMae pursed her lips and whistled softly. "The old coot was smarter than I thought." Then she shook her head. "But I don't think it had anythin' to do with June. That girl never did care much for money. Don't figure she minded a bit."

"Damn. Are you sure?"

"Sure as I can be. She don't like clothes, and she don't buy fancy cars. 'Sides, she's got the money off her books."

She was right. June didn't seem to care about money. Before June had bought a briefcase she'd carried her manuscript in a paper bag; it was all the same to her.

I tucked the information away to think about later, and moved on to the next subject. "Okay, then what about the Judge and Julio Chavez? That was just the opposite case. We found out that the Judge bought some land from Chavez and took a real beating on the price. Do you know why?"

"The things you're bringing up, Jolie! Lord, it does take me back."

"Then you do remember?"

"Well, I don't like to gossip."

"Both the men involved are dead," I reminded her.

"Yeah, but if anyone was to come back and haunt me, it'd be one of them for sure." For emphasis, she stubbed her cigarette out in a battered tin ashtray.

"It can't hurt them anymore."

IdaMae leaned forward, suddenly serious. "Jolie, it could hurt other folks, so you got to swear that you won't go spreadin' this around."

I couldn't promise and I didn't want to lie. "IdaMae, it might be too important to keep quiet."

She stared at me, her lined face stony.

"Please, IdaMae," I said, leaning forward. "Just tell me. It's the only way I can stay in Purple Sage. And if it's not important, I won't tell anyone; you know that."

After a long pause she said, "Okay, I'll tell you, but I'm trustin' your good judgment on this one." I nodded and she went on. "Well, it's like this. And you keep in mind that don't no one know this whole story. Not no one alive in Purple Sage, at any rate."

"I'll remember."

"Okay." She took a breath and started in slowly. "Well, the Chavezes was in pretty bad financial trouble if I remember rightly. Most of the laborers was 'cuz the factory'd shut down. Oh, it was a good year for the farmers so some of the men got hired on as field hands, but the money was kinda poor, if you know what I mean. Anyhow, Julio, Maria's dad, was pretty hard put for money, and he was about to lose that land. It was pretty much just scrub anyway, wasn't good for much except for running stock and he didn't have any. He might've had it leased out, I don't rightly remember, but if he did, the lease didn't cover the payments. You know."

"I understand." Families in Purple Sage were often land poor.

"Anyhow, so the Judge bought it, and from what I heard, Julio made enough to pay off the note and still walk away with a couple of thousand dollars. That was a lot of money in them days."

I was nodding, following along, but her story was too simple. There were things she wasn't telling me. "But, why?" I asked, leaning forward. "Why would the Judge do that? And why would Julio Chavez commit suicide just two weeks later?"

There was a long silence again.

"Are you sure you got to know all of this?" IdaMae asked.

"Didn't the whole town know?"

She snorted. "They did not! I told you, them that knew is dead. All except for Maria's mother, and I don't suppose you could rightly call her alive anymore."

"IdaMae, I promise, if it doesn't have to come out, I won't say anything."

"Okay," she said with a long breath. "The Judge did it 'cuz he was crazy mad for Aurelia Chavez."

"He was in love with Maria's mother?"

"Yeah. Oh, she was something to see in those days. I mean, really beautiful with them high cheekbones and dark eyes. There was something real high-class about her, too. She was a real lady. Just the same, though, she was as crazy for him as he was for her. They was always sneakin' around spending time together."

I shifted in the rickety plastic chair, letting the story soak in. Maybe that was why the Judge had never married. "Couldn't she have gotten a divorce?"

"Nope. Devout Catholic," IdaMae said, as if that explained it all. Her face became sad. "Oh, and who knows, it might have all turned out different, but then Julio found out and—well, you know what happened."

I knew: Julio Chavez had committed suicide.

It wasn't hard to imagine how that had affected Aurelia Chavez, especially considering her religious beliefs. She would have devoted her life to her children, and all the while the guilt would have eaten at her. It would have colored her love for the Judge and eventually killed it. Perhaps her illness now was a blessing; it took her back to happier times and relieved her of the shame that had no doubt been a cruel burden for too many years. Especially in a small town.

Then I remembered that IdaMae had said no one knew.

"IdaMae, are you sure that people in Purple Sage didn't know about Mrs. Chavez and the Judge?"

"Oh, I'm sure."

"Then how did you find out?"

"Honoria!" She spat out the name with a vengeance. "She was a friend of my daughter, Helen's, and she was Aurelia's best friend. She took care of the children while Aurelia was out with the Judge. Honoria thought it was just some mad romantic adventure! Every time Honoria came around to see Helen she'd have this shit-eatin' grin on her face, and I knew she was up to somethin' but I never could figure out what. She was always hurryin' off and so secretive!" She shook her head and let out a sigh. "When Julio killed hisself, Honoria damn near went crazy. I found her cryin' on my back door one day, just about all done in. She was just a kid then, only twenty-five or so, hell, they all was kids, and she just never thought it could get so serious. I must have held Honoria for hours while she cried." And then, very softly she added, "I wonder if anyone held Aurelia."

Sadness swept over me. How easy to see them slipping around behind her husband. And how easy to understand that it had been partly a game, at least for Honoria. Maybe for the Judge and Aurelia, too. One that ended in a tragedy that deprived Maria of a father. One that had taken a life.

I had to clear my throat before I could talk. "Thank you for telling me, IdaMae. I promise, I won't say anything unless I have to."

IdaMae was all business. "I trust you. Besides, I already decided that protectin' the dead is no excuse for hurting the living. If that story leads you to the Judge's murderer then you use it, 'cuz you need to be watchin' out for yourself and Jeremy."

"I will," I said, rising and picking up my purse. "And thanks."

"You take good care, you hear?"

"Promise," I said.

I had trekked back to my car, my mind still haunted by the story IdaMae had told me, before I remembered Jeremy. He hadn't been in the bakery and obviously he wouldn't find me, so I had to go find him.

I looked up Main. He wasn't on the sidewalk, nor did I see him anywhere on the hill.

"Damn." I got in the car and cruised up the hill slowly, looking to both the right and the left. I still didn't see him.

He wouldn't have gone far; he knew I was expecting him. There was the slight possibility that I'd missed him in the crowd at the bakery, so I hung a U-turn and let the Mazda coast down the hill. With any luck Jeremy would be outside of the bakery by now.

He wasn't. I rolled past IdaMae's, still searching for a lone figure on a skateboard. A lone figure walking. Anything.

I circled the square and started back. There was still no sign of Jeremy and no parking places, so I slid the Mazda in behind a little VW, on the theory that the owner would be little, too.

Just then Jeremy came out of the bakery, a scowl on his face. He spotted me.

"Where have you been?" he asked. "I looked everywhere for you."

For a moment I just stared at him. "It doesn't matter," I said, reaching over and giving him a hug. "Let's go home."

We climbed in and I headed for the house. I wanted desperately to talk with Diane. Or maybe Matt. Unfortunately, I knew neither one was available. Actually, it was probably a good thing since I couldn't tell them what I'd learned anyway.

After a few minutes I became aware that Jeremy was watching me.

"What's the matter?" I asked.

He screwed up his face. "Well, it's just that I kind of wanted to talk to you, but I'm not sure that now is a good time."

"It's a great time," I said. "No phones and no TV. At least you'll have my undivided attention. What did you want to talk about?"

"Well, see I'm not sure that you're going to be happy about this, but I think you should be. Well, actually, I guess I don't know if you should be or not, but you shouldn't get all hyper about it, either."

I rounded a corner. "Jeremy, I hope this rambling is not a habit you picked up from me," I said. "Spit it out."

"Yeah, well, I'm going to, only..." he paused, looking out the window.

We turned onto our street. "Yes?" I said.

"Hey, look. Matt's back! That's great."

My heart had jumped at the sight of the Bronco, too. I tried to control it as I said, "Jeremy, you're making me a crazy person. What did you want to tell me?"

We pulled into the garage and Jeremy jumped out of the car. "I'll tell you and Matt together."

I followed him into the house and into the kitchen, where Matt was pouring a cup of coffee. He looked wonderful that morning, a little tired but so much more relaxed. I had to stop myself from going straight into his arms. Not in front of Jeremy, until I was sure.

"You're back," Matt said, his eyes taking me in. "I was worried when I didn't find you here."

"We just went to the bakery," I said, and then caught the tiniest wink from him. When I was sure Jeremy couldn't see, I winked back.

Matt looked down at my empty hands. "No doughnuts?"

"Sorry, it was too crowded."

"Oh."

"But I'm glad you're here," I said. "Jeremy has something he wants to tell both of us. Come on, Jeremy. You've kept me in suspense long enough. Tell me."

While Matt and I watched, Jeremy looked down at his sneakers, then back to us. "Well, see, I don't want either of you to get mad...."

I grabbed his arm. "Tell me now or I'm going to hurt you."

He grinned at me, not even pretending to be worried. "Yeah." Then he looked at Matt. "I saw all that stuff that you guys were working on last night, about the murder, you know. And I kind of got to thinking about it, and so this morning, I read the notebooks. I thought that maybe I could help."

"Absolutely not, Jeremy," Matt said firmly. "We don't want you involved."

Jeremy took a breath. "Well, I kind of already did it."

"Did what?" I demanded.

"Talked to someone." He straightened up. "See, I know all about how the Judge was murdered, and I got to thinking that the Captain lives right across the street from the Judge. I wanted to go to his house this morning, but I didn't get a chance." He shifted his shoulders. "I guess it didn't matter, though, because I saw the Captain anyway."

"He was by the bakery," I said. "And that was why I couldn't find Jeremy. "But, wait a minute. The Captain doesn't talk."

"Sure he does," Jeremy said. "Oh, not a lot, but he comes around the baseball field sometimes. He's really pretty cool."

Matt cleared his throat. "Jeremy, I don't think it was wise."

"It wasn't," I agreed. "But we'll get to that later. What did the Captain say?"

Jeremy looked at us. "He said that nobody went to the Judge's house."

"No one?" I couldn't believe it.

"Is he sure?" Matt asked.

Jeremy nodded. "Yeah, he said he went out on the porch just as Maria was leaving, and that was early. Oh, about four-thirty or five, and he sat outside until almost six-thirty, just watching the sunset. He said no cars stopped at the Judge's house at all."

"Cars," I said, thinking hard. "Maybe someone could have walked up. Or ridden a bicycle."

Jeremy shook his head. "The Captain said no one came to the house. No one."

There was a quick knock at the front door and then it flew open. "It's just me," Diane called as she came in. "I've been saved. I have to cover at the museum this afternoon, so Trey went to get Randy instead. Oh, and have I got a great theory!" She stopped in the kitchen doorway and looked at the three of us. "I'm sorry, did I interrupt something?"

I shook my head. "You're just in time. Tell her, Jeremy."

Jeremy repeated what the Captain had said.

"A locked room mystery?" Diane said in disbelief. Then she rolled her eyes upward. "Why us, Lord?"

TWENTY-SEVEN

"WAIT A MINUTE," Matt said. "What is a locked-room mystery? What does that mean?"

"It's a classic," Diane said, pulling out a chair and sitting down. "The murder is committed in a locked room, or someplace where no one could get to the victim."

"I don't get it," Jeremy said, opening the refrigerator. "If the room is locked, then how can someone be murdered?" He took out the orange juice, and Matt handed him a glass.

"It's actually pretty simple," I said, taking a seat at the table. "Diane, do you want something to drink?"

"Oh, no thanks."

Matt sat beside me. "So, explain how a murder is committed in a locked room."

"There are a number of ways, actually," Diane said. "There was one case where the murderer locked the dead bolt with a string that he pulled after he closed the door. Then he slid the string out under the door behind him, so there weren't any clues."

"Ellery Queen wrote it," I said. "But usually, the person who supposedly finds the body actually does the killing. They make up a story about the victim being dead and the doors locked, but in truth, the victim was still alive when they got there."

"Hey, cool," Jeremy said. "So who found the Judge dead?"

"What?" I'd been too busy puzzling over it even to hear his question.

"I asked, who found the Judge? You know, Mom, who was the first person there?"

"Andy!"

Diane mirrored my surprise. "There goes my theory!"

"Andy? Wait a minute," I said, getting serious about the idea. "It could have been Andy. Rhonda said the Judge was sick, he needed transportation to the hospital. Okay, but maybe he was just sick, not dying like everyone thinks. Maybe having a heart attack, or just gas, who knows, I mean, he was old. And when Andy gets there, he finds the perfect opportunity to stick the Judge with his poison-tipped pin."

"Maybe we're making too much of this. There are other ways into the Judge's house." Diane closed her eyes to think. "We're missing something." She looked up at me. "The perfume. Remember, there was perfume on the pin?"

"So what?" I said. "Andy could have picked up a sample of the perfume at some department store in Houston. Maybe an old girlfriend left it at his house. He could have gotten it somehow."

"Motive," Matt said. "Andy had no motive for killing the Judge."

"Remember the disagreement they had?" I asked. "Well, what if that kind of thing went on all the time? What if Andy really was incompetent and the Judge knew it? Diane, when you talked to your cousin did he say that Andy had a clean record or that he was a good cop?"

"A clean record! There's a big difference, isn't there?"

"Exactly," I said. "Matt, you were going to talk to Andy this morning. Did you?"

"I did." He didn't sound happy about it.

"It's bad news, isn't it?"

"Depends on how you look at it."

"Matt," Diane said, firmly, "what did the man say?"

"He said that he's getting nowhere with the investigation. He knows exactly how it was done, thanks to Jolie, but he can't seem to find anyone who was there. No fingerprints, no telltale hairs, nothing. Dead end."

"Oh, hell," I mumbled.

"It's not so bad, Jolie," Matt said, patting my hand to comfort me. "At least he's not convinced you did it anymore."

"So what? Half the town will always believe I killed the Judge."

Jeremy had remained quietly in the background, but now he put his hand on mine beside Matt's. "Don't worry, Mom. Somehow we'll figure out who did it."

I tried to sound tough, but I was too discouraged to put much effort into it. "You can't get involved, Jeremy."

"But maybe I can help. Let me at least listen, okay?"

I looked at Matt and made my decision. "Okay, Jeremy, you can stay, but you can't talk to anyone about it. If I hadn't talked to the wrong people I never would have been attacked."

Jeremy slid into a chair quickly. "I promise I won't mention this to anyone."

Diane was drumming her hands on the table. "Jolie, whatever happens, we don't have a choice now. We've got to get this thing figured out and settled."

I was ready to swear an oath with my boiling blood. "You're right, we can and we will." I sat up, determined. "So, Diane. Do you think it was Andy or someone else?"

"I think it was Rhonda."

"Why?" Matt asked.

Her answer was quick. "Because of Buddy Wayne. The way I'd worked it out, somehow the Judge found out about Rhonda and, uh . . ." she paused with a look at Jeremy.

Jeremy finished the sentence for her. "Morris. I read it in Mom's notes."

Diane shook her head and went on. "Right. Anyway, so the Judge was threatening to tell Buddy Wayne. To save her marriage, or her neck, Rhonda killed the Judge."

Rhonda the robot. The coolness of the murder method fit Rhonda's personality. Then I remembered that Rhonda also had a passionate side, at least when Morris Pratt was around.

"It makes sense, and it doesn't," I said, putting my hands flat on the table. Something about Rhonda as a murderer didn't seem right, but I couldn't say exactly what.

"What about June?" Matt asked. "She's a good candidate."

Diane demanded to know why, and Matt explained about the land Theodore Ingram had sold to the Judge. "Since only part of the Ingram land was flooded, the rest became shorefront property. Over the years the Judge has made probably close to a million dollars on that land. Some of it he sold at the time, the rest he hung on to. The pier is just leased to the operators. I did some checking at the courthouse this morning, and even last year he was still selling lots. Now they're going for forty-eight thousand apiece. And there are several lots in an acre.''

"How did you get into the courthouse this morning?" I demanded.

Matt almost smiled. "I asked the right people to let me in." More Wyatt clout.

"But June doesn't care about money; she doesn't need it," I said.

"Maybe not," Matt said. "Does she make a lot off her writing?"

I looked at Diane and she shrugged. "No idea," she said. "She should be making anywhere from twenty thousand a year to a hundred."

"But June doesn't care about money," I said again.

Matt disagreed. "Maybe not for herself, but it takes a lot to keep up a ranch like hers. She's not running cattle, and she can't be making much off her horses recently."

"You're right! And that does change things," Diane said.

"Well, I think Maria did it," Jeremy said. If she was the last person to be at the Judge's house, she could have killed him."

We all thought about it for a moment.

"Too much time passed after she left, and before the Judge got sick," I said.

"And there's motive, again," Diane added. "She didn't have any motive that we can find. Oh, wait, Jolie, your notes said that Maria was furious with the Judge the night he died. But that was about housecleaning. Who would kill someone over a dirty house?"

I had my mouth open, all ready to pour out the story IdaMae had told me, but I caught myself in time. I'd promised not to say anything unless it was necessary, and this didn't seem necessary enough. I closed my mouth and sat back.

"You know," Matt said, "the Judge was actually very kind to the Chavez family." He got up and began to move around the room. "Since the Chavez land eventually ended up being underwater, Julio Chavez was one of the few people in town who got the better of the Judge.''

Diane shook her head. ''Then why did Julio Chavez commit suicide just two weeks later? That doesn't make any sense at all.''

''Maybe his death didn't have anything to do with the land,'' Matt said. ''Or maybe Julio felt remorse over the deal.''

''Then why didn't he just give some of the money back?'' Diane stood up, too, and began to pace behind her chair.

I watched them passing each other as they walked.

''We've got too many suspects and too many motives,'' Diane said. ''Like Liz. We haven't really pursued that angle.'' Diane finally stopped moving. ''I feel like we've got all the pieces except the crucial one. I keep wracking my brain, but I can't figure it out.''

Even knowing what I did, I had to agree with her. ''Maybe if we quit trying so hard to figure it out, something will come to us.''

''No, I've got to think it through,'' Diane said, grabbing up her purse. ''If I don't my brain's going to explode. I'm going home to spend some time on it.''

''I don't think any of us should be alone right now,'' Matt said. ''It's just too dangerous.''

''I won't be there very long. I have to cover at the museum from one until four.'' She glanced at her Rolex. ''It's quarter of twelve now.''

''I could go with you,'' I volunteered.

Diane shook her head. ''I appreciate it, Jolie, but we'd end up talking and I need to think. I've got to be alone to really concentrate.'' She began digging through her purse for her keys.

''I'm at least going to follow you home,'' Matt said. ''I'd hate for you to get there and find our murderer waiting for you.''

''And I'll stay with Mom,'' Jeremy volunteered.

He made it sound like the Old West was rising again, with the big tough men protecting the weak little women.

After Matt left, Jeremy braced a chair under the front door knob. I hated to shatter his illusions of heroism by pointing out that any murderer with half a brain would come in through the jalousie windows in the sunroom, but I did anyway. The macho stuff didn't become him.

Jeremy thought about it. "You're right," he agreed, stationing himself on the couch in the sunroom.

I started printing out a final editing draft of my book. While the printer clacked away, I wandered the room, trying to make sense of everything we knew. It just wouldn't fall into place. I couldn't even figure out exactly how it had been done; then I had an idea.

I picked up the phone and dialed the police station, asking for Andy.

When he came on the line his voice was crisp and professional. "Detective Sawyer."

"Andy, hi, it's me, Jolie," I said quickly. "I have a quick question for you."

"I'll answer it if I can."

"Two questions, actually." I don't know why, but the hardest one slipped out first. "I heard a rumor that the Judge was uh, well, unkind toward you about some burglary case. I wanted to find out if it was true."

"What the hell! What kind of a question is that?"

"A fair one," I said, hoping I sounded firm and rational. I believed that just because Andy was a police officer he wasn't above the law. Or above investigation. "You've been investigating me because I had a disagreement with the Judge, and because I knew all about using Pest Out for murder. I found out that those two things are true of you, too."

"Jesus! Is that why half your writers' group has been poking around asking me questions?" He sounded stunned and angry.

"What do you mean 'half my writers' group'? Who? Who else has been asking questions?"

A sharp intake of air. "Damn it, Jolie, I'm not bound legally or morally to answer any of your questions, and if you'll remember, this is the second time you've made this kind of accusation. I resent the hell out of it."

My anger flared. "Then you know exactly how I've been feeling! It seems to me, Andy, if you don't have anything to hide there's no reason not to tell me what I want to know."

His voice turned stony, each word separate and distinct. "I had no reason to kill the Judge. I did a damn good job of investigating that burglary case; it's not my fault if some fancy-ass lawyer from Dallas made a fool of the DA! Everyone in the department knew that the Judge's accusations were off base."

"I didn't mean to offend you. I just needed to know some things and you're the only one who could tell me." I let out a long breath. "Why don't we just level with each other?"

He took so long I thought he'd hung up, but eventually he spoke. "Look, Jolie, this is a police investigation and I'm legally bound to keep information confidential." Then he said firmly, "But you do need to know one thing. I didn't kill Judge Osler. I uphold the laws; I don't break them."

The hell of it was that I believed him; so why didn't he believe me?

I rubbed my forehead. "I'm just so sick of this whole thing," I said.

He must have heard the distress in my voice, because he seemed to soften. "I know, and I'm really sorry this has been so tough on you. I've heard how people are treating you and Jeremy and it's a damn shame."

"Thanks, Andy."

"Look," he went on, "maybe I could answer a question or two if it isn't crucial to the investigation. What did you want to know?"

"Nothing major, but does everyone in my writers' group have an alibi?"

"Yeah, they all do. Some better than others, but the Judge had to have gotten the poison between five-thirty and six-thirty to die at five 'til seven, and they're all accounted for."

"Did you find any of the poison on the Judge's shirt or coat? And where was the pin when you found it?"

He hesitated, but he answered. "Dr. Baxter noticed the pin on the floor at the hospital after they undressed the Judge, so I don't know for sure where it had been. As for the poison, yeah, there was some on the back of his shirt collar." He stopped. "I think I see what you're getting at."

"Good. Maybe it will get me off the hook." I said, "Oh, and Andy, one more thing. Who in my writers' group has been asking you questions?"

"All of them. Or damn near. Rhonda, of course, but she's always nosing around. Maria has been here, too. Seems she's using this investigation as research for her next book; she says it's going to be a mystery. Even June Ingram stopped by the other day to have a 'little chat.' Oh, and your ex-husband."

I felt as if I were getting close. At least now I knew how the murderer had done it, and still had an alibi. "Thanks, Andy," I said.

"Yeah, you're welcome."

We said our good-byes and hung up.

I heard the front door knob rattle.

I ran for it, and got there the same time as Jeremy.

"Who's there?" Jeremy demanded in a gruff voice.

I looked out the window. "It's Matt," I said. "Just a minute, Matt," I called. "Jeremy, move the chair."

Between the two of us we finally got it out of the way so Matt could get in. By that time the phone was ringing, and Jeremy leaped for it.

"Matt, it's Bart. He sounds upset."

"Oh, hell." Matt went to the phone and I followed him into the kitchen.

"Bart," he said into the mouthpiece, "are you all right?" He listened, nodding. "It's no problem. No, I'm on my way. You go back to bed and don't worry about it. I'll keep trying to get him on the car phone. Okay. I'll be there in a few minutes." Matt hung up and turned to me. "One of the cows is calving and she's having some trouble. Bart says it's breech, so we'll have to turn the calf."

"He can't get the vet?"

"No, and Bart's too sick to be out there. I'll have to go. I'll need some help." He called out, "Jeremy?"

Jeremy responded with a "Just a minute," but he didn't appear.

"You can come, too," Matt said.

I shook my head. I still wasn't ready to face the ranch; it was like some visible proof of my past failure. Just the thought of it made my stomach begin to roil. "Matt, I can't go. The printer is running and you don't have time to wait. I'll go over to Diane's."

Matt was already digging in his pocket for his keys. "She's leaving for the museum in a few minutes."

"Then I'll go there. Don't worry about me. I'll be very careful, I promise."

He slid his arms around me. "I don't like this."

"It's broad daylight and I won't be here alone for more than two minutes."

Jeremy came in then, and he must have been surprised to see Matt and me wrapped up in each other's arms. "What's going on?" he asked.

"Nothing," I said, breaking away from Matt. "You've got to go out to the ranch with Matt."

"How come?"

Matt was already moving toward the door. "I'll explain on the way."

I waved good-bye and Matt turned back to say quickly, "Jolie, call me on the car phone as soon as you get to the museum, okay?"

"Promise."

Then they jumped into the Bronco and left. I locked the door carefully and went to check the printer.

TWENTY-EIGHT

AS SOON AS the printer was done, I turned it and the computer off, then grabbed up my notes on the Judge's murder and put them with my purse. Diane and I could go over them again at the museum. Then I hurried into the kitchen, where I threw a sandwich together. I wrapped it in a paper towel and shoved it in my purse. I was moving at top speed, not out of any fear, but because I'd promised Matt. I had a lot to live for and I wasn't taking any chances.

The last thing I did before I locked all the doors was change the message on the answering machine to say that I could be reached at the museum. That was in case Diane called looking for me before she left.

It had turned muggy outside, the air warm and cloying. I went to the garage, and as soon as I opened the door I could see that there were no shadowy figures lurking near my car. Still, I got in quickly, locking all the doors before I drove off toward the museum. By that time it was twelve-thirty, and I was torn between feeling silly for all the precautions and being nervous because I was alone. There had been no threat to me recently; I was beginning to believe that the attack had been some sort of mistake. Or maybe just a random mugger. It simply didn't seem real.

I cruised down Main, hurrying for no good reason on the nearly empty street. By Saturday afternoon most of the stores in Purple Sage were closing, so things were quiet. The courthouse square seemed deserted and the old red-brick jail with its tower looked faded in the bright sunlight as I pulled into the lot. Diane's car wasn't there yet, but I knew the place wouldn't be empty; some faithful volunteer would be on duty to help the tourists.

The door creaked as I pushed it open. It was hot and dim inside, and it took a moment for my eyes to get adjusted. When they did, I saw June Ingram staring at me from her seat at the oak table. She was wearing a calico dress and bonnet, standard uniform when you're manning the museum, but I'd never seen June in hers before. Even with her close-cropped gray hair hidden by the bonnet she was out of sync with the costume; she looked too tough.

"Jolie?"

"Hi," I said, suddenly nervous. "I was looking for Diane. Isn't she here yet?"

June shook her head, then glanced at the clock. "She should show up soon to relieve me."

"It's hot in here."

"The air conditioner is on the blink again. Shut the door, you're letting the last of the cool air out."

It seemed cooler outside, but I didn't argue. I stepped inside and closed the door behind me. "So, how's it going?" I asked, moving slowly across the wood floor.

"Fine, I guess."

June watched me as I hung back. I straightened up. "How's your writing?"

"Just fine. Jolie, what's wrong with you?"

"Nothing." I pulled out a chair and sat down, trying to behave casually.

She pinned me with a stare. "Well, you're damn sure up to something."

"Me? No, of course not," I said. "Well, I am a little nervous. Matt and Jeremy are delivering a breech calf." I heaved a big breath like I was beginning to relax. "I guess watching them race out of the house, and then worrying, made me more tense than I realized."

Her eyes seemed to narrow. "So you're going to wait for Diane?"

"Well, I'd planned on it, but..."

June jumped up and I flinched.

Then she whipped off her bonnet. "Then you won't mind taking over for a few minutes, will you?" She peeled herself out of her dress, revealing a T-shirt and jeans underneath. "My niece is in town, and if I hurry I can join her for lunch," she said. "Diane shouldn't be more than a few minutes."

June was already wadding her dress into a ball and shoving it into her big bag. "I guess you'd better put on one of these dresses if you're going to be here."

"What?" I looked around. "But I don't—"

"In the back closet in the kitchen. The one next to the broom closet. Betsy Winkler's should fit you. It's the blue dress with a matching bonnet." She picked up her hat and handed it to me. "If you don't mind, you can hang this up while you're in there."

I took it from her. "Sure."

"If any tourists come, just give them a brochure and tell them to look around. Show them upstairs, that's all they really want to see anyway." She got to the door and turned around, her back against it. "Before I leave, I have some unfinished business with you."

There was nothing for me to do but nod dumbly as the sweat collected on my body.

She took one step toward me. "I'm sorry about this, Jolie, but you have to realize some things. If you'd taken my advice and kept your nose out of the police investigation, you never would have been attacked Tuesday night. I know because I asked Andy about it and he agreed with me."

"You're right."

June went on. "Well, I'm glad you agree with me. Now I can save my lecture and go meet my niece." She turned around and opened the door, saying over her shoulder, "See you Tuesday." Then the door closed and she was gone. I sank down into a chair. For just a moment I had thought . . .

With resolve I stood up and started for the kitchen, where the phone was hidden from tourists. I needed to call Matt and let him know that I was safely at the museum. Or maybe more truthfully that I was at the museum.

The phone rang before I was halfway there. Even through the closed door it was piercing. I hurried into the kitchen and picked up the receiver of the yellow wall phone. "Purple Sage Museum."

"Jolie?"

"Diane? Where are you? You're supposed to be here."

"I know," she said, sounding harried. "But my mom called and she's decided that since I didn't go there, she's coming back with Trey so we can visit! Do you believe that? Now, of all times! Anyway, I've been getting the guest room ready, and I totally forgot the time, but I'll be there, honest."

"When?"

"Soon. I have to run to the store and pick up a few things. Can you cover for me?"

I extended the phone cord until I could open the closet door. There was an array of dresses, but only one blue. It was a muted print with tiny flowers and cutesy ruffles at the neck, cuffs, and waist. With much disgust, I pulled it off the hanger. "I'm already covering for June, so I guess it doesn't matter."

"You're an angel, but what are you doing there?"

I closed the kitchen door and began unbuttoning my shirt. "I was waiting for you," I said as I pulled off my shirt, the air feeling cool on my sticky body. I wedged the phone between my shoulder and my ear. With great care I stepped into the dress. "Just don't take too long, okay?"

"I won't. Not more than half an hour. Matt's there with you, isn't he?"

"No," I said, wrestling with the dress.

I stopped at some muted noise in the next room. "Wait just a second." I put down the phone and got my arms into the sleeves, pulling and tugging to get myself covered. Then I peeked out of the kitchen door. The room was empty, but the old wall air conditioner was making a clicking noise in a valiant effort to turn on.

I let out a sigh of relief and picked up the receiver. "I'm back."

"What's going on?"

"Nothing. The air conditioner is making odd sounds and I can't get Betsy's dress on. She must be anorexic!" The starched lace ruffles on the cuffs were scratching my wrists and I was already feeling hampered by the tightness.

"So where's Matt?"

"Delivering a calf; he and Jeremy went out to the ranch."

"Oh, hell. I'll go even faster. Don't worry, some tourists are bound to show up, so just keep them around for protection."

"Right," I said. "Just hurry."

"I will. 'Bye."

After I finally got the zipper up, I got out the blue bonnet and tied it on; it was the final insult. Just one more thing to blame on the Judge, since he was the one who'd insisted that the volunteers wear period costume. Everything seemed to be his fault. The Patron Saint of Purple Sage, my ass. He had created more problems in my life after his death than he had when he'd walked the streets.

The Judge and his life. The Judge and his death. Things started to come back to me. Little things people had said about the Judge. About his murder.

The reception room was hot and quiet as I went to the oak table and opened my notebook. I read through each page slowly, letting the information filter into my mind. I began making some additional notes. I closed my eyes and thought back over things that people had said. Things they had left unsaid. Their reactions.

Then I remembered a direct quote and it negated all my other facts. I concentrated hard on that statement. The more I thought about it the more puzzled I became.

And then I realized that it was a lie! Murderers do lie.

When I opened my eyes, I knew who'd killed the Judge.

TWENTY-NINE

I JUMPED UP and called the police station. My voice sounded high-pitched as I asked for Andy.

"I'm sorry, ma'am, Detective Sawyer is out. Can I take a message?"

Oh, God. "When will he be back?"

"He's off the rest of the afternoon," came the bored response.

I gulped back an expletive. "Look, it's crucial that I talk with him right away," I said. "Is he in a patrol car? Could you reach him on the radio? Could I call him at his house?"

"I don't know where he is, but he doesn't have one of the cars. If it's that important, I could send a patrolman."

A patrolman. It would take too long to explain. "No, but please, try to contact Andy. This is Jolie Wyatt and I'm at the museum. Tell him I need to talk to him immediately."

"Immediately?" He sounded suspicious.

"I know who killed the Judge."

He became a little more interested but not much. Apparently the dispatcher had already decided who'd killed the Judge, and he was talking to her. "Sure. I'll do what I can."

"It's urgent," I reiterated.

"Yes, ma'am, I'll do my best."

I hung up the phone and went into the reception area to pace. If anything I felt even more vulnerable with my newfound knowledge. I picked up my notebook and looked over the pertinent entries. I had to be clear and concise when I talked to Andy, so I dug a hot pink highlighting pen from my purse and began to mark all the important clues. While I was doing that, I watched the clock, willing Andy to hurry. Or Diane. Someone!

When the door opened, I jumped up, half in hope, half in fear. It was a road-weary family of four, and in my relief, I pushed aside the notebook and greeted them profusely.

"Hello, there! Welcome to the Purple Sage Museum."

A boy of about seven, hyper and obviously tired of being cooped up in a car, began to move around the room, fingering everything he could reach. "Was this a real jail? It doesn't look like a jail."

His mother frowned as he jumped up to touch a glass case containing examples of old barbed wire.

"Billy, calm down," the woman said.

I picked up a brochure and handed it to her as I addressed the little boy. "It was a jail. It was used for a long time to hold prisoners in Purple Sage. The cells are on the second floor, and there's even a gallows up on the third floor."

"A real gallows?" he asked with suspicion.

"A real one," I said.

The father, carrying a little girl of about five, started forward. "Why don't we look at them, Billy?"

But Billy had discovered the rolltop desk and was pushing and pulling on the slats that formed the rolling cover.

"I'm hungry," the little girl whined.

"Don't be a baby," the boy said. He tugged at the top again, and I reached over and took his arm.

"Come with me," I said. Regardless of how active Billy might be, I was thankful for their presence. "I'll show you upstairs."

The mother shot me a grateful glance as I led them all to the stairs.

"You'll like this part," I said, hiking up my skirt so I wouldn't trip. We reached the top, and there was a landing with a heavy double-thick metal door with a barred window. I pushed it open, understanding now why the museum committee had removed all its locks. Obviously so kids like Billy couldn't accidentally get locked in, although . . .

I kept my hand on him as we went inside the room. "Billy, help me hold the door for your family."

He squirmed but reluctantly agreed. "Okay."

Once they'd trooped past us I let the heavy metal door clang shut. In front of us were eight cells in two rows of four with a brick wall running down the center for separation. A walkway went around both sides, giving the jailers access to the barred metal enclosures. On the walls were wanted posters, mounted and framed for protection against people like Billy.

"Was he in here?" Billy asked, pointing with his free arm at a poster for Billy the Kid.

Probably a cousin, I thought. "No, he wasn't."

"So, who was?" he asked, squirming to get free of me.

I smiled, ignoring his movements. "Nobody famous. Just criminals."

"Murderers?"

Even seven-year-olds seemed to know about murderers.

"Yes," I said, "at least one that I know of."

Billy twisted again and broke free, making a dash for the inside of the last cell. He bounced on the metal cot, then turned on the water in the pitted freestanding sink.

"Is this all they got?" he asked.

"That's all," I said.

"Let's go look at the gallows," his father suggested.

"It's over here." I lifted my skirt and led them to another door and opened it wide.

Billy shot past his dad then stopped at a half-size door imbedded in the wall. "Hey, it's just my size. What is it?"

"It leads to the area below the gallows," I said.

"Wow!" Finally he was impressed, although it didn't last long. He examined the door carefully, then dismissed it to race up the stairs. His mother gave a tired shrug and followed him. I went up behind her.

The small square room that held the gallows was almost like a tiny theater, with a row of wooden chairs on the far side. I took my place near the door to explain, while surreptitiously running a finger under the scratchy ruffle at my neck. "The chairs were for officials who were here to witness or preside over the hanging. The executioner stood here, where I am, in this enclosed area. This metal lever controls the mechanism that releases the trap beneath the gallows themselves."

A rope, complete with hangman's knot, hung over an open area in the center of the room. New railings secured the area to protect visitors from an accidental fall.

Billy climbed the rail and ran directly under the rope, staring up at it. "So, who'd they hang?" he asked.

"A man who killed a rancher," I said. I glanced at the heavy lever and checked to see that it was in the locked position.

"Well that stinks! All murderers should hang."

All murderers should hang. I shivered.

"Let the lady finish the tour," Billy's mother said.

I knew the rest of the spiel; I'd heard Diane give it once and she was magnificent. I didn't try anything so dramatic, but I did attempt to give them the whole show.

"If you'll all take seats, I'll give you a demonstration."

"Let's put a dummy in the rope," Billy suggested.

"No, let's not," his father said firmly. With his free hand he took a hold of the boy and pulled him over to one of the chairs. "Sit down and watch."

I took a firm grip on the lever. "The prisoner was brought up here in the custody of the sheriff. He'd already eaten a last meal, and was given a few minutes with the minister of the First Church of Jesus Christ. Then, with his hands tied, the officials placed him on the center of the trapdoor. The noose was fastened securely around his neck, and the spectators took their seats." I paused for dramatic effect. "That's when the lever was pulled." I did so, and the flooring under the noose fell away with a loud whooshing noise.

Billy jumped off his chair to peer down.

"Get back here!" his father snapped. Then he too looked down and realized that someone with great foresight had placed two mattresses below the door just in case someone did fall.

"Can I jump?" Billy asked.

"No," his mother said, grabbing him by the shoulders and pulling him up. "We're going to eat now."

I raised and secured the trapdoor, putting the lever back into its locked position. By the time I was done, Billy had already raced past me and headed out.

When we got to the reception area, his father thanked me for my time. "We really appreciate your patience," he said.

"I enjoyed it," I said, realizing that when they left, I would be alone. "Would you like to look around here? This desk is a superb example of an antique rolltop."

"I can see that," the father said, taking Billy's hand and leading him to the outside door.

"And the barbed-wire collection is one of the finest in the state," I went on, trying to hold them a little longer. "We have samples that go back to the eighteen-hundreds."

The mother glanced at the glass cases and shrugged. "We'd really better get some food for the kids."

"But you haven't signed our guest book!" I said, jumping to get it from the top of the desk. "It won't take but a second," I urged.

"I'm hungry," Billy said plaintively. "Can't we go?"

The father opened the door and Billy dashed outside. The father shrugged at me and followed his son. A muggy heat seemed to seep into the room.

"Another time," the mother said. She started out, too, turning back only to say, "Thank you for the tour."

I trailed after her. "Oh, you're welcome. Come back anytime." Then I waited at the door while they piled back into their dusty car.

"Thanks," the father called.

I waved until they were gone, just like we were old friends, and then I turned back inside with a feeling of dread. Slowly I made my way back to the table and looked around for my notebook. I would use the time before Diane got there to finish highlighting my notes.

The notebook wasn't where I'd left it, so I looked underneath the table. Nothing there, not even dust.

I was sure I'd been writing in it when Billy and his family had arrived. I'd been compiling my information so that when I talked to Andy my arguments would be clear.

Had I dropped it in the desk when Billy was playing with the top? I went over and rolled up the cover, making a loud clattering noise. Inside were some brochures, a couple of pens, and a writing tablet. Not my notebook.

"Looking for this?"

I turned around and found Maria standing between me and the doorway with my notebook in her hand. The bright pink stripes of highlighting seemed to scream at me from across the room.

"Maria," I said stupidly.

"Pretty careless of you to leave this lying around. Anyone could have come along and read it. Even the murderer."

I tried to smile. "It's just conjecture, no firm conclusions, yet. What are you doing here?"

"I called your house and found out that you were here. I was going to ask you to come with me to Fredericksburg. I thought you'd like to get away for a while."

My hand clutching the edge of the table felt cold and numb, like the rest of my body. "I can't leave. I'm only waiting for Diane. She should be here any minute. Then Matt's expecting me at the ranch."

"Busy day," Maria said, flipping through the notebook in her hand. "But I wouldn't hold my breath waiting for Diane. I just saw her going into the grocery store and it's packed. Should take her an hour at least to get out of there."

"Oh."

I waited, hoping she'd hand me the notebook and leave. She stayed planted firmly between me and the door.

The ticking of the clock seemed to grow louder. I willed myself not to look at it as Maria and I faced off across the room like two gunfighters. Maybe Matt would show up. Or Andy.

The silence stretched and grew as my muscles became taut with the waiting. Maria just watched me, her face impassive.

When I couldn't take the stillness or the waiting any longer, I said, "Can I have my notebook back?"

Maria smiled then, almost angelically. "I don't think so, Jolie. I'm afraid I'm going to have to burn this." She reached behind her, and without looking, clicked the lock on the front door. "It's your own fault, though. You ruined your own perfect murder."

Even as I tensed for the fight, some part of me felt relief. There would be no more games.

"No, you ruined the perfect murder," I said. "You carried it out."

"But no one can prove it. No one knows all the things you found out." She looked at me curiously. "How did you find out everything? My mother didn't tell you, did she?"

"You gave yourself away," I said, wondering if I could overpower her, and at the same time knowing I was constricted by the dress. "Your need for money. Remember on the way to Brownwood I asked if you'd gone to anyone else for help? You looked angry for just a moment. I think I knew something then, but it didn't really register. Then when I found the connection between your family and the Judge, I figured out you'd asked him."

"So what if I did?"

"And he turned you down?"

"The asshole! He owed us! But would he help? Hell, no!" she said, her old fire showing through. "He said he'd already bailed my family out once. That was bullshit! He's the reason my father committed suicide. If my father were alive, I wouldn't have to support my mother. The Judge owed all of us."

"And you couldn't just let it go," I said softly, very aware of the ticking of the clock.

"Why should I? My mother told me all about how that bastard seduced her! She kept calling me Honoria, and crying about my dad." Maria swallowed the emotion and her face turned icy. "The Judge deserved to die. He was a murderer." She watched me for a while, neither of us speaking, then she said, "So, what else did you figure out?"

I shrugged, trying to seem casual. "You lied. You said that a writer was coming to visit the Judge. That wasn't true."

"I lied? Well, fuck me!" Sarcasm bit through every word. "What a terrible thing. I lied. And that's how you figured it out?"

"Partly. It had to be someone who knew me, because of the murder method. And the rumors." I added, "That hurt, Maria."

She threw back her head and snarled, "So what? Somebody put down Miss Rich Bitch, high-and-mighty Jolie Wyatt! Big fucking deal! Grow up, Jolie! You've had everything handed to you all your life: a nice family, a rich husband, and plenty of money. So just once you had to face a little unpleasantness. If you think I feel sorry for you, you're full of shit," she spat. "All my life I've had to struggle. How do you think I felt when everyone in our group bragged about how productive you were? How much writing you did? Of course, because you had time to write! You didn't have to work like I did. You didn't have to take care of a mother who's half crazy!"

I wanted to defend myself, but I had no words. "I'm sorry."

"Yeah, you and everybody else in this town. What do you think it was like, being Hispanic and growing up in Purple Sage? Never quite as good as everybody else? Never having the right clothes, or a nice home? I had to work hard for everything I had, taking care of my brothers and my mother. I worked all through high school to support my mom, and I still graduated third in my class, but do you think anybody noticed or gave a shit? Hell no! And then a couple of weeks ago I found out about the Judge; I just wanted a little of what was due me."

I took a step backward, as if moving away physically would set me free of her stream of venom.

"It wasn't the Judge's fault," I said.

"He was a bigot! If we'd been Anglo he'd have married my mother."

"Maybe she wouldn't marry him," I suggested.

"That's bullshit! She loved him, and he used her. Used his power and his position to take advantage of her and then when my father found out and killed himself, the Judge walked away."

"You can't know that for sure."

"Oh, but I do! My mother's living those days again, telling me everything. Talking to me as if I were her friend Honoria."

I took a step toward her, speaking gently, "Maria . . ."

Maria smiled again, coldly and cruelly. "Save your pity. It's too late."

I shifted position. "Maria, I don't know what you think you're going to accomplish. If I figured it out, Andy will, too."

"Not likely," she laughed sarcastically. "The police investigation is all but closed."

I shook my head slowly, while I looked around the room for some way to escape. There was none.

"Then why did you attack me?" I asked, stalling for time.

"Because I knew you and your methodical ways; you wouldn't give up until you found out the truth. I was going to kill you then, but Jeremy came out."

"And you took some of my Pest Out."

"Jesus! Now I'm a thief, too!" she said. "Too damn bad, Jolie, because you're not going to tell anyone about it. I'm going to kill you." She sounded pleased.

My head snapped back to attention. "Then they'll convict you of my murder," I said.

"No, I don't think so, and believe me, I've thought about this a lot. Everyone knows how the town has turned against you. You don't have a job, your marriage is over; you don't have a reason to live anymore. No one's going to be surprised when you kill yourself the same way you murdered the Judge."

She dropped the notebook on the floor and I saw that in her hand was a pin. A long, thin, old-fashioned hat pin, the tip glinting in the dim light. No doubt it was covered with nicotine. If it pierced my skin I would die.

"Sorry about this, Jolie, but you brought it on yourself."

I glanced at the door and then back to Maria. She took advantage of the moment to lunge at me. I didn't stop to think; I ran.

The only way out was up. I took the stairs two at a time, clutching the long skirt to keep it out of my way. At the top of the stairs I flung open the door, raced inside, and slammed it shut. I tried to hold it closed against her, but my tennis shoes kept slipping on the slick floor and Maria was throwing her entire weight into her efforts. The door was opening more each time she did it.

The cells were useless. There was no way I could get her in one, and there would be no safety for me. The keys hung on a peg downstairs.

"Give it up, Jolie," Maria shouted, flinging the door open even farther. "It's too late. You lost."

Locks, there had to be someplace that locked. Or another way out. And suddenly I knew.

I waited until she shoved one more time, and as soon as the door closed, I ran up the stairs that led to the gallows. I didn' stop to think; I raced inside and grasped the lever, pulling it hard. The trapdoor fell away and I started over the railing.

Maria was close. She grabbed at my dress and I twisted quickly.

The pin! Where was that damn pin?

I heard the waist of the dress give as I wrenched myself out of her grip. We both went down on the wooden floor just a few feet from the trapdoor.

"Dammit!" Maria swore.

I slithered across the floor until my legs were dangling through the opening, then I let go. I tried to relax as I hit the mattresses, but the jolt caused an instant flash of pain through my neck. I didn't have time to cry out. I was up in a second, ripping over the skirt as I fell off the mattresses.

Maria came crashing down just moments behind me.

I was already fumbling at the small door that lead to the cell area. It was jammed, and I heard myself swearing. "Open, damn it!"

The door gave way and I skidded out onto the floor, racing for freedom. I got to the metal door and pulled it open, but Maria was right behind me. She grabbed my skirt and wrenched me back. Without thinking I swung at her and caught her in the chin. She fell back without ever loosening her grip on my dress.

I clutched at the doorframe, literally pulling myself through it. Then, with a terrific lunge I started down the stairs. There was a crash behind me, and Maria gave a little cry that seemed to break off in the middle. By the time I reached the bottom I realized she was no longer hanging on to me.

I glanced around; Maria lay on the landing but she was already fighting her way to her feet.

I gathered up the skirt and flew to the front door. It opened as I reached it and there stood Andy. He looked at me, and then followed my glance. Maria had risen to her feet and was watching us from the top of the stairs.

"It's her," I said as I gasped for much-needed air. "Maria killed the Judge."

Andy started forward but Maria stopped him by holding out the pin. "Don't move!"

His hand lingered over his holster. "Just be calm, Maria."

She looked from Andy to me, then back to Andy. "You be calm." She raised the pin; the light caught its sharp point. It was so small, and yet so lethal. "I'm not going to prison."

Then she brought the pin down, gently sliding it under the golden skin on her bare forearm.

THIRTY

MATT KEPT REACHING over to touch me as the Bronco bounced along the ruts of the caliche road. Maybe he was afraid I'd change my mind about moving back with him, although there was no chance of that.

Or perhaps he was just glad that I was still alive. I was certainly glad that I was still alive. Maria had done her best to kill me, but her best hadn't been enough. Her futile attempts at the museum had been spur-of-the-moment after she'd come in, noticed my notebook, and read over my conclusions. Her effort lacked her usual careful planning and attention to detail.

I was still amazed that she had carried another lethal pin in her purse, tucked away in a perfume vial just like I'd thought. If anyone had checked her purse she would have been caught. But Maria, smug after her first success, had figured no one would. She'd been right, at least about that.

"What are you thinking?" Matt asked, looking over at me.

I shrugged. "Nothing."

He touched my leg and said with a little smile, "Now that's not very communicative."

I tried to smile back, but I couldn't. "I was thinking about Maria."

He increased the pressure on my leg, just enough to let me know that he understood. "It's over, Jolie. Thank God, it's over."

"Oh, I know. But she's dead." I shook my head sadly. "I know it sounds crazy, but I'll miss her. I feel so sad, and . . ."

"And, what?"

There was more, but it hurt to say it out loud. "I guess it's hard to accept that she hated me so much. Hated me enough to try to blame the Judge's murder on me."

"She also tried to kill you."

"I don't know why, but that isn't as bad as what she said about me."

"It wasn't really you," Matt said gently. "It was what you represented. You were a more productive writer. She resented your time and dedication."

"No, she was just as dedicated, Matt. It's just that she was under a terrible burden with her mother being sick. She's actually got a book out with an editor. Wouldn't it be ironic if they decided to publish it? I hope they do. Maybe June can write the editor or something. Do something that Maria couldn't." I shook my head, wishing I could understand why life had dealt Maria such a rotten hand. "It seems so unfair. Life isn't fair sometimes."

"But she had choices."

I nodded, remembering the way she'd looked when they'd loaded her into the ambulance. Fiery, angry, bitter. She was too young to be that way. And it was all because she refused to let go of her old resentments, or maybe they wouldn't let go of her. I only knew that they had ruined her life, and nothing seemed worth that.

I reached down and touched Matt's hand. "I'd feel even sorrier for her if she hadn't hurt Jeremy and my friends."

"But she did," he said. "Maybe that was unintentional."

"I'd like to think so. It would be easier to take if the rumors were just caused by the slip of a tongue, although Maria didn't have many of those." It seemed so strange to be talking about her in the past tense.

"Did she tell Andy the whole story?"

I nodded. "A deathbed confession, Andy called it." And while that had been happening at the hospital, I had waited at the police station, knowing that she was dying, unable to cry, or feel anything but a terrible numbness.

I'd called the ranch but Matt was busy with the cow who was calving. By the time Matt had arrived at the police station, Andy had been back for almost an hour, and we'd finished all the formalities. He'd also told me that, at the last minute, just before she died, Maria had asked him to apologize to me. I could only shake my head when I thought about it.

It had been a long afternoon, and now the sun was low in the sky, promising us a spectacular sunset.

Matt touched my hand. "Would you mind telling me the rest of the story? If it's not too painful..."

"I don't mind," I said. Maybe talking about it would be a catharsis. I'd already told him about the events at the museum. "It all started when Maria's mom got so sick and started living in the past. Mrs. Chavez thought Maria was her old friend, Honoria, and she kept asking her why the Judge hadn't come calling lately. Maria told Andy that when she'd finally pieced together the whole story she was angry, and that's when she asked the Judge for money." I sighed. Her behavior had been so foolish, and so typical of Maria. "When the Judge said no, she was furious. Knowing Maria's temper, there was probably a real battle, but maybe not. Maybe she didn't say anything, just went home and planned the whole thing. Planned it very carefully."

The two sides of Maria. Fire and ice.

"It doesn't seem to me that much planning was needed," Matt said. "She just borrowed your murder."

"And some of my Pest Out." It was one of the things that still galled me. "I'll bet she got everything ready in advance. Andy told me this morning that Maria asked her mother's sitter to stay for dinner that Tuesday night, the night of the murder, and that was unusual. The nurse was Maria's alibi. And Maria made a big thing of the time, hurrying to fix that green punch for the reception the next day."

Matt nodded, then asked, "What I don't understand is how she got close enough to the Judge to stick him with the pin. Did she explain that?"

"No, but I've got a pretty good idea. In my book I had the murderer sneak up on Winston, the victim, at a crowded party, but Maria couldn't do that. I think she used her charm. She was probably terribly sweet when she went back to the Judge's house the next week. And then, when she'd convinced him that she wasn't angry anymore, she just told him that his collar was wrinkled, or something simple like that. While she pretended to fix it, she was actually putting the pin through it."

"And after that there was enough poison left to kill him?"

"Just barely, but the Judge was old. His system didn't take much."

"It seems pretty chancy. The pin might have worked its way out without harming him."

"All he had to do was turn his head sharply one time. But if the pin hadn't eventually stuck him, well, so what? She could simply try again." I sighed. "But it did work."

"And now, it's all over."

I watched the scenery for a minute, realizing how close we were getting to the ranch.

"Except for Maria's funeral." Maybe Diane could tell me if it was appropriate for me to attend. Then I remembered something else. "And the election. It's this Tuesday. Only two more days to wait."

"I wouldn't worry about that," Matt said. "I talked with Trey this morning and he's pretty well decided it's not that important to him anymore. If Bill wins, it's going to be on a sympathy vote."

"Then we'll be stuck with Bill Tieman as mayor."

"And how much do you think he's going to get away with now that Trey's made his interests clear? Besides, it's only a two-year term. Then Trey can run again and you can work with him to make sure he's elected. I doubt that next time there will be a murder to complicate things."

He turned in at the wide gates to the ranch and my muscles tightened. Matt must have sensed the change in me.

"There's nothing to be nervous about," he said. "It's just a house."

"Your house," I said.

"Our house. And you can do whatever you want to make it seem like home. As I told you before, Jolie, it's whatever you want. However you want it."

But I was still nervous. I kept telling myself how silly it was to be afraid to face a house, especially after everything I'd been through, but the fear remained. Even as we drove through the front pasture filled with wild licorice and Johnsongrass, my muscles were taut.

Matt took the last curve slowly and there it was. Just a rambling old ranch house with a wide green lawn, enclosed by a white-railed fence. All around the outside of the fence there were wildflowers stirring gently in the mild breeze. Feathery green stalks dotted with delicate yellow flowers. Mustard flowers.

As Matt stopped the car, I turned to him in surprise. "Mustard. You've got a field of mustard flowers! When did you plant those?"

Matt helped me out of the Bronco. "*We've* got a field of mustard flowers," he corrected. "And I didn't plant them. They're volunteers that come up every couple of years. You haven't seen them before?"

"Never," I said.

Jeremy ran out the front door. "Finally you two are home."

I looked at Matt. "Now that's an entrance cue if I ever heard one."

He laughed and took my hand as we walked toward our house.

SARA PARETSKY
RUTH RENDELL

AND OTHERS...

3RD CULPRIT
A Crime Writers' Association Annual

First Time In Paperback

NEW YORK TIMES BESTSELLING MYSTERY AUTHORS

Crime in all its devious incarnations is presented in this treat of murderous morsels dished out by old pros and promising newcomers. Artfully crafted and impossible to put down, each story bountifully demonstrates why these authors are crème de la crime.

"Celebrates nothing but good crime writing."
— *Publishers Weekly*

"An excellent anthology."
— *Booklist*

Available in September at your favorite retail stores.

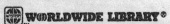

THE BLUEJAY SHAMAN

First Time In Paperback

LISE McCLENDON

An Alix Thorssen Mystery

MURDER AMONG THE SACRED

There is no artistry in slashing a woman's throat. Alix Thorssen, art dealer and forgery expert, knows that much. Whoever killed Shiloh Merkin hated her and wanted her dead. Her brother-in-law, Wade, is accused of murder.

Wade, an Indian activist and zealous defender of Native Montana land, despised Shiloh's New Age women's group. His knife is the murder weapon.

With help from a local cop, Alix follows a trail of sex, moonlit rituals and legendary artifacts...as another murder leads her to a chilling confrontation with a killer.

"Reminiscent of Tony Hillerman at his best."
—James Crumley, author of *The Mexican Tree Duck*

Available in September at your favorite retail stores.

 **WORLDWIDE LIBRARY®**

BLUE

HARLEQUIN®

I N T R I G U E®

THAT'S INTRIGUE—DYNAMIC ROMANCE AT ITS BEST!

Harlequin Intrigue is now bringing you more—more men and mystery, more desire and danger. If you've been looking for thrilling tales of contemporary passion and sensuous love stories with taut, edge-of-the-seat suspense—then you'll *love* Harlequin Intrigue!

Every month, you'll meet four new heroes who are guaranteed to make your spine tingle and your pulse pound. With them you'll enter into the exciting world of Harlequin Intrigue—where your life is on the line and so is your heart!

Harlequin Intrigue—we'll leave you breathless!

INT-GEN

...A DANGEROUS THING
BILL CRIDER
A Carl Burns Mystery

First Time in Paperback

PAINFUL CORRECTNESS

The new dean of Hartley Gorman College arrives with an agenda of political correctness that hits Professor Carl Burns where it hurts: Shakespeare, Milton, Homer, Wordsworth—all of his DWEMs (Dead White European Males) must go.

True, the new curriculum at HGC has wrought some controversy, but when a popular professor takes a fatal flying leap out a window, it's death by anybody's definition.

Between grading papers and vying for the affection of the librarian, Burns discovers a sordid tangle of lust, scandal and secrets that draw him into a chase for an elusive and unlikely killer.

"An amusingly self-effacing...mystery series."
— *New York Times Book Review*

Available in October at your favorite retail stores.

WORLDWIDE LIBRARY ®